"Are you s
take a lover,
his deep voic
across the su ~~skin.~~

"To let another man touch you?"

Lifting her chin, she kept her own narrowed gaze locked in tight on his burning one. "I'm not threatening. I'm stating a *fact*. You either stop this archaic bullshit you've been pulling, protecting my virginity like it's something you expect me to keep for-freaking-ever, or I'll end it for you."

Cian drew in a deep breath, then slowly exhaled, his shoulders seeming even broader as he came another step. "You really think I'll allow that to happen?" he rasped in a low, almost silent slide of words.

"Just try to stop me," she finally whispered, unable to shout when everything inside her was aching and raw. Incapable of enduring another moment in his presence, she turned and walked away from him. Though she was dying a little more with each step that she took, she kept her chin high, refusing to look back, even when he growled her name in that deep, delicious voice.

BLOOD WOLF
DAWNING

RHYANNON BYRD

MILLS
BOON

Rhyannon Byrd is an avid, longtime fan of romance and author of more than twenty paranormal and erotic titles. She has been nominated for three RT Reviewers' Choice Awards, including Best Shapeshifter Romance. Rhyannon lives in the beautiful county of Warwickshire, with her husband and family. For information on Rhyannon's books, visit her website at rhyannonbyrd. com, or find her on Facebook.

To my amazing editor, Ann Leslie Tuttle.
Mountains and oceans of appreciation for all that
you've done for this series.
It wouldn't have been the same without you!

Prologue

If this was what falling for someone did to a person—
what *craving* them felt like—then Sayre Murphy wanted
no part of it. *Ever.* She might be young, as well as inex-
perienced, but she was a woman, damn it, and she knew
when she was done.

When she had finally had *enough*!

With her back straight and her hands fisted at her
sides, she stood in a moonlit Maryland forest, high on
the mountain that the Silvercrest Lycans, her brethren,
had owned for centuries. And she wasn't alone. Standing a few yards in front of her was the most magnificent, infuriating, arrogant male she had ever known.
One who treated her as if she were nothing more than a
child and interfered in her life time and again, making
it painfully clear that he never had any intention of seeing her as an adult female capable of making her own
choices. It was an antiquated attitude—completely fitting with his dominant, alpha personality—and one she
was entirely sick of.

Honestly, who cared that she was only eighteen? Did
that make her a child? Hell no. A handful of weeks ago,
she had fought beside her loved ones in a bloodthirsty
war to protect their homeland. Had used the unique pow-

ers she possessed as a rare Lycan witch and sent grown male werewolves to their deaths. If that didn't make her an adult in his eyes, then she wondered with frustration if anything ever would.

"I've had enough of this insanity," she told him, determined to keep her voice from shaking. "It ends. Now."

The tall Bloodrunner approached her, his dark-assin hair gleaming in the moonlight, narrowed silver eyes burning with fury. "You do not dictate to me," he snarled, his lilting Irish brogue thicker than she'd ever heard it before. "Not now, not tomorrow and not the day after that. You will *never* control this. You understand me, lass?"

"I'm not interested in controlling you," she shot back, fisting her hands even tighter, while deep within she felt the fiery heat of her power swirling with energy, desperate to break free. A rising power that she only managed to hang on to by a thread. "I'm simply making my position clear. You're the one who's been acting like a jealous ass. Not me!"

"I'm protecting you!" he roared in a voice that held dark, dangerous things that were so much more than human. As a male who was half werewolf, he was as deadly as he was beautiful. But she knew he would never cause her physical harm, even when he was glaring at her with such raw, seething fury.

The safety of her heart, however, was a different matter.

"I don't need your protection. I never have." Words rushed up into her mouth that were revealing and intimate—words she knew would make her vulnerable the moment they were spoken—and yet, she couldn't stop them. Couldn't hold them back. "I…I just need *you*," she whispered, loving the way the muscles in his strong, corded throat moved beneath his skin as he gave a hard swallow, his blistering gaze fixed on her tongue as she nervously wet her lips. He watched her mouth with the hungry avidity of a predator who wanted to play and claim and mate, his body expanding with need, his rigid biceps straining the sleeves of his T-shirt. But the human half of him was too stubborn to give in.

"No," he bit out, the denial emerging like a bitter piece of gravel stuck in his throat as he shook his head. And then again. *"No."*

"Finally take what's yours, or I'm finished," she warned him, tired of the maddening double standard that existed between them. Of the way he could sleep with endless numbers of women, and yet, she wasn't allowed to have a simple conversation with another male without him interfering. "I have friends," she snapped. "Good ones. *Male* ones. Lycans who won't reject me. Who won't be so opposed to the idea of enjoying my body if I offer it to them."

His head jerked back as if she'd suddenly struck him with her fist. Then his gaze sharpened and a muscle began to pulse rhythmically in the hard line of his jaw, while his breaths became rougher, eerily stark in the heavy stillness of the forest. The woods were unusually quiet, as if every living creature were tuned in to their argument, waiting with bated breath to see how it would end. This was a storm that had been brewing between them for months, its fury finally unleashed in a torrent of anger and hurt and maddening frustration.

"Are you seriously threatening to take a lover, Sayre?" he demanded, his deep voice causing chills to race across the surface of her skin. "To let another man touch you?"

Lifting her chin, she kept her own narrowed gaze locked in tight on his burning one. "I'm not threatening. I'm stating a *fact*. You either stop this archaic bullshit you've been pulling for months now, protecting my virginity like it's something you expect me to keep for freaking ever, or I'll end it for you."

He drew in a deep breath, then slowly exhaled, his shoulders seeming even broader as he came another step closer, his nearness causing her own breath to quicken. "You really think I'll allow that to happen?" he rasped in a low, almost silent slide of words.

Sadness stabbed her right through the chest as she stared up at him, seeing his resolve in that piercing metallic gray, the phrase *He'll never want you…need you… accept you* looping over and over within the darkness of her mind. She had asked him to meet her tonight so that she could make a final bid for her sanity. Had offered him her body, with no strings attached, desperate for a measure of relief from the incessant hunger rushing through her veins, her need for him growing stronger each day, until she was ill with it. But he'd turned her down, refusing to give her what he so casually gave to so many others, and all because fate had decided to screw with them for a laugh. The connection between them was nothing more than a sick, costly joke, and she and the Irishman were the ones who would pay.

But *she* was the one paying the most. Because while he eased his hunger with countless others, he refused to allow her to do the same. And though she didn't want another male—how could she when she so desperately wanted *him*?—she was tired of playing the pathetic pawn in his twisted game. Tired of being alone. Of sleeping in an empty bed when his was always full.

"Just try to stop me," she finally whispered, unable to shout when everything inside her was aching and raw. Incapable of enduring another moment in his presence, she turned and walked away from him. Though she was dying a little more with each step that she took, she kept her chin high, refusing to look back, even when he growled her name with that rough, delicious accent. She could feel the burning, savage intensity of his stare pressing against her skin until she was finally shielded from his view by the lush flora of the forest, the leaves and branches feeling as if they were reaching out to embrace her. She normally took comfort in the verdant plant life, loving the way its rich scent filled her head and soothed her nerves. But tonight she was too cold. Too shattered.

She would give him the rest of the night to brood and rage…and hopefully think over what she'd said. But that was all.

Pressing a trembling hand to her stomach, her next breath stuttered out on a broken sob, and yet, she refused to give in. She'd already cried enough over the stubborn male. All she could do now was pray that he would make the right choice and alter his path, embracing what they had, even if it were just for one night, instead of doing everything in his power to spurn it. But she was terrified that this was it. That it was over. Whatever *it* was.

Oh, God. Had she honestly thought that she could hold the tears inside? The hot, salty wetness on her cheeks was proof that she'd been wrong. But as awful, empty and alone as Sayre felt at that moment, it was nothing compared to what was coming. To the pain that waited for her, lurking like a killer in the darkness, ready to cut and rend…and completely destroy her.

Because when the sun rose over Maryland the following morning, the Irishman was already gone.

Chapter 1

Five years later

Morning sunlight glinted through the treetops as Cian Hennessey pulled onto the paved mountain road that led into Bloodrunner Alley. He tried to stay focused on what he was about to face, but his last night in the picturesque glade he'd called home for so many years kept playing through his mind. After his disastrous meeting with Sayre in the woods, he'd known he was done there—that he couldn't stay. He'd waited until everyone had gone to bed, and then he'd packed his Land Rover with as many of his belongings as he could. His plan had been to take off before anyone noticed, but Eli Drake, a badass Lycan mercenary who had recently returned to the Silvercrest werewolf pack after years of banishment, had found him before he could get away.

"You can't run from fate, man," Eli had lectured him. "Take that from someone who knows. Even when you try to convince yourself that leaving is the right thing to do, it's nothing but a goddamn lie. And it all comes back to bite you hard in the ass when it finally catches up to you."

That had been five years ago. If he'd known just how

true Eli's words would prove to be, he might have paid more attention to them. But he'd been so sure he knew what needed to be done. That the path he'd been set on taking was not only the right choice, but also his *only* choice.

In the end, Cian had finally realized that he hadn't known a damn thing. All he'd managed to do was postpone the inevitable. But he'd been around long enough to understand that there wasn't any point in wishing for a do-over. What was done was done, and nothing he could do would ever change that. He just had to chalk it up as another entry on the long list of regrets that he lived with, and focus on how to make the best of the situation at present.

So here he was, returning to the only place he'd ever truly thought of as home. At least since he'd left his childhood behind. The scenery might not be as dramatic as the craggy seaside cliffs near Killian's Mount in Ireland, where he'd been raised as a boy, but the mountains held an undeniable beauty. And the half-human/half-Lycan hunters who lived there were not only his friends, but also his family in the truest sense of the word.

Hell, the Runners were more like family to him than anyone who still walked this earth and shared his blood. And yet, he'd turned his back on them because of *her*. Because of a little slip of a witch named Sayre Murphy. Until today, he hadn't seen or spoken to them since he'd left that fateful night. Not even an email or a text. So there was no telling what kind of reception he was about to receive from the men and women who protected the Silvercrest pack from its enemies.

He only knew it wasn't likely to be a warm one.

Parking the black Audi he'd arranged to have waiting for him at Dulles in the grass at the side of the road, he turned off the engine and climbed out, his narrowed eyes taking in his surroundings while he shut the car door and slipped the key fob in his front pocket. As he drew in a deep breath of the crisp mountain air, the scent of the surrounding forest was so achingly familiar that, for a moment, he felt as if his chest might crush inward from the force of regret pressing in on him.

But despite the familiarity of that woodsy scent, the Alley hadn't remained unchanged in his absence, the passage of time marked by differences that were both big and small. He hadn't been there to see the picnic tables repainted, or to help with the completion of the impressive cabins that now stood at the far end of the glade. Had missed the paving of the road and the additions that had been built onto many of the original cabins, where his friends and their mates lived. He could have undoubtedly spotted more changes, but the sight of the tall, auburn-haired Bloodrunner headed straight for him diverted his attention.

The welcoming party, it appeared, was on its way. Though there definitely didn't seem to be anything remotely welcoming about it. No, if he were reading the situation correctly, his former Bloodrunning partner, Brody Carter, looked more likely to throw a bone-crushing punch than he did to go in for a bro hug, and something sharp twisted in Cian's chest.

What did you expect? the wolf part of his nature grumbled inside his head. *He might have been our best friend, but you destroyed that when you turned your back on him. Asshole.*

Knowing damn well how true the beast's snide words were, he hardened his jaw, determined to take whatever

Brody felt like dishing out without retaliating. He pushed
his hands in his pockets and waited as Brody closed in
on him, surprised to see that the guy looked even bigger
than he'd been before. Brody had always been muscular, but now he was cut in a way that was truly impressive, his tall body rippling with power as he stalked
toward him. The Runner's auburn hair was long again,
but pulled back from his scarred face. And there were
little laugh lines that crinkled at the edges of his green
eyes, attesting to the fact that he was a happily married
man who loved his life—even if those green eyes were
currently narrowed in fury. Not that he could blame
him. If Brody had bailed on the Alley the way Cian had,
he would have been so angry it'd be hard to hold back.

Behind Brody's broad shoulder, he spotted the guy's
human wife, Michaela, as she came down the porch
steps of her and Brody's cabin. The Cajun's dark hair
was still long and curly, and even from that distance
Cian could tell that she remained incredibly beautiful.
Marriage obviously suited the two of them, and he found
himself remembering back to the obstacles they'd faced
when they'd first gotten together.

During the last months that Cian had lived in the
Alley, there were times when he'd felt like one hell of a
matchmaker. On several occasions, he'd even gone so
far as to claim that he wouldn't make the same mistakes
he'd watched his friends make when his own woman finally came along—but in the end, it'd been nothing but
talk. Talk he couldn't back up, because happily-ever-
after had never been an option for him.

Instead, finding *his* woman meant he should run as
far and as fast as he could in the opposite direction,
and never look back. The kindest that fate could have

been was to connect him with a female who wasn't a part of the Silvercrest. One he could ignore and keep his distance from, without leaving his friends. But that hadn't happened.

No, he'd been linked with beautiful little Sayre. That right there just proved that the universe had an exceptionally sick sense of humor.

Though he tried not to fixate on her, he kept scanning the Alley beyond Brody, searching for that familiar heart-shaped face and strawberry-blond hair. But she wasn't there. Besides Brody and Mic, the place was unusually empty. He'd texted Brody's old number when he'd landed, warning him that he was coming, and had naturally assumed that Sayre would be waiting for him. She no doubt had a hell of a lot to say to him, after the way he'd left. Not to mention the fact that he hadn't once tried to contact her in the last five years. But there wasn't any sign of her. He told himself not to panic, that she most likely didn't live in the Alley and was probably up in Shadow Peak, the mountaintop town that the Silvercrest Lycans called home, which was only a few miles away. Hell, she could be on her way down to see him at that very moment.

But when he pulled in another deep, searching breath, his heart started to hammer even harder as he realized that Sayre's mouthwatering scent was *nowhere* to be found. Not even the slightest trace. It made a cold sliver of fear begin to coil through his insides, keeping company with his tension. From the moment her older sister, Jillian, had moved down to the Alley to live with a Bloodrunner named Jeremy Burns, Sayre had been a constant feature at the couple's cabin. So what was keeping her away now?

Looking at Brody, who had just come to a stop no more than five feet in front of him, he cut off whatever the Runner was going to say with a rough, impatient burst of words. "I know you want to tell me to get lost, and after the way I left, you have every right. But I came back for a reason. I need to talk to Sayre. Where is she?"

Brody's green eyes burned with an even brighter surge of anger. "You think she's with the pack?"

Cian scowled. "Where else would she be?"

God, if she'd found someone and moved away with him he was going to completely lose it.

Michaela reached her husband's side, a concerned look on her beautiful face as she said, "Cian, Sayre doesn't live with the Silvercrest anymore."

Thinking this must be some kind of ploy to either screw with him or protect the young witch, he held Michaela's troubled gaze. "I'm not here to make things hard for her, Mic. I just…I came back because I need to talk to her."

Though human, Michaela possessed the unique ability to psychically "read" others' emotions, and Cian could only imagine what she was picking up from him at that moment: frustration, fear, guilt, anger, regret and, beneath it all, a seething, never-ending need for something he could never have. She slid Brody a quick glance, then delicately cleared her throat as she looked at Cian and said, "We're not lying. As much as I hate to say it, she honestly isn't here."

So many raw, visceral curses suddenly crowded into his throat, he thought he might choke on them. He swallowed a few times, then finally managed to scrape out a single word. *"Why?"*

His insides twisted when he noticed the way they

glanced at each other again, as if neither of them knew how much to tell him. Or *what* to tell him.

"After you left," Michaela finally murmured, taking a careful breath, "there were…well, some things changed."

"What kind of things? What the hell are you talking about?"

He'd kept up on the pack enough through third parties to know that the Silvercrest had flourished in the past five years, thanks to the hard work of the Runners. They might have still been recovering from their war against the neighboring Whiteclaw pack when he'd left, but it'd been clear even then that they'd become a force too powerful for anyone to mess with. Nothing had happened in these mountains that should have necessitated Sayre leaving. Not unless it was something personal, and the secrets he could see burning in his friends' eyes were seriously pissing him off.

"Stop worrying about how I'm going to react," he said, "and just spit it out."

Michaela sighed. "Cian, Sayre isn't the same." At his darkening look, she hurried to explain. "Not long after you took off, Sayre went into a decline and suffered a…breakdown. Not only was she wrecked because of the way you abandoned everyone, but she'd also been dealing with some pretty powerful issues in private. Her powers had been increasing at an abnormal rate, but she didn't want to worry anyone and tried to hide it as much as she could. But after the war, it eventually got to be too much for her, and she had to get away and be on her own. She hasn't lived here in over four and a half years."

Four and a half years? Reeling, he tried to suck in a sharp breath, but his lungs had locked down. He was sealed in a goddamn vise of disbelief, the roaring in his head making him flinch. *No. No, damn it. This can't be happening.* He didn't want to believe, but he could tell by the looks on their faces that they were telling him the truth.

Somehow, he managed to choke out, "Where. Is. She?"

"It's too much of a strain on her system when she's around other people, so she lives by herself just over the border, in a cabin in West Virginia."

His throat was so tight with fear he could barely speak. "And there's no one there to help her? She's completely alone?"

Brody jerked his chin up and scowled. "She doesn't like to be around anyone. Even Jillian and Jeremy. It physically pains her to pick up on others' physical and emotional energy."

Cian paced away from them and lowered his head, staring at the tips of his heavy black leather boots. He shoved his hands into his hair, pushing it away from his face as he squeezed his skull, working everything he'd just learned through his head. *Christ*, all this time he'd thought she was safe, surrounded by her family and friends, when he couldn't have been more wrong. She was alone, damn it. On her own in the middle of fucking nowhere!

Rage seared its way through his veins in a thick, eviscerating spill, and he lowered his arms and fisted his hands at his sides as he turned back around and took an aggressive step toward Brody. Five years ago, he'd left a single message for his partner that read: *Take care of her.* But that obviously hadn't happened.

Locking his furious gaze with Brody's green one, he snarled, "I trusted you."

"Yeah, I trusted you, too," the Runner shot back, curling his upper lip. "But that didn't stop you from running like a coward, did it?"

Cian struggled to control his temper and calm his harsh breaths, but the darkness inside him was rising, and he knew it wouldn't be long before he lost the fight against it. Which meant he needed to get the hell out of there. "I need directions to where she is," he growled. *"Now."*

Brody snorted and shook his head, looking at him with disgust. "It's been *five* years, Cian. Why the sudden hurry?"

Before he could respond, Michaela reached into the pocket of her long skirt and pulled out a small piece of paper. "You both just need to calm down. This isn't going to help anyone." Offering him the paper, she said, "I already wrote the information down for you after you sent Brody that text."

Her husband shot her a disgruntled look. "What the hell, Mic?"

She slid Brody an apologetic smile. "I'm sorry, honey, but she deserves the chance to deal with this on her own."

Cian didn't speak as he grabbed the tiny slip of paper from Michaela's hand. A quick glance showed that she'd written down a brief set of directions along with several names and phone numbers.

"The others will be sorry they missed you," she told him. "They've taken all the kids down to the beach for two weeks in South Carolina. But we chose to stay home because Jack's still too young for that kind of thing."

He opened his mouth, a hundred different questions on his tongue. Jack? Kids? Exactly how many did his friends have now? What were their names, ages and genders? His curiosity was strong—but his fear for Sayre's safety was stronger.

Snapping his mouth shut, Cian turned and headed back to the sleek sports car he'd left parked in the grass. Just as he opened the driver's-side door, Brody grabbed his shoulder and jerked him around, getting right in his face. "What the hell are you up to, Hennessey?"

"I'm bringing her back where she belongs."

The three thin scars that slashed across Brody's tanned face turned white as he grimaced. "She won't come back with you. We *begged* her, but she was adamant. You really think you'll be able to change her mind after leaving like you did?"

"The difference is that I don't plan on asking, or begging. I'm not giving her a choice," he ground out, digging the key fob from his pocket. "I'll tie her up and throw her over my shoulder if I have to, but one way or another, she *is* coming back to where it's safe."

The Runner's green eyes widened with comprehension. "What aren't you telling us?" he demanded, tightening the brutal grip he had on his shoulder.

Looking his former partner right in the eye, Cian said, "I don't have the time to get into this, Brody. But I *will* explain when I get back."

"Are we in danger?" he asked in a low voice, showing no signs of backing down.

Cian shook his head, hoping like hell that it wasn't a lie. But he had no reason to believe that the Runners were targets. If that were the case, something would have happened a long time ago, when Cian had been one of them.

A knowing light started to burn in Brody's eyes. "Is Sayre in danger? Is that what this is about?"

"If she is, what is it to you?" he growled, hating the way that Brody was looking at him—with years' worth of fury and hurt and disappointment that made him feel completely worthless.

Deep voice vibrating with rage, the Runner said, "It's important to me because I was your partner and your best friend, asshole. So that was on *me*. You don't think I felt responsible when you just up and ran? I had to watch that girl deal with your betrayal while everything was falling apart for her, and felt guilty as hell for not figuring out what you were up to. Because you can bet that if I had, I would have saved her from having to deal with whatever bullshit you've brought down on her head *now*."

Struggling to hold on to his control, he forced his response through his gritted teeth. "I don't have time for this, man. You want to beat me down when I get back with her, then fine. Go for it. I'm sure it's exactly what I deserve. But right now, I've got to go."

"You want to leave," Brody seethed, his towering height allowing him to go nose-to-nose with Cian, "then you tell me what's going on. *Is* Sayre in danger?"

Through the thrashing of his pulse in his ears, he heard himself say, "She's been in danger from the moment I first realized she was *mine*."

"From who? *You?*"

"No," he grunted, choking back the bile that rose in his throat. "From an old enemy of mine."

"What *old* enemy? What the hell does that mean? Don't we all have the *same* enemies?"

Jerking free of the Runner's hold, Cian climbed into the car and slammed the door. Brody banged on the window with his fist, but he ignored him as he cranked the engine, then twisted in his seat to look over his shoulder and floored the accelerator as he reversed down the road.

He felt exactly like the asshole Brody had called him for leaving like this, knowing they were going to worry. But, damn it, he didn't have time to waste on explanations. He needed to get to West Virginia, to the girl he'd left behind, before it was too late and he lost his chance.

Your chance to do what? Save her life? his wolf muttered. *Because that's the* only *thing you have a chance in hell of saving when it comes to you and her. You've screwed up too badly for any "second chances" with the girl. And don't think I'm ever going to let you forget it.*

He ground his back teeth together, not wanting to hear it—*any* of it. Then he felt something slick and cold stir to life inside him, meandering its way through his veins, and suddenly the beast's nagging seemed the far lesser of two evils. Yeah, the wolf part of his nature might be a pain in the ass at times, but at least it was noble. Hard and vicious and animalistic, yes; but it lived its life according to a code.

Unfortunately, the wolf wasn't the only thing living beneath his skin, and Cian wanted to claw at his heart until he could rip the blackened organ from his chest. Because that was where the "other" part of him lived. And it wasn't noble or honest or loyal. It was nothing but hunger and rage and greed. An evil so twisted he'd always hated its existence. Had hidden it away, even from those who were closest to him. Who'd fought at his side, and put not only their lives in his hands, but also the lives of those who meant the most to them.

But now there was no more running. No more avoiding the inevitable…or his past…or those parts of his life that he wished he could simply erase from existence, like a hard rain could wash away grime and filth.

He could search the world over, but he wasn't ever going to find a rain that came down hard enough to wash *him* clean.

Glancing over at the passenger's seat, he spotted the crumpled bit of paper he'd tossed there earlier, the handful of words penned onto its surface carved into his memory like a blade scoring flesh.

Cian,
I imagine you'd hoped I wouldn't learn your secret, but I have. I'll give you a head start—though you better hurry. It's time for the little witch and me to play.
A

It was a message that had chilled him to the bone the instant he'd woken in his Dublin apartment and found it waiting on his bedside table. His worst nightmare had come to life, because it meant that his oldest enemy had finally learned the truth about Sayre. That she was *his*. His *life mate*. The one female in the world who had been created for him and him *alone*.

And now his bastard of a brother intended to kill her.

Chapter 2

Sayre Murphy stiffened at the sound of a car smoothly rumbling its way through the quiet forest that surrounded her home; a noise she didn't often hear these days. She pulled off her gardening gloves and moved to her feet, turning away from the flourishing herb garden she'd been tending to cast a worried look toward the narrow dirt road that led right to her cabin. It wasn't even noon yet, but the heat was already oppressive, which was why she was dressed in a pair of cutoff shorts and a tank top and nothing more. She no longer had any need to dress for company, and she sure as hell hadn't been expecting any. Jillian and the others knew better than to show up unannounced, which meant that whoever was coming up her drive wasn't going to be anyone in her family.

And that meant they could be looking for trouble.

She dropped her gloves beside a leafy, aromatic patch of basil and flexed her hands at her sides, confident that she could deal with any threat that might be approaching. As a Lycan witch, she didn't possess the ability to shape-shift like the others in her pack—but with the strength of her powers these days, it didn't matter. She could zap any person or creature that tried to get near her with a jolt of pure energy that had brought grown Lycans to their knees.

"Ohmyfreakinggod." The hoarse words slipped past her lips as a sleek black sports car came around the last bend in the road and she caught sight of the driver. Stunned, she lurched back as if she'd suddenly been kicked in the stomach. Cian Hennessey was the *last* person she'd ever expected to see, and she shuddered, every blasphemy she could think of screaming through her head. Gripping the front of her tank top, directly over the thundering beat of her heart, she pushed down as if she needed the physical pressure to keep the racing organ inside her chest.

His pale gray eyes were locked hard on hers as he killed the engine, opened the door and unfolded his long, powerful body from behind the steering wheel. The sight of him had her stumbling back again, and she nearly fell on her bottom when the right heel of her hiking boot connected with the wooden edge of a flower bed.

The morning sun was behind him now, shining directly into her eyes. It was difficult to make out his features as he headed directly for her, his long-legged stride making short work of the yards that separated them. But she *felt* him with every part of her. The pull between them was so strong she could have counted his thudding heartbeats down to the minute, or his quickening intakes of air. The closer he came, the more heightened her sensory perception grew, and she really hoped that it didn't work in the reverse. She didn't want this man reading her. Didn't want him to feel the rushing of her pulse or the heat gathering beneath her skin, warm and thick and wild.

And she sure as hell didn't want him to know that

there was a part of her breaking into sharp, jagged little pieces deep inside just because she was looking at
him, breathing him in, completely and embarrassingly
glomming on to every exquisite detail, after believing
for so long that she'd never see him again. She knew
there wasn't a man alive who could make jeans, a black
T-shirt and boots look so unbelievably good—his body
appearing even harder than it'd been before, as if he'd
spent the past five years engaged in brutal combat.

"What are you doing here?" she demanded as firmly
as possible, when he came to a stop no more than ten
feet in front of her and she finally managed to find her
voice. The way his long-lashed silver gaze swept hotly
over her figure, taking her in from head to toe as if he
had every right to what he saw had her vibrating with
pure, volcanic rage. The freaking nerve of the guy! "No,
scratch that. I don't care why you're here. Just get back in
your car and go away, Hennessey. I don't want you here."

He didn't respond to her outburst in any way other
than to take a step closer, and she was surprised when
she found herself pulling in even deeper breaths of air
through her nose, just so she could soak in that sexy-as-
sin scent of his. A heady combination of the outdoors,
musk and salt, it sat on her tongue like something she
wanted to savor and suck on, and keep it there forever.
She'd always enjoyed the way Cian had smelled, even
when he carried the faint scent of cigarette smoke on
his skin, but...*whoa*, her reaction had never been this
intense before, as if she wanted to rub up against him
like a kitten and get that mouthwatering scent all over
her. More than a little rattled, she snapped, "Well? Are
you going to stand there staring at me all day or are you
at least going to say something?"

"Sorry," he rasped, the lilting sound of the brogue she knew he'd developed while growing up in Ireland even stronger than she remembered it, making her wonder where he'd been living. His tongue touched the corner of his mouth, and his thick lashes lowered over eyes she could have sworn had started to glow like melting metal, despite the tiredness she could see in them. "I just...you surprised me," he added gruffly. "I didn't expect you to be even more beautiful than you were before."

Wearing cutoff denim shorts with a threadbare tank top and scuffed boots on her feet, her long hair in a crazy swarm of curls around her shoulders and dirt probably smeared on her cheek? Um, yeah, like she was really rocking an attractive look at the moment. Shaking her head, she snorted at his lame-ass attempt at flattery. "We've never lied to each other before, Cian. It would be pointless to start now."

"I'm not lying, lass. You're..." He trailed off as his breath left his lungs on a sharp exhalation, and he cursed as he slowly rubbed one of his hands over his wide mouth. "You were always pretty, but the only word I can think of that does you any justice now is *stunning.*"

The scowl on her face became a little fiercer, and she wanted to tell him to take his bullshit and shove it up his backside. She knew she looked different than the scrawny eighteen-year-old he'd left behind—she was curvier now, her hair was longer and wilder, and God only knew she had more freckles on her nose and shoulders thanks to all the hours she spent outdoors— but she didn't look *that* different.

And he was...damn him, he was still just as gorgeous as ever. Other than the shorter cut of his hair, he didn't look as if he'd changed at all, even though he had to be pushing close to forty by now. His features were still chiseled, but ruggedly male, the shadow of stubble on his lean cheeks and square chin giving his already dangerous good looks an even sharper, more aggressive edge. All broad shoulders and masculine lines, ripped and lean and deliciously cut. The kind of guy that women acted like idiots over, losing their self-esteem somewhere down around their ankles, right along with their underwear.

Then there was his bravery and intelligence and his wicked sense of humor. His undeniable loyalty to his friends and family.

Well, that last bit could no doubt be scratched from the list now, seeing as how he'd turned his back on them as completely as he had on her. But before that…God, before that, Cian Hennessey *could* have been exactly what she'd wanted.

If he'd only wanted her in return.

"Cian, please," she said as carefully as she could manage, praying her voice wouldn't tremble. "Say whatever you came to say and then leave. I honestly don't want you here. It isn't…it isn't good for me."

She watched his throat work as he swallowed, his voice low and rough in a way that had never failed to make her shiver from the inside out. "There's a lot I need to explain. I know that, Sayre. But we don't have the time. We need to leave this place."

"Not a chance," she said, wondering if he'd been hit over his gorgeous head with a crazy stick. "*We* don't need to do anything. I live here; you don't. Whatever you want from me is nothing but a waste of your time. I don't give second chances."

Frustration shot through his narrowed eyes, making

them as dark as smoke. "You never even really gave me a first chance, much less a second one."

Amazed by those quiet, almost bitter words, she slowly shook her head, then pulled her shoulders back and glared. "That's total crap and you know it. And don't make it sound like you even wanted one."

"Then don't act like you know what I wanted," he argued roughly, "because you never had a goddamn clue."

Her control shredded like a cheap pair of tights, and she heard herself snarl, "You made my life hell!"

He came another step closer. "Right back at you, Sayre."

"Then why are you even here?" she shouted, watching his eyes widen as he slowly looked her over again. Oh...*hell.* Her power had just slipped free of her hold with the galvanic rise of her temper, skittering around her body in a fine spray of tiny, golden sparks.

Damn it, it was just her luck that she looked like a freaking sparkler every time she lost control of her emotions these days. With her hands fisted at her sides, she waited for him to comment on the bizarre display, knowing it was shocking even in their nothing-is-normal world.

But he didn't.

Instead, he rubbed his hand over his mouth again, almost as if he were wiping away whatever words were waiting there. Then he cleared his throat, muttered a low curse and looked her right in the eye as he said, "There isn't time to explain, but you *can't* stay here, Sayre. I'm taking you back to the Alley, where you belong."

She blinked back at him, unable to believe his arrogance. He acted as though he had every right to just stroll back into her life and take control. "Cian, even if

I *wanted* to go back to the Alley, I couldn't." Her voice almost shook with a telling tremor as she added, "I can't stand to be around other people."

It occurred to her, as soon as the words left her lips, that she wasn't experiencing any pain—at least physically—while standing there with *him*. If he didn't mention it, then she sure as heck wasn't going to. But he was staring at her so intently with those incredible metallic eyes, she felt as if he were trying to take an intimate stroll through her mind, to dig out all her secret thoughts and emotions and truths, and in a sudden change of heart, she almost wished that he could. It would serve him right, because while he wouldn't have any trouble finding her desire for him, he'd also witness firsthand just how deeply her anger and disappointment ran. And it was deep. As deep as her freaking soul.

Finally, he pulled in a somewhat ragged breath, slowly exhaled and broke the tension-filled standoff. "I went to the Alley this morning," he confessed in a low voice. "Brody and Mic told me why you had to leave." His tongue flicked against the corner of his mouth again, and he shook his head a little. "I didn't know, Sayre. All this time, I thought you were still *with* them. That you were protected."

"Don't," she muttered, realizing that Michaela hadn't even called to warn her that Cian was coming. She couldn't believe her sister's friend would do that to her. The traitor! "I don't need your pity, Cian."

His mouth twisted, and she couldn't help but stare, thinking about what it would be like to feel those sensual lips against hers. She might not know many things about pleasure, but she knew how to kiss. She'd kissed her share of cute boys in her teens, and had enjoyed the hell out of it, though she'd never been willing to go further than that. Turns out it'd been a stupid choice. Back then, she'd had her girlish head filled with the idea of an everlasting, romantic love when she found her life mate, like Jillian and Jeremy had. Not that their road to happiness had been all sunshine and roses, but she wanted what they'd worked so hard for and had found in the end. Wanted it so badly that she'd been willing to fight for it, too. To earn it. Cherish it. Him. *Her man.*

Then fate had played the cruelest joke possible, and given her the Irishman. Yes, he was the most insanely sexy and gorgeous and powerful male she'd ever encountered. But he was the worst womanizer in existence. Sayre had heard all the rumors about the pack females he'd bedded until they could barely walk straight. Of his extreme intensity. His talent, skill and stamina, and the way a woman was never quite the same after she'd experienced his bed…or any of the other hundreds of places Sayre had heard he'd taken them.

She'd wanted a man who would love her and build a life with her. And, instead, she'd been given the one who'd always looked at her as if he couldn't quite stand to be in her presence.

She still remembered the moment when she'd finally realized why there was so much tension between them— the moment she recognized *exactly* what he was to her. They'd been in a roomful of people, surrounded by their friends, and she knew he'd already picked up on what was between them, or at least suspected it, when he looked over at her and caught her stunned expression. She'd been torn between agony and a need that was so strong she'd had to reach out and brace herself against the wall. Her eighteenth birthday had already come and gone, but he'd looked at her as if she were nothing more than an annoying child.

In that moment, Sayre had been so frightened of how badly he could hurt her. Of the pain he could inflict—not to her body, but to her heart. But then, standing there across from him in that crowded room, her conscience had chided her for being judgmental and not even giving him a chance. For one brief, incredible moment, hope had flooded her system, filling her with heat, and she'd given him a tentative smile. One that no doubt said, *I think you're beautiful and you're mine and I vow to do everything I can to make you happy. Everything I can to make you want me...make you love me.*

He'd answered her unspoken message by taking his phone out and holding her stare as he called someone. She was too far away to hear what he was saying, but she could read enough of the words on his lips to know he'd just called one of *them.* A woman he would take to his bed and bury himself inside, giving her what belonged to Sayre.

Her girlish heart had died a little that night. And then a little more with each night that went by and he lost himself inside female after female, never attempting to hide what he was up to.

Over the weeks and months, life on the mountain had become intolerable because of him. It was obvious that he had no intention of ever acknowledging the connection between them, and yet, he hadn't liked her spending time with other males. Not even with Max Doucet and Elliot Connors, who were her closest friends, and the youngest of the Bloodrunners.

The final straw had come a few weeks after the war they'd won over the neighboring Whiteclaw pack. Finally deciding she was done with whatever stupid game he'd been playing with her, the next time Sayre got him alone, she'd given him an ultimatum: he could either stop acting like a jackass and take her virginity, or she was going to say to hell with it all and give it up to the first of her male friends who agreed. He'd been livid at her threat, but she'd refused to back down.

Instead, she'd left his ass standing there in the forest, and had walked away.

What had happened that night had been the most difficult thing she'd ever done, putting herself out there like that, but she'd been fueled by ridiculous hope that it would make a difference. A hope she'd refused to admit even to herself at the time. But now, looking back, Sayre knew she'd been gambling her pride on the idea that if she could just get Cian to touch her, he'd realize she was all he needed and that they were meant to be together.

God, she'd been such a pathetic little fool.

In the morning, she'd heard that he'd left the Alley and nobody knew where he'd gone, or if he would ever return. Her heart had been completely shattered, but within a few days it became clear that more than just her heart had been altered by his absence. And while the others had become aware of her increasing problems with her powers, none of them had ever figured out her secret—and she sure as hell never planned on telling them the truth.

Now, after everything that had happened and all the time that had passed, she could hardly believe he was standing in front of her. All the pain she'd tried so hard to bury these past years came rushing back in a surge of emotion, cutting its way through her insides like a scalpel, and she shuddered as she took another step back from him, shaking, no doubt turning as pale as a ghost. She watched his eyes darken with sympathy, and her palm tingled with the urge to slap his beautiful, faithless face.

"I didn't know," he said again, the rough words sounding scraped from his throat. "I would have come home sooner, Sayre. I wouldn't have stayed away. I was only trying to—"

"Stop!" she snapped, cutting him off. "Just stop. I don't want to hear it, because if you say you left to protect me from your big bad self, so help me, God, I just might have to kill you."

He pulled in a sharp breath, nostrils flaring as he shoved one of those big hands back through his thick, dark-as-midnight hair. She'd never seen it as short as it was now, the ends only just brushing the back of his collar. "You know, I *should* have left for that reason. But I wouldn't have. I wouldn't have had the strength. As bad as I am, Sayre, I left to protect you from something even worse."

"Oh, God, that's funny," she said with a choked laugh, wrapping her arms around her middle. But no matter how tightly she squeezed, she still felt like she teetered on the cusp of falling apart. "What could be worse than *you*?"

He flinched at that brutal assessment, but didn't back down. "It's a long story and we don't have the time to get into it now. I just…I need you to trust me."

"Cian, just stop," she said with a derisive snort. "I honestly didn't know you could be this freaking hilarious."

"This isn't a goddamn joke," he muttered, giving her a look that seemed to say he was thinking of putting her over his knee and swatting her backside. And, God, did that piss her off. He'd lost the right to even think about putting his hands on her.

"You're damned right it's not a joke," she seethed, crackling with so much energy she was in danger of singeing her beloved garden. "Now get the hell off my land!"

"Sayre." He said her name on a long, drawn-out sigh, sounding too much like an adult who'd lost his patience with an unruly teen, and she felt her fury tip from emotion…right into action. Bathed in a fiery shower of sparks, she reached behind her and whipped out the gun she always kept tucked against her lower back when she was outside on her own. Just because she didn't need the weapon didn't mean it didn't come in handy. Especially when dealing with rowdy human males who wandered onto her land, thinking they could cause trouble with the woman who lived there on her own. And right now, it felt unbelievably sweet to point the gleaming barrel directly at Cian Hennessey's no-good heart.

He shot her a dry look and slowly arched one of his raven-black brows. "It's a pretty toy," he drawled, the lazy way he crossed his muscular arms over his chest telling her he didn't believe for one second that she'd shoot him. "But you know that bullets won't kill me, Sayre."

"They might not kill you, but they'll hurt like a bitch."

"You really think I could believe that you'd pull the trigger? You're a healer, not a—"

"Seriously?" she laughed, cutting him off as she unlocked the safety with a practiced flick of her thumb. "You might have watched me grow up, Cian, but don't for an instant think that you know what I'm capable of as a woman. I've had to deal with more crap since you left than you could ever imagine. People change. *I've* changed. So when I pull a gun out, you can bet your ass that I plan to use it."

His sexy mouth pressed into a hard, irritated, challenging line. "Then do it."

She aimed for less than an inch from the toe of his right boot, and fired a perfect shot.

"Shit!" he cursed, jumping back a step. "What the hell, woman? Have you lost your bloody mind?"

"I told you I'd do it." She kept her tone hard and cold, determined to make him see that she meant business, and slowly raised her aim. "So tell me, Cian. Do you really want to play this game?"

He worked his jaw for a few seconds, no doubt cursing her to hell and back. Then his scowl smoothed out, and his eyes narrowed to the point that it was impossible to read the look in them. Whatever he was thinking as he calmly turned on his heel and headed back to his car— the back view of his tall, powerful body damn near as mouthwatering as the front—was something he didn't want her to pick up on. And *that* made her nervous.

When she called his name out, just as he was opening his car door, he looked back at her over his broad shoulder, and she gave him a sharp, icy smile. "If you like your body without any extra holes in it, *don't* bother coming back."

Chapter 3

Knowing Sayre needed some time to calm down, Cian climbed back into the Audi. He drove nearly a quarter of a mile down the mountain, then pulled over into a flat grassy area on the side of the road and parked. Though he never would have believed it, the beautiful little witch *had* been ready to put a freaking bullet in him. He'd have been incredibly proud over the way she'd stood up for herself, if her target had been anything other than his own body...and the circumstances weren't so serious.

But they were, which was why there was no way in hell he was tucking his tail between his legs and running. This was nothing but a change in strategy, and a good hunter always knew when to step back and regroup. So while he might have let her think she'd won the first round, he was already focused on the second, determined to be the one who came out on top in the end.

On top of her, *you mean*, the wolf's gravelly voice rumbled in his head, and he rolled his eyes at the beast's wishful thinking. Not that it wouldn't have been nice— and by nice he meant fucking exceptional—but he knew that sex was the last damn thing he could afford to think about in connection with Sayre. Too much of that al-

ready took place when he finally allowed himself to
sleep.

Though he'd tried not to, Cian had been dreaming
about Sayre Murphy from the moment he'd walked away.
Hell, even before that, when he was still living in the
Alley and fighting his need for her on a daily basis. But
the dreams had been…*evolving* over the last few months,
and while many of them were more nightmare than fantasy now, the erotic ones were becoming shockingly intense. Not that they'd ever been tame—but there was a
feverish, visceral edge to them now that had him strung
so tightly he was surprised he hadn't snapped. Over the
past few weeks, he'd awakened so many times thrusting
and clawing at his sheets that he'd started to feel like a
perpetually randy teen again, and God only knew he'd
spent too many years perfecting *that* testosterone-driven
stage of his life.

But even his dreams hadn't done the reality of her
justice.

Sayre at eighteen had been beautiful. But Sayre at
twenty-three was enough to make him want to sell his
goddamn soul for the chance to touch her. She was *that*
incredible. So earthy and warm and sensual that it'd
taken every ounce of his strength to claw on to his control when he'd approached her, instead of taking her
down to the ground and claiming every inch of her lush
little body for his own.

Only the certainty that she'd hate him in the end had
enabled him to fight that fierce, possessive pull. That…
and the fact that he had no business touching her when
he could never give her the things she deserved. Christ,
he couldn't even give her next month, much less promises of love and a family and forever.

Careful to stay hidden, he made his way back up the mountain on foot and studied her cabin from the shelter of the woods. The place was small but pretty, surrounded by a large, colorful garden that was obviously well tended. But the location couldn't have been more remote if she'd moved to the wilds of Alaska, and it twisted his insides to think of her being stuck out here all alone. It was the last thing in the world he would have expected for the girl who'd always greeted everyone with a smile and a hug; she'd always been an effortless little social butterfly who people couldn't help but want to be around.

Though there were a lot of Lycans who went away to attend university among the human population, he knew that Sayre had planned on going to a local school for a degree in environmental studies. He hadn't understood why she was so determined to stay with the pack while she continued her education, but now he thought that maybe he did. If her powers had been increasing to the point that she was having trouble dealing with them, she might have worried over what would happen if she were too far away from her family. He hated that she'd carried that kind of burden back then; girls in their teens didn't need to be worrying about such serious issues. But Sayre had fought in the war right along with the rest of her family, and it'd been apparent even then that her powers were...different. She'd already been capable of firing powerful bursts of light from her hands, and had taken down the enemy with a skill that had completely shocked him—though young, she'd shown no mercy to those who would have harmed her loved ones.

And now this. Instead of finishing her studies and starting to find her way in the world, she was living like a recluse in the goddamn mountains, all alone. No family. No friends. He felt to blame, even though he hadn't been there. But wasn't it better for her to be alone than to be with someone like him?

Not wanting to think about the answer to that question, he glanced at the thick, military-grade watch on his wrist, surprised she hadn't come down to check that he'd followed her orders and left. Did she actually believe he would just turn and walk away when her life was in danger?

Only you never actually got around to telling her that part, did you? his beast muttered, making him scowl. He didn't need the animal telling him what he already knew. Yeah, he should have explained the seriousness of the situation to her right from the start, but he'd had his reasons for holding back.

At first, he'd simply been too dumbstruck by how she'd changed, and he couldn't blame himself for that. He'd all but been knocked back on his ass by the sight of her. But then he'd told her there wasn't time to explain, which was bullshit. He could have *made* the time, but the fact was that he simply hadn't been ready to spill the whole sordid story. Telling her meant giving her one more reason to hate him, and she already had enough of those.

But no matter how angry she was, or how much the situation sucked, he wasn't leaving this mountain without her. He might have turned his back on her before, but only because he'd thought it was the best way to keep her safe.

Only…the danger had found her anyway, hadn't it? Which meant that for all his running, he was still stuck in the same destructive loop, and there didn't seem to be any way out of it. Not until Aedan no longer hung over his life like a malevolent shadow, ready to wreak pain, terror and death on anything that he wanted for himself.

The minutes moved by in a slow crawl, the air hot and sticky with humidity, though he barely noticed, his attention completely fixated on Sayre as the witch went about her daily routine. Every now and again, he would pick up the muted sounds of her voice as she talked to herself, the low words edged with anger and frustration. He'd definitely pissed her off by coming there, which meant that she was still angry about the way he'd left and hadn't gotten over it. That she hadn't forgotten him. And as wrong as it was, he liked that she'd been thinking about him all these years. That he'd made a big enough impact on her life to be remembered.

You're her life mate, dimwit, his wolf grunted. *Not like she can just forget that little tidbit.*

"Piss off," he muttered, knowing damn well that the beast was right.

Are we going to just stand out here all day? the animal persisted. *Because we belong over there with her. We belong* inside *her.*

He choked back a curse, the need searing through his veins making him sweat even more than the heat. He'd never so much as kissed Sayre, and yet, he strongly suspected that sex with her would be unlike anything he'd ever known. Just the fantasy of it overshadowed every woman he'd ever been with, and there'd been so many. *Too many.* Faces and bodies and names that he wouldn't have been able to recall to save his life—which only made him that much more of a bastard.

The wind finally picked up, but he was far enough away that he didn't need to worry she would scent him on the air. Though Lycan blood pumped through her veins, she was unable to take the shape of a wolf, which meant she didn't have the same heightened abilities as the rest of them. Instead, the women in her bloodline were known as witches, or healers. They were each powerful in their own right, but he'd never felt the charge of energy surrounding a Lycan-born witch like he had with Sayre. She was truly in a class of her own, and he couldn't help but wonder how those powers would mature as she grew older.

He seriously doubted that she needed the gun. Though he'd once been able to force his way through her power, when they'd been in the heat of battle and he'd been hell-bent on protecting her, she was stronger now. If she'd wanted, he was sure she could have blasted him with enough energy to put him out of commission for the rest of the day—and Christ, that was sexy. Everything about the woman was…intoxicating. He'd always thought she was beautiful in an ethereal, fey kind of way, and had been intensely attracted to her. But now…*Jesus*. There honestly weren't words to describe the way she affected him. Her curly hair had to be a good seven inches longer, reaching the middle of her back, the color a deeper red that was shot through with streaks of gold, no doubt from all the time she spent outdoors. Her once thin, coltish body was now deliciously curved, her breasts and ass a little fuller, giving her slender figure a more lush, womanly look. He couldn't help but imagine what this new shape of hers would feel like spread out beneath him, all that sweet, creamy flesh his for the taking.

But his attraction to Sayre Murphy had always been about more than her looks, and that hadn't changed. If anything, the force of her will held an even deeper draw for him now, her fiery spirit when combined with her tender nature creating an alluring package that would entice any man, but especially the one chosen by fate as her perfect match. Everything about her was designed to please him, and a gruff, troubled burst of laughter softly fell from his lips as he scrubbed a hand over his face, knowing he was in some seriously deep shit. Even if she weren't the sexiest thing he'd ever set eyes on, he'd have wanted her. The fact that her innate sensuality was even more prevalent now, her mouth and scent and the husky sound of her voice calling to him on every primitive level, well…that was just overkill. A play of the universe to make the coming days as excruciatingly painful as possible. Hell, at this rate, he was pretty sure he'd feel like he'd gone ten rounds in a medieval torture chamber by the time this nightmare was over. And he'd no doubt bear the scars to prove it, on his skin as well as his blackened heart.

Keep her alive and keep my hands to myself. That needed to be his new mantra—but the second part wouldn't be easy. When she stood up after tending another colorful flower bed and lifted her arms over her head to stretch her back, the little tank top she wore rising up to reveal her sexy tummy and a tiny, dark tattoo that was scrolled around her navel, he realized it would be damn near impossible.

Sweet little Sayre had a tattoo?

Holy…shit. He was fairly certain that his jaw had just dropped down to somewhere around his ankles, his cock so hard he probably wasn't going to be able to walk straight. He didn't know what the intricate symbols of the tattoo meant, but he'd have sold his damn soul in that moment for the chance to drop down on his knees

in front of her and press his open mouth to that provocative little piece of artwork. And he sure as hell wouldn't
stop there. Trailing his tongue down the center of her
body, he would keep going until he was breathing in the
sweet, humid scent of her where it would be the rich-
est. Like hot, wild honey on his tongue, melting down
his throat, making him hunger in a way he didn't think
any human male could ever completely experience. A
hunger that went deeper than his flesh—that bled down
into his veins and his bones and pumped through the
very heart of him.

A drop of sweat slid down the searing heat of his temple, stinging the corner of his eye, and he shook himself
out of his thoughts, painfully aware that they weren't
leading to any place he'd be able to go. And damned
if it weren't enough to make him want to bawl like a
friggin' baby. Or howl at the rising moon.

When she reached for something in the back pocket
of those short-as-hell shorts and started to walk around
the back of the cabin, Cian pushed off from the tree
he'd been leaning against, ready to change his position
so that she wasn't out of his sight. But he froze when
his cell phone suddenly vibrated in the front pocket of
his jeans, his brows lifting with surprise. He was un-
used to anyone trying to contact him, since the number
was one he'd gotten after he'd left five years ago, and
there were only a few informants he'd employed over
that time who he'd given it to. They rarely contacted
him, and how was he even getting reception out here?

This is so ridiculous. I know you're out there. Leave. Now.
Before I go all West Virginia on your ass.

The text was from Sayre?

How the hell did you get my number?

I asked Mic for it.

Ah, that's right. He'd texted Brody that morning, so his number was in the Runner's phone. All Mic had to do was—

Enough stalling, his beast snapped, cutting him off. *Text her back!*

How did you know I'm out here?

That's not the issue, Cian. Leave. Like I told you before, I don't want you here.

He rubbed the back of his neck, wondering just how strong her powers had gotten over the last five years. Christ, she couldn't read his mind, could she? No, if she could, then she'd know about the danger from Aedan, which meant she'd understand how serious he was about taking her back to the Alley, where the others could help him protect her.

Knowing he just needed to get it over and done with, like ripping off a bloody bandage, his fingers flew across the keypad as he typed in his response.

I can't leave, Sayre. I'm here because you're in danger. You need to give me the chance to explain.

She didn't text back right away, and he hoped she was finally taking him seriously. Then his phone vibrated again.

No explanations needed. If that's true, then I can take care of myself. Just go.

He cursed, hesitating, then forced himself to write:

I can't. It's because of me.

Huh. So what did YOU do? Do I have some psychotic jilted lover coming after me now? Did you accidentally let it slip that you have a mate? Should've told the poor woman you want nothing to do with me. She's wasting her time.

Oh, Jesus. He barked out a dry laugh, even though there was nothing remotely funny about the situation. Not want her? There were parts of her he wanted so badly he was surprised the need hadn't permanently damaged him.

Would serve you right, his beast muttered with disgust, as disappointed in him as everyone else who had ever meant anything to him.

You're damned right I am. And you sound pathetic.

Irritated that the animal had just called him out for taking part in an embarrassing private pity party, he started to make his way toward the cabin, ready to face the wrath of Sayre *and* her gun, when he and his beast both instantly realized something was wrong. While the wolf chuffed in his head, Cian lifted his nose and sniffed the mountain air, searching for what had snagged his attention, and promptly finding it. Two…no, three human males were closing in on Sayre's cabin from the north, and Cian stealthily headed in their direction, until he could pick up their muted conversation.

"Oh, man, he didn't tell us she was such a hot little piece. I'm thinking we need to try this one out before we deliver her," one of them said, obviously eyeing Sayre through the trees.

"I get her first," argued a second male.

"Like hell you do," a new voice cackled. "You always break them and then they aren't any fun for the rest of us."

"But I've got a thing for redheads," the second one whined.

"We don't give a shit. You can wait your fuckin' turn."

Cian moved silently through the trees, drawing nearer, every part of him completely focused on his prey. Did these idiots actually think he was going to let them get close to her? Did they have any idea what they were walking into? Either way, it didn't matter. Their fates had been sealed the instant they voiced their intentions.

"Let's spread out, blocking her exits. That asshole who hired us said it might be a few days before he showed up to collect her, and I'd rather spend the time we've got with her having fun than running her down."

One of his friends snickered. "That's just because your bum knees don't hold up anymore. But I kinda like the thought of chasing her down like a bitch."

In that moment, Cian almost regretted the necessity of killing them quickly. It no doubt made him a brutal bastard, but he would have enjoyed making these assholes suffer long and hard before he finally finished them off.

He quickly texted Sayre, ordering her to lock herself inside the cabin. Then he shoved the phone in his pocket, and released his long, lethal fangs and claws, the sharp tips piercing through gum and skin with a brief but familiar bite of pain. Without the light of the moon, this was as much as his body could shift form, but it was more than enough. Whatever weapons the humans possessed, they weren't going to be any match for his speed and skill.

In normal circumstances, he would have never revealed the deadly, animalistic side of his nature in front of humans, since the Lycan race's existence was a carefully protected secret from the vast majority of the population. But these weren't normal circumstances, and these assholes weren't ever going to leave this mountain.

Relaxing his tether on his beast, Cian allowed the wolf to prowl closer to his surface, the animal's possessive, visceral need to protect its mate punching deeper into his system, ramping his adrenaline at the same time he shifted into a state of total focus. His objective was extremely simple: destroy the threat by any means necessary. With a deep breath and a flex of his claws, he launched his attack.

It took only seconds to find the first male in the line of trees behind her cabin, the vile stench of body odor impossible to miss for someone with Cian's acute sense of smell. He slashed his claws across the human's throat and swiftly retreated to avoid as much of the thick, crimson spray as he could. Its rich scent had his pulse ramping up, the blackened part of his soul that he hated with such ferocity awakening with the rush for *more*. For that wet, slick spill to slide down his throat and feed the darkness. Forcing himself to abandon the kill and move on, he quickly closed in on the second human from behind, the bastard never even knowing he was there until he felt the sharp press of Cian's blood-covered claws tearing across his throat as his body crumpled to the forest floor.

Two down, one to go.

The third male had made his way around the eastern edge of her property, intending to cut off Sayre from the south. Following the scent of cheap beer and stale sweat, Cian easily found the human standing between two towering trees as the last vestiges of sunlight held on, not yet ready to release its claim to the day. There was a nauseating leer on the bastard's face as he stared at her cabin, his tongue slicking across his lips while he tapped the blade of a hunting knife against his thigh. Cian was giving private thanks that Sayre had actually listened to him and gone inside, when she suddenly stepped out from behind the small shed not ten yards away from where the man stood, holding a rifle in her arms. He heard the click of the gun a fraction of a second before she fired a bullet into the male's thigh. The force of Sayre's shot sent the human crashing to the ground, and Cian quickly finished him off with a fatal swipe of his claws before turning toward the headstrong woman who apparently didn't know how to follow orders to save her life.

It took him six strides to reach her, and while she lowered the gun, she didn't even try to run. Retracting his blood-drenched claws, he ripped the gun out of her hold and tossed it aside. Then he quickly gripped her upper arms, yanked her up onto her toes and roared, "What the hell, Sayre? I told you to stay inside the cabin!"

"Like I give a rat's ass what you told me to do!" she shouted back at him.

"You got a death wish, little girl?" He got right in her

face, his voice dropping to a sibilant hiss. "Because that was the dumbest move I've ever seen anyone make."

Shaking with fury, she began using her power to try and make him release her, but he refused to budge. If he'd been human, the palms of his hands would have no doubt been blistered within a few seconds, unable to endure the searing burst of heat she was generating without letting go. He growled at her, but she didn't so much as bat an eyelash, and he realized this female— *his female*—was a woman who would never cower before a man. Raging, intense pride and lust fired through his system, his blood thickening low in his body, while his heart thundered like something trying to break its way free.

With another rough, guttural growl, Cian forced himself to slowly set her back on her feet as he loosened his grip on her arms. He knew that if he didn't put some distance between them right then, there was a strong chance he was going to take her to the moss-covered ground beneath their feet and drive himself so deep inside her he wouldn't ever find his way back out.

"Who were those men?" she demanded, ripping out of his hold.

"My brother," he grunted, only to realize that his words didn't make any sense. "I mean, none of those men were Aedan. But I'm guessing they were working for him."

She blinked up at him with dark, gold-tipped lashes. "What are you talking about? You don't have a brother."

"It's a long story, but I'll explain on the road." Well, he'd explain some of it. No way in hell was he telling her everything.

"Cian."

"Listen. Next time, he won't send a bunch of human thugs. Those guys were just a game to him, Sayre. A message meant to let us know that he's found you and has you in his sights. But he won't play the game for long. Eventually, it will be *him*, in the flesh, and I know you don't trust me, but you can believe me when I tell you that going head-to-head with Aedan isn't something we could walk away from without paying for it first. Not here. Not alone."

She cut her gaze to the side and frowned. "I—"

"Damn it, Sayre, look at me!" He worked his jaw as her narrowed gaze locked with his, then grated out, "I can't let that happen. I *won't*. I will throw you in my damn car and tie you up if I have to, though I'd rather you come on your own. I don't want to hurt you, but there's no way I'm letting you stay here. He's *not* getting you."

She opened her mouth, then snapped it shut. He could see the indecision shadowing her gaze, her intuition battling against her desire to be rid of him. He could understand her anger, but he couldn't let it get in the way of keeping her alive.

"If not for yourself, then think about Jillian. About Jeremy and their kids," he told her. Jillian had been pregnant when he'd left, so he knew the couple had at least one child. "You don't think he'd go after them if he thought it would hurt you?"

Color leached from her face, making the spray of freckles across her nose stand out in stark relief. "What the hell do me and my family have to do with any of this?"

"He wants to hurt me, and he thinks you're the way to do that."

A bitter laugh burst from her pink lips, and she shook her head in disbelief. "Then he's a fool. I didn't even mean enough to you to fuck. I was just a troublesome little girl you wanted out of your way."

Christ, she couldn't have been more wrong, but he couldn't tell her that. And he sure as hell couldn't let himself think about that four-letter word that had just fallen from her lips—a word he'd never heard her say before. "Sayre, we don't have time to argue. We need to be on the road ten minutes ago."

She stared up at him as the seconds stretched out, each one seeming to last longer than a lifetime while his hands itched with the need to reach out and grab her so that he could get her to safety. "Fine," she finally agreed, looking as if someone had just thrown her firstborn off a cliff. "I hate it, but I'm not going to cut off my nose to spite my face."

"Smart girl," he murmured with relief.

"*Woman*, Cian. Smart *woman*. I'm no longer a child."

"Uh, yeah. Got it." Then he tacked on a "sorry" for good measure.

Jabbing him in the center of his chest with her finger, she said, "You're damned right you had better be sorry. Because this is *all. Your. Fault!*"

Guilt settled heavily in his gut, and he knew he needed to tread carefully. "I know, and I'm sorry. But can we please just get on the road?"

Shaking her head, she said, "No."

"No?" He sucked in a sharp breath, struggling not to shout at her again. "I thought we just went over this."

"I believe that you've landed me in the middle of a freaking problem, but that doesn't mean I'm running back to the Alley. However—" her voice sounded like she'd swallowed a handful of razor blades as she held one hand up to him in a hold-it-right-there gesture "—I'm willing to let you come inside and talk to me."

"I'm not letting you stay here alone, Sayre."

"Then you had better not piss me off," she huffed as she walked over to where he'd tossed her gun and picked it up, "because I was planning on letting you take the sofa until we have this figured out."

Shit, he thought, shoving a hand back through his hair. Staying here wasn't what he wanted. He needed her in the Alley, where he knew it would be easier to protect her. "It's safer there, Sayre."

With the gun propped on her shoulder, she turned back to him, her expression impossible to read. "That may be. But I'm not going to let you rush me into any decisions right now. I will give myself some time to process this, and then I'll let you know what I've decided to do."

He closed his eyes for a moment, dropping his head back on his shoulders, and counted back from ten.

"While you're struggling with whatever's going through that thick head of yours," she told him, sounding as if she were gloating a bit, "I'll just run inside and grab my keys, then take you down the road so that you can grab your car and bring it back here."

Opening his eyes, Cian lowered his head and watched her walk away, wondering how she made the money to pay for the truck and the cabin, knowing she wasn't the type to live off her parents. Then again, the truck that was parked beside the shed was fairly ancient, so he knew she hadn't unloaded a ton of cash on it.

"You were wrong," he said in a low voice, when she came back outside, keys in hand.

"About what?" she murmured, keeping her gaze focused straight ahead as she made her way over to the faded blue Ford.

"When I first saw you today," he muttered, following after her, "you said we'd never lied to each other. But we did. *I* did. I lied to you all the time."

She didn't ask what he'd lied about as she opened the driver's-side door and climbed behind the wheel, and he wondered if she knew.

He'd told her time and again that he didn't want her.

And each time, it'd been a lie.

In his entire life, he'd never wanted anything like he wanted Sayre Murphy. In his bed. Under him. Completely full of him, his body packed so deeply into hers she could feel him in every part of her. Every cell and breath and thought.

He just didn't want the rest of her.

The last thing in the world that Cian needed was a woman's heart, because he knew exactly what he'd do to it. And while he might not love Sayre Murphy, he liked her too much to want to see her crushed, which is what would happen. It wasn't arrogance or his ego talking; it was a simple fact. She was too young to clearly separate sexual need from higher emotion, and he knew that if he touched her, she'd likely end up thinking she was in love with him. Wasn't there a saying about how hate and love were simply two sides of the same coin? So while she might hate him now, that feeling could be twisted into the other. After everything he'd done, he owed it to her to keep that from happening.

Does that mean you plan to keep your hands to yourself? his wolf demanded, prowling beneath his skin. *'Cause I gotta tell you, that doesn't work for me. If*

*given the chance, I plan on getting between those per-
fect thighs of hers and staying there, where we belong.*

He made a gruff sound in the back of his throat, wishing the animal would just shut up and leave him alone.

And by the way, I still think you're an idiot. Jackass.

Irritated, tired and at the end of his rope, his grip
tightened on the passenger's-side door handle until he'd
nearly ripped it off, the beast's guttural laughter echoing
through his head as he climbed up into the truck. It knew
it'd gotten under his skin, and he wondered if his friends
all had this much trouble with the possessive predators
who lived inside them, or if it were only him. Seemed
just his luck that his wolf would not only be a pain of
the first order, but a sarcastic son of a bitch, as well.

"Cian?" Sayre said as she cranked the engine and slid
him a curious look. "Are you going to sit there growling
at your door all day or are you going to shut it?"

He didn't bother to respond. He didn't dare. He didn't
trust anything that might have come out of his mouth
at that moment, and his pulse was thrashing in his ears
too loudly to carry on a conversation anyway.

Instead, he slammed the door shut, rolled the window down and focused his attention on the surrounding woods, knowing that Aedan could very well be out
there, watching and waiting, slowly biding his time. The
human thugs had been his brother's first play, but they
wouldn't be his last.

And now the clock was ticking.

Chapter 4

As soon as he parked the Audi behind Sayre's truck and climbed out, a terrible sense of doom settled over Cian, hanging around his shoulders like a leaden weight. It sounded embarrassingly dramatic, but there was no denying the emotion. It was like a thundering death knell echoing in his head, warning him that nothing about this situation was going to end in the way that he wanted it to. He *knew*, damn it…and yet, he couldn't turn back.

Instead, he simply followed her into the small cabin, doing his best to keep his attention focused on their surroundings and not on how tight her little ass looked in those too-short-for-his-sanity shorts.

Seriously? You sound like an old man who doesn't even know how to get it up anymore.

"Fuck off," he muttered under his breath, mentally giving his wolf the finger. It wasn't a question of not being able to get it up. It was knowing how quickly she'd have his friggin' balls kicked in if he let the sight of her in those shorts take hold of him.

While she closed the door behind them, he did a quick survey of the room. The cabin was built with an open floor plan, the walls lined with row upon row of packed bookshelves, the bindings on the books creased from use. A hallway on the right led to what he assumed would be her bedroom and the bathroom, the kitchen located off to their left. There was a high-tech sound system on a small table in the corner of the main room, but no television. If she watched movies, it was likely on her computer or iPad, and he recalled Jillian once talking about her sister's penchant for comedies.

A scowl twisted his brow as he tried to recall the last comedy he'd watched. It'd no doubt been something he'd caught down at one of the cinemas in the human town of Covington with Brody before he'd left, but he couldn't remember the title. Just that he hadn't felt like he got even half of the jokes, and he'd hated how old that'd made him feel.

He hated it even more now, when there was a so-beautiful-she-hurt-his-eyes twenty-three-year-old walking away from him as she headed toward the kitchen. She would probably laugh her ass off if she knew he'd "technically" be pushing fifty in a few years.

His body might be young—he halted the aging process when consuming blood as one of his main food sources—but his spirit felt freaking ancient, as if he'd lived three times that long.

As she washed her hands at the kitchen sink, she looked at him from over her shoulder, eyeing his blood-spattered jeans and T-shirt, and jerked her head in the direction of the small hallway. "You're messier than I am. Why don't you go ahead and grab your shower? It's the first door on your left. Towels are under the sink."

Taking a few steps toward the kitchen, he said, "Actually, I should go and bury the bodies first."

She turned around as she dried her hands on a towel, blinking back at him with those big, storm-colored eyes.

"Um...of course. I wasn't...I don't know why I didn't think of that."

Because she wasn't a natural born killer, like he was. And because she was also probably a bit in shock, after everything that had happened. She might have grown up in the hard, often brutal world of the Silvercrest, but Sayre Murphy had always been a dreamer at heart. And dreamers weren't the kind of girls who were accustomed to burying three dead bodies out in the woods behind their homes.

"Is there a shovel in your shed?"

She pulled her lower lip through her teeth and nodded.

The sight of her white teeth on that plush lip had him sweating, and he cleared his throat a little as he swiped his arm over his forehead. "Then you go ahead and grab your shower," he told her, the roughness of his voice telling him he needed to get back outside and cool the hell off. "This won't take me long."

Her eyebrows lifted slightly. "Don't you need help?"

Shaking his head, he said, "I'm not letting you anywhere near them, Sayre. But I won't go too far. I'll be close enough that I can hear you if you need me."

He turned and walked back outside before she could say anything more, and pulled in a deep breath of the humid air as he headed for the shed. A half hour later, he was shoveling the last scoops of dirt over the place where he'd buried the bodies, the grave situated between two thick blackberry bushes that would quickly grow over it. He'd checked all three males' clothing before putting them in the ground, looking for anything that might give him a clue about Aedan's plans, but wasn't surprised when the search turned up nothing. His half brother might be seriously twisted, but he was too smart to make a dumb-ass mistake by trusting anyone like these jackasses with vital information. That was why Cian hadn't bothered to keep one of them alive for questioning.

That…and the fact that he'd been too bloody furious to let them live.

After putting the shovel away in the shed, Cian made his way back inside the cabin, locking the door behind him. He couldn't hear the water running, so he knew Sayre was out of the shower. The sound of a hair dryer clicking on told him she'd be busy for a while longer, so he washed his hands in the kitchen, then went through the French doors that opened onto a small deck and took out his phone. After scrolling through his contacts, he called Brody's cell phone number.

Within two rings, the Runner answered the call. "Where the hell are you? I thought you were bringing her back."

"That's still the plan," he said in a low voice, unsure how much of this shit storm he should explain over the phone. "But it looks like we're staying here tonight."

Brody exhaled a rough breath. "I told you she wouldn't do it."

"Yeah, well, she doesn't have a choice. We ran into some trouble, which I've handled, but this place isn't safe enough for her in the long term. I need her *in* the Alley, with all of your full security measures in place."

"I've sent Michaela up to Shadow Peak with our kids, since you wouldn't tell me what's going on. And I've told Jillian to stay up there, as well, right now. The others are going to stay down in South Carolina until we know it's safe for them to return with their families."

"That's good," he murmured, wondering what had kept Jillian behind. Had the witch had a premonition that her sister would need her?

Brody's next words pulled his attention back to the conversation. "Max and Elliot have been out on a Bloodrun, but they'll be back in the morning. And the mercs have been working a job over in Tennessee, but they're expected back in the next day or two. So we'll have security covered, and I'll have the scouts from up in Shadow Peak double their patrols. But we need to know what we're dealing with."

At the mention of the mercs, Cian's already tensed muscles coiled even tighter, and he pinched the bridge of his nose between his thumb and forefinger. The mercenaries were four badass warriors who had worked with Eli Drake for years, and had decided to stick around once Eli had returned to the Alley and married Carla Reyes, the only female Runner in the group.

"This silence is getting kind of tiring, man. You there?" Brody asked.

"Yeah, I'm here," he muttered, keeping a careful eye on the surrounding forest.

"You ready to tell me what's going on?"

He swallowed so hard he could feel the movement all the way down his throat. "This...it's not something I want to get into over the phone, Brody." Hell, it was something he'd rather avoid altogether. But that wasn't going to be an option. "And before you try to argue, don't. You're just going to have to trust me on this."

Brody's deep voice was gruff with frustration. "Yeah, well, it was easier to trust you before you disappeared for five years."

He bit back a guttural curse, knowing there wasn't

anything he could say to that particular piece of truth. Part of him was eager to prove to his friends that he was still the same man he'd been before, while another part kept wondering what the point would be, when he would only leave again when it was all said and done.

"Cian, man, I'm serious. You better talk to me or you won't be welcome back in the Alley. I hate to say that, but I don't know where your head is anymore."

He scrubbed his free hand down his face, his insides knotting. So many emotions roiled through him, clashing like warring, blood-drenched sides on a battlefield, that it was impossible to keep them straight. "I swear I'll tell you everything when we get back. I just…" He worked his jaw as his words dried up, hating that he couldn't simply avoid this problem forever. With a tired sigh, he said, "In all honesty, Brody, I need some time to figure out how to say it all."

Silence met his admission, followed by a rough, quiet burst of words. "It's that bad?"

"Yeah. But I won't leave you in the dark. I give you my word on that."

"Then we'll talk when you get back," Brody muttered. "But I need to know if Sayre is okay. Jillian gave Mic and me an earful for not warning the girl that you were coming for her. Jilly's been trying to get her on her cell phone, but Sayre won't take the calls. Just texted back that she was fine and would be in touch later."

"She's good. Pissed, but she's all right."

"Okay then. You need any backup on the road when you head back?"

Unable to resist having her all to himself for just a little longer, he said, "Thanks for the offer, but I think we've got a few days before we need to worry."

"Then keep me updated."

"I will. And stay sharp. There's no reason for you to see any trouble when she's not there, but it's better to be safe."

"On it," the Runner murmured, then disconnected the call. Shoving the phone in his pocket, Cian walked back inside just as the bathroom door clicked open, releasing a wave of warm, Sayre-scented air into the cabin. He couldn't see into the hallway from where he stood, but what was probably her bedroom door snapped shut a moment later. He debated going back outside for a smoke, but decided to simply wait her out, loving the way that intoxicating scent was filling his lungs, working its way through his system.

He spent the next moments looking over the titles on her bookshelves, surprised she was into gritty suspense novels, many of the books ones he'd already read. He lost track of time as he walked around the room, soaking up all the telling details like a sponge with water, hoarding them in his mind. They were like tiny clues that he needed to unlock the mystery of her life, his brain cataloguing everything from the scent of her candles to the type of pen she'd left sitting on top of a notebook. The sofa was off-white and deep, his mind easily picturing her cuddled up among the matching throw pillows with a book, while the evening sunlight touched on the feminine curves of her body. The sensual slope of a shoulder. The lithe shape of her thighs. He stood in the middle of the room, each breath drawing more of her provocative scent into his lungs, while his hands flexed and released at his sides. His tension just kept winding tighter…and tighter, until he nearly stumbled from the jolt of hunger that slammed into him when she came back into the room a few minutes later.

Christ, he thought as he got a good look at her. *Is she trying to kill me?*

The cutoffs had been exchanged for a pair of jeans that hugged her curves like a second skin, her tight black T-shirt molding to a pair of breasts so perfect they made his mouth water. Her skin was still dewy and pink from the shower and the sun, and he had to physically hold himself back from her. Had to fight the animalistic urge to yank her against him and run his tongue up the slender column of her throat, taking all that salty warmth into his mouth. Summer heat had never looked so good on a woman, and he knew he needed to get out of there before he did something stupid.

"Shower's all yours," she told him, her gaze focused on the base of his throat instead of his eyes.

"Thanks." His voice was gruff, but he couldn't help it. She'd taken a step toward him, bringing her into the last wash of sunlight that spilled through one of the front windows, the shimmering beams highlighting the strips of gold buried in all those waves of strawberry-blond. He wanted to search out every strand…wind the long skeins around his fist…and hold her tight. Pull her to him. Into his arms. Until she was trapped there.

And that's my cue to get the hell out of here.

Grabbing the leather bag he'd left by the front door, Cian headed toward the bathroom without so much as another glance in her direction. But it was hardly any better once he was alone in the tiny white-tiled room. Her scent lingered in the steamy air, and he pressed his shoulders against the door as he dropped the bag on the floor, his head pressed back against the wood as he squeezed his eyes shut and clawed on to every ounce of self-control he could find. He needed it like an alcoholic standing before an open bar, the shiny bottles tempting him with *drink me...drink me...drink me*. Though in his case, the words were coming from Sayre's soft lips, her husky voice curling around him like sensual tendrils of heat.

It actually hurt a part of him deep inside to be near her like this. And, yeah, it'd been pure hell to be so far away from her for so long. But this....*Jesus*. This was torture on a level he'd never experienced before, and he still hadn't managed to get a handle on the right way to deal with it.

He ended up taking the coldest shower of his life, knowing if he lingered he was liable to take matters into his own hands. And he instinctively knew it wouldn't be enough.

Fifteen minutes later, when Cian headed back out into the living room, it felt like he was walking into some kind of surreal new reality that didn't fit in his world. The delicious scent of sizzling vegetables and Asian spices drifted to his nose, and he looked toward the kitchen, surprised to see Sayre standing with her back to him as she stirred something in a pan on the stove.

What the...? Was she making him *dinner*?

A slight flush warmed her cheeks as she glanced at him over her shoulder, sweeping those big eyes over the clean clothes that covered his body. "It's getting kinda late, so I figured I should throw something together for us to eat."

"Thanks."

"It's not much," she murmured, her gaze seeming to

linger a bit on his chest before she quickly looked away. "Just some veggie stir-fry and salad."

"That sounds great, Sayre. Anything I can do to help?" he asked, biting back the words he really wanted to say. *Lose your clothes and let me touch and lick and nibble on every mouthwatering inch of you* wasn't the kind of thing he needed to be thinking when it came to this woman, much less saying out loud.

He joined her in the kitchen, the two of them working in silence as she finished the noodles and he pulled down plates and glasses from the glass-fronted cupboards. Though they weren't speaking, he could see her clever mind working overtime as he watched her from the corner of his eye, the hammering pulse at the base of her throat telling him she was anything but unaffected by his presence.

"Do you want to sit outside?" she asked him, once the stir-fry and salad had been dished onto their plates. "It's probably cooler out there."

"It'll be safer inside," he replied, carrying his plate and glass of iced tea into the living room.

"Suit yourself," she said, taking a seat in one of the chairs while he sat on the sofa. "But I don't have a TV for you to veg out in front of."

"Not a problem." He never watched TV much anyway, which seemed to be something they had in common. He preferred to be outdoors, his time indoors usually spent in a bed. Though since he'd left the Alley, he'd gotten damn good at losing himself in a book, during those brief periods of time when he hadn't been searching for Aedan.

He was nearly halfway through the delicious meal, enjoying simply being in her presence without arguing, when she finally looked over at him and said, "Your accent seems stronger now. Have you been living back in Ireland?"

"I've traveled a lot, but I have an apartment in Dublin."

She swallowed a bite of salad, then sighed. "I bet it's beautiful."

"Dublin?"

Sounding more than a little wistful, she said, "Ireland. All of it. I've always wanted to go, but…well, traveling isn't something that really works for me now."

He took a drink of his tea, then slid his gaze back to hers. "That sucks," he offered in a low voice, wondering why he was stating the friggin' obvious. Of course it *sucked*. She'd basically been living like a recluse up on this goddamn mountain, and on that note, he muttered, "I can't believe Brody and the others didn't put anyone on you for protection out here."

"They tried," she said flatly, turning her attention back to her plate. "But no matter how sneaky they were about it, I could still pick up on them. When they realized they were only hurting me more, they finally just let me be."

Since hearing that made him want to destroy something with his bare hands, he forced himself to change the subject and think of something positive to say. It wasn't easy, considering all he felt like at that moment was kicking his own ass for all the mistakes that he'd made, but he finally came up with a worthy compliment. "You've turned this into a beautiful place, Sayre. The, uh, garden is incredible."

Her mouth twisted with something caught between a wry smile and a grimace. "Thanks. It keeps me busy."

"Well, you're obviously amazing at it."

Shrugging one feminine shoulder, she kept her attention focused on the noodles she was twirling around her fork. "They like my touch, so it's easy."

His chin shot up like he'd just been clipped on it. "Your touch?"

"Yep," she replied, lifting her gaze. "I've always had a green thumb when it comes to growing things."

"Yeah," he murmured, shaking his head a little. He was *not* going to get jealous over a bunch of leafy green shit, damn it.

Keep telling yourself that, his wolf laughed. *I, for one, would give anything to be a mother-lovin' daisy if it meant I got to feel her hands on me.*

He grunted under his breath, and they finished eating, then carried their plates into the kitchen. He dried while she washed, trying like hell to take shallow breaths, since her scent was seriously screwing with his head. Unable to take it anymore, he set the towel down after drying the last pan and muttered, "It's getting late, Sayre. You should get some rest."

Propping her hip against the counter, she gave him a look that said she didn't like being told what to do. "I'll go to bed when I'm ready. Right now, Cian, we need to talk. Not chat about mundane crap. We need to actually discuss something important."

Figuring he knew exactly what she wanted to discuss, he tried to find the words to come clean, but couldn't. He swallowed, struggling for the right way to explain, but nothing was there. It was like the fucking well had just dried up, his tongue thick in his mouth. Shaking his head with frustration, he somehow managed to rasp, "I know we need to talk, but…I'm not ready to tell you everything. Not yet. I need a little more time."

A quiet, bitter laugh fell from her lips. "That's such a jackass attitude, seeing as how I seem to have been thrown into the middle of some bizarre family feud you have going on with some *brother* none of us ever even knew existed. But that's not what I was getting at."

Relief swept through his system as he leaned back against the opposite counter. "What then?"

"It's the Alley. I'm not exaggerating when I say that it's hell for me there these days."

"I'll be there with you, Sayre."

"You'll be there with me, huh?" She laughed again, shooting him a baffled look of amazement. "Is that meant to make me feel better?"

He flushed, grinding his molars together so hard he was surprised they hadn't cracked. "I just meant that I'll do whatever I can to help make it easier for you there. But we don't have any other choice at this point, because we *need* the protection."

"And when you're gone?" she asked softly, her slender brows slightly raised in challenge.

"Let's just get through the present. We can worry about the rest later."

"Seriously? That's all you're going to say? You don't even think I deserve the courtesy of a full explanation?"

"Jesus, Sayre. I don't want to talk about this right now," he growled, his heart hammering so hard he wondered if he were on the verge of a friggin' panic attack. And the more she stood up to him, the harder it was for him to remember why he had to keep his goddamn hands to himself.

Brow knitted with a fresh wave of anger, she said,

"Yeah, I picked up on the fact you don't want to talk. But guess what? I don't give a damn!"

"You *should*," he argued, his voice rising. "Because there's a good reason for why I want you to just shut the hell up. Every time you open your mouth, I want—" He broke off, cursing at his crumbling self-control as he shoved both hands back through his hair so hard he nearly ripped it out. "Christ, woman. If you knew what I want to do to you, you'd run screaming all the way back to Maryland. So just let it go for tonight!"

Given the situation, Sayre knew that "letting it go" was probably a damn good idea, but she couldn't do it. Not when Cian Hennessey was suddenly looking at her as if she were the embodiment of every primal sexual fantasy that he'd ever had. "Wait. Are you...are you saying that you *want* me?"

"I *always* want you."

The gritty words were so sharp with emotion she almost felt cut by them, and she slowly shook her head in wonder. "But you *always* said I was too young for you."

His hands tightened into fists until his knuckles turned white. "You're no longer a child, Sayre."

"And I wasn't a child at eighteen," she snapped, sick of this archaic attitude he had about her age. "If I was old enough to go to war for my pack, then I was old enough for sex, Cian. But you left me anyway."

"That was only part of the reason I left," he said roughly, his chest expanding with each of his hard, ragged breaths.

Narrowing her eyes at him, she kept her tone deliberately calm. "I left, too. But not right away. I lived in the Alley for nearly six months without you there, and it was nice to learn that there were *some* men on that mountain who didn't think I was too young for what they wanted."

An immediate scowl twisted his brow, his silver gaze going dark and diamond-hard. She could feel the powerful force of his anger surrounding her, blasting against her, but unlike with the others, Cian's emotions didn't cause her physical pain or discomfort. They simply fed her own, making her feel…charged, like a draining battery that had finally been given a potent boost. The jolt was as stunning as it was delicious, raising the fine hairs on her skin, and the fact that it felt so freaking good only made her angrier. So furious, she didn't even flinch when he straightened to his full height and snarled, "What exactly are you saying, Sayre?"

Crossing her arms over her chest, she threw him a taunting look that she knew would rile him, her voice a soft, sultry drawl. "That really isn't any of your business, is it?"

He advanced on her so quickly he was there before she'd even noticed he was moving, getting right up in her space until he was looming over her and she had to crane her head back just to see his face, his expression one of pure, seething fury. "Everything about you is *my* business, little girl. And if any male has put his hands on you, I will fucking *kill* him. Am I clear?"

Sayre blinked up at him in a mild state of shock, unable to believe he was actually reacting this way—as if he truly gave a crap about what she did or who she did it with. Sure, he'd acted like a jealous ass before he'd abandoned the Alley, but the guy had dropped off the grid for *five* years. That was half a damn decade! For all he knew, she could have run off, married some amaz-

ing man and started a family by now. He'd had no way
of knowing what she was doing or who she was doing
it with. His actions couldn't have made his feelings toward their connection any clearer than if he'd looked her
right in the eye and told her she meant *nothing* to him.
Not a single goddamn thing.

Though the women he'd taken back to his cabin in
front of her had certainly gotten the message across
before he'd left. Nothing like watching your life mate
hook up with an endless stream of females to make it
clear he didn't want you.

Pulling in a deep breath, Sayre took a few steps back
to put some much-needed space between them. "What
I'm clear on is that you'll never know what I've done or
who I've done it with. So this is a pointless argument,
Gramps."

His eyes widened at the name she'd used for him, and
she had to bite back a satisfied smirk. Now that she'd
found a chink in that titanium-plated armor of his, she
was sure as hell going to exploit it. Heck, she might even
look up old-man jokes online just so she could have them
in reserve, ready to use when needed.

He opened his mouth, then closed it, his nostrils flaring as he pulled in a sharp breath of air. The seconds
stretched out, each one heavy and weighted with possibility and tension, until he finally cursed something
thick and guttural under his breath and stalked around
her, making his way toward the front door with long,
angry strides. Then, without so much as a backward
glance, he slammed out of the cabin. She waited, wondering if she'd hear the roar of the Audi's engine, but
his shadow moved across the curtained window a few
moments later, and she realized he was outside pacing.

A brief spot of flame sparked as he paused to light a cigarette—the first one she'd seen him smoke all day—and then the pacing resumed.

It wasn't anything to necessarily be proud of, but she'd have been totally fibbing if she'd said it didn't feel good to know that she'd gotten to him. *Hah! Score one for the witch! In your face, wolf boy!*

But as she turned and headed back to her bedroom, she had to face the harsh reality that he'd gotten to her, as well. Her body ached a little deeper with each step that took her away from him, her heart thudding to a jarring, painful beat that sounded suspiciously like *go back...go back...*

And the sex-hungry wild woman living inside her was practically screeching her head off, furious that Sayre wasn't giving her what she wanted. Unfortunately, Sayre pretty much felt the same way.

She might be a twenty-three-year-old virgin, but damn it, that wasn't by choice. And while she might still be innocent, she embraced her sexuality. Had learned to touch herself and make it feel good. Liked reading about sex and imagining what it would feel like when she could finally give her body the freedom to enjoy it one day. After Cian had left, if there'd been a man she'd wanted, she would have gone to bed with him. But there hadn't. So she'd taken care of herself, and hoped that one day that would change.

The last few weeks, however, had been...different, her need becoming sharper, more focused, until she'd wondered if it weren't time she invest in some "things" to help her out. She wasn't thrilled about walking into a sex shop, because while she might be a modern woman, it was still probably going to make her blush. Even the idea of ordering something online and having it delivered to her PO box in town made her cheeks warm. But now...now she wondered if maybe her body had started quickening in preparation for *this*. For his return. For the man she'd always wanted showing up out of the blue and acting all protective, as if he actually gave a crap about her.

Was she really willing to let him walk away without taking everything that she could from him before he went?

She didn't know, but she needed to figure it out, and fast. There was no telling how long he would stick around this time. She couldn't count on forever. And after the way he'd treated her, she no longer wanted a lifetime with him anyway.

But she needed to decide if she could go all in for nothing more than a good time. If she could use him for that mouthwatering, kick-ass body of his for as long as she dared, and then turn around and walk away before he got around to it.

Would the pleasure be worth the inevitable pain that would follow?

As she crawled onto her bed and turned out the light, Sayre could have sworn she heard a voice in her head murmur, *How will you know if you never give yourself a taste?*

Chapter 5

For Sayre, the following morning put the phrase *leap of faith* in a whole new light. One that was up close and personal…and as exciting as it was terrifying.

Cian had prowled outside the cabin until just after two in the morning, then finally dragged himself inside. Sayre had dozed off at that point, too, awakening later than usual after a restless night's sleep. Dressed in soft cotton shorts and a tank top, she padded out to the living room and stopped at the end of the hallway when she saw that he was still asleep on the sofa. His long legs hung over the end, one powerful arm thrown across his face to block out the morning sunlight flooding in through the French doors.

As she stood there with her shoulder propped against the wall, staring at his sunlit body sprawled across the off-white cushions, she knew she'd made her decision. Knew what she wanted. And while things usually went to hell in a handbasket when people started making decisions based on what they felt they deserved, rather than on what was smart, she didn't care. She figured this was her one shot at joining the masses and being a "normal" girl. Even if it were just for a brief moment in time.

But there was more on the line here than her need for

sexual discovery and satisfaction. More than her need to finally get herself a "little somethin'" before she ended up a crazy old recluse who had nothing but chipmunks and squirrels for company. She needed to think about what the right answer was for their current safety situation. Not so much for herself, because she knew that while Cian might be an ass when it came to women and relationships, he would do whatever it took to protect her. His coming back to the States was a clear indication of his determination to keep her safe from this unknown brother of his. But she was most likely putting him in a dangerous situation by making him face it alone, with only her to help him. If they went back to the Alley, he would have others to watch his back and ensure his own safety.

And as long as he was there with her, she had a feeling she would be able to deal with the issues her powers created. When she'd mentioned how difficult it was for her there during their argument the night before, she'd been thinking more of the emotional strain it would put her under—not the physical one. Being there with Cian, when everyone knew how he'd just upped and left her, was going to be anything but peachy. She didn't plan on actually spelling any of this out for him, though. It would simply be a lie by omission, and she could live with that.

Plus, she knew most of the others were on vacation at the beach with their kids, enjoying a summer getaway, so the group would be small. Brody and Mic were there, and Jillian had had to stay behind, because she was needed in town to help deal with several premature babies who had been born within the last few weeks. Sayre was aware of the details, because her sister had been blowing her phone up with texts since yesterday. Instead of calling Jillian back, like the texts had begged, she'd replied that she was fine and would be in touch, and left it at that. Yeah, it was bitchy, but she didn't have the energy for the guilt she knew she'd feel when she heard the worry in her sister's voice that was always there whenever they spoke.

And God only knew Jillian would have a lot to say about Cian showing back up in her life. Cian's leaving had drastically altered her sister's perception of the Irishman. Words like *bastard, selfish* and *coward* were the ones Jillian used to describe him these days, whenever he happened to come up in conversation. And Sayre had always agreed with her.

But now…now she didn't quite know what to believe. Sure, there were parts of her that still felt he was all of those things and more. But she was starting to see that the "more" part had a lot more to it than she'd ever realized. That there were things about Cian's life, like this so-called brother he'd mentioned, that she and the others had never been told about. A brother who for some reason wanted to harm her simply because of her connection to Cian. Who was crazy enough to have hired those human assholes to come up here on her mountain and mess with her. It made her wonder what other secrets Cian had been keeping from them—and why he'd felt he needed to keep them in the first place.

Unable to resist this stolen moment, where she could stare at him at her leisure and simply soak him in, she pushed all of that to the background and padded quietly into the room, until she stood only a few feet away from where he lay. His ebony eyelashes were long and thick and ridiculously beautiful—the kind of lashes most women would have killed to have. His brows slashed arrogantly across a face that pretty much left her breathless. And then there was the long, powerful body, his tight skin wrapped around chiseled muscles that would make any hot-blooded female a little weak in the knees. It wasn't fair for him to be this mesmerizing, as if everything about him had been designed to draw in a woman and make her *want* him. *Crave* him. *Need* him in a way she'd never needed anything in her entire life.

And the fact that fate had chosen him as her perfect match meant that Sayre felt those things in the extreme, as if they were two magnetic fields being drawn together with incredible force—even when he so obviously wanted to fight it. That particular little fun fact made her long to slap him as desperately as she wanted to lean over that fallen-angel face of his and kiss him until he forgot his own blasted name. Until he was as lost in her she'd always ached for him to be, his need matching hers in a way that was guaranteed to burn the cabin down around them, it was so freaking hot.

As if he sensed her presence, he made a low sound that rumbled deep in his chest and lifted his arms over his head as he stretched out his big, muscular body. He'd thrown his shirt over the back of the sofa and taken off his boots and socks, leaving him dressed in nothing but those low-slung jeans he'd changed into after his shower. Every mouthwatering inch of his wide chest and ripped abdominal muscles were on dazzling display, and she actually had to lift her hand and wipe the corner of her mouth, the rush of her pulse pounding in her ears like the warning blare of a siren. *Get back! Be careful! Don't touch!* The guy was just too beautiful for his own good.

Damn it, even his bare feet were sexy!

She tried to be strong and walk away. She really did—because using him for pleasure was different from mooning over him like a lovesick idiot. But the way he suddenly turned his head, those sleep-heavy eyes warming with pleasure when he blinked them open and saw her, his wide mouth curling in a slow, sin-tipped smile, was just too much. Too perfect. Too freaking emotional. And the way that for just that single instant he looked genuinely happy to see her…damn it, it broke her stupid heart all over again. Put foolish, dangerous thoughts in her head. Made her dream, when that was the last thing in the world she should be doing where he was concerned.

"You okay?" he asked in a low, sleep-rough rumble, his accent even thicker than when he was fully alert.

She wet her lips, took a shallow breath and searched for her voice. "I…I'm fine. I still need to get dressed, but first…I just wanted to let you know that I'll go back with you. We don't need to have another argument in order for you to convince me."

He pushed up on an elbow, looking like something on a goddamn hunk calendar. Only Cian was more gorgeous and rugged and sexy than any model she'd ever seen photographed. Sounding a bit more awake than he had before, he said, "I'm glad to hear it, lass. But what changed your mind?"

"I don't want your death on my hands," she murmured, wrapping her arms over her middle, her confession making her feel even more exposed than her skimpy sleepwear. "You'll be safer there."

He sat up and swung his legs around until his feet were flat on the floor, confusion joining in with the surprise and relief she could read on his handsome face. "It's *you* I'm worried about, Sayre."

She slowly arched one of her brows. "Are we really going to argue about this, or are you going to just be happy that I've decided to make your life a whole lot easier? Would you prefer it if I threw a tantrum and refused to leave?"

"Hell no."

Her lips twitched as she took a step back. "Then get up and get dressed so that you can help me."

Pushing his hair back from his face, he shot her a wary look. "What are we doing?"

"I might be able to suck it up and endure a visit, but I'm no more moving back there permanently than you are. So I need to make sure things are in good working order around here before I go."

His jaw got tight, as did the skin around his eyes. He didn't like hearing that she would be coming back to the cabin. Though why it would matter to him, she couldn't understand.

"This place is that important to you?" he asked, as he leaned forward and rested his elbows on his parted knees.

"The garden here isn't just a hobby, Cian. It's my job, because I run a blog called *The Green Witch*," she explained, wondering why her body felt the ridiculous need to blush as she revealed this information. "My income feeds in from my YouTube subscribers, as well as the companies that advertise on my site. I use my garden to make instructional videos on how to do everything from planting and general maintenance to horticultural design."

He blinked a few times, then scratched the shadow

of stubble on his jaw. "Hell, Sayre. That's pretty damn impressive."

"I'll never be a millionaire, but I don't need to be. I just need a roof over my head and money for the bare essentials."

His look of admiration slipped into a grimace, and she shook her head, wondering what his problem was. Before she could ask him, he switched gears and said, "*The Green Witch*, huh? Cute name."

She smirked. "What the humans don't know about the truth in the name won't hurt them."

A deliciously low laugh rumbled up from his chest, the corner of his mouth kicking up a bit. "I guess not."

That laugh, as well the freaking lopsided smile that went along with it, was about to put her in meltdown mode, so she quickly retreated, mumbling something about needing to change clothes and would he please put on some coffee.

When she came back out not even ten minutes later, dressed in denim shorts and a white T-shirt, he'd thankfully thrown his shirt back on, and they quickly ate some toast and cereal before heading outside. It took her the better portion of the day to get the automatic watering system set up, as well as the wire netting that would protect her precious plants and flowers from hungry animals.

By the time they finally had the place secured enough that Sayre felt comfortable leaving it, Cian gave off a vibe like he was coming out of his skin, his attention constantly focused on the surrounding woods. She knew the delay in leaving had pissed him off, but he'd been smart enough not to voice his complaints out loud, understanding she was stubborn enough to change her mind. Not that she was going to. Cian's tension had rubbed off on her to the point that even *she* was anxious to get the heck out of there. She didn't know much about this mysterious brother of his—okay, she knew next to nothing—but the fact that he worried the Irishman was enough for Sayre to know he was going to be a crapload of trouble.

After they'd wolfed down a late lunch of sandwiches and chips, she locked up the shed, grabbed her things and they climbed into the Audi.

"Nice car," she murmured, stroking her hand over the sumptuous leather. The seats in her truck were so cracked that she'd covered them with a quilt her grandmother had made. Her parents, as well as Jillian and Jeremy, had tried to buy her something newer, but she'd refused, unwilling to take their charity. They'd already done too much, helping her remodel the cabin up there in the middle of nowhere, when she'd needed to get away before she suffered a total breakdown.

Her brows pulled together as the memory of how helpless she'd felt during those dark days pressed in on her, and she mentally shoved it to the back of her mind, along with all the other things she didn't want to think about at the moment. Things like the fact that even if there had been someone she'd wanted to sleep with before she'd left the Silvercrest, like she'd warned him she would do, the problems with her powers would have likely made it impossible. That despite hoping her powers might one day mellow out enough that she could return home, there was a strong chance that she would *always* be this way. That Cian Hennessey's absence from her life meant she would forever be alone. That fooling around with him might very well be the *only* chance for intimacy that she ever had, and boy did that thought suck, seeing as how he'd admitted to wanting her...but clearly hated that he felt that way.

Knowing Cian, he was probably terrified she'd mistake passion for love and start following him around like an adoring puppy dog, constantly begging for his attention.

God, I'd rather die a virgin!

Since she desperately needed to get out of her negative head space, she pressed forward with more chatter about the car. "When do you have to have it back to the rental company?"

"It's not a rental," he murmured, handling the powerful engine with ridiculous ease as he took the winding mountain roads. And looking entirely too freaking sexy while he did it.

She whistled under her breath at his response, shocked that he'd spent so much money on a car. The Runners were all financially comfortable, but they didn't have the kind of wealth that made them able to throw around the amount of cash it took to buy a set of wheels like the Audi. "So what's the story with that, then? You win the lottery while you were gone?"

He shifted his long body in his seat, his energy moving from relief that they'd finally left to restless again. "Didn't need to," he muttered under his breath.

Sayre sensed he'd be happy if she dropped the topic, but given the situation between them, she wasn't particularly interested in giving him what he wanted. "Then how did you afford it?"

He worked his stubble-covered jaw a few times, then exhaled a sharp breath through his nose before he admitted, "I used money from my trust fund, which I finally started to spend after I quit Bloodrunning. And since I didn't know how long this thing with Aedan was going to take, I didn't see the point in renting anything when I could just buy it."

Her mouth actually hung open for a moment. "Trust fund? Are you serious?"

He grunted in response, and she had to laugh. No wonder the guy had always seemed a little out of place in their small mountain community. He was probably used to living in a freaking mansion, rather than the rugged beauty of Bloodrunner Alley.

She didn't know much about Cian's family, other than that his mother had been a member of the pack who'd fallen in love while on vacation in Ireland and had never returned. But Cian never talked about her much, and she couldn't recall him *ever* talking about his father. "Do the others know?"

He slid her a shuttered look that was impossible to read, then shook his head and returned his attention to the winding road. He'd explained when they set off that it would likely take them hours to reach the Alley, since they'd be avoiding the main roads, taking smaller ones that were less traveled...and less likely to be monitored by his homicidal brother. She let the conversation about money go, thinking instead about the possible reasons for the Hennessey brothers' apparent feud. Was it over a woman? The family money? Or something even darker than that? Wouldn't it have to be, if Aedan wanted to hurt his brother badly enough to kill over it? And that was definitely the point of all this. Cian's behavior made at least that much apparent.

"So," he murmured, his deep voice startling her when

neither of them had said a word for the past half hour. "I was wondering what your powers are like now."

Her shoulders lifted in a brief shrug. "Oh, you know. Just typical witch stuff."

He shot her a look before turning his attention back to the road. "Can you go into a little more detail than that?"

A quiet laugh slipped past her lips. "I can't read your mind, if that's what's worrying you."

"It wasn't," he remarked in a dry tone, "but thanks for clarifying."

"I can sometimes do that with animals, though, and communicate with them. But it's pretty rare, and usually only when they need my help."

"Like with the snakes?" he asked, shifting the Audi into a lower gear as he took a particularly tight turn in the road.

"What?"

"When Elise first came to stay with Wyatt, he and I came back from being out on security patrol one evening and found all the women freaking out because some rattlesnakes had wandered into the Alley. But you were as calm as could be when you came outside and spotted them. Instead of screeching, you just lifted your hands in the air, your eyes all glowing and bright, and those fucking snakes listened to whatever you told them, slithering back into the forest."

"I remember that," she said with a small smile. "Chelsea was so pissed at Eric because he couldn't stop laughing at how ridiculous her and the others looked, jumping up and down on top of Brody's truck and screaming their heads off."

He gave a low laugh. "It was one of the craziest, funniest damn things I've ever seen."

"You calling me crazy?" she asked, playfully smacking him on the arm.

A sensual smirk curved the firm line of his beautiful mouth. "Only in a good way."

Sayre rolled her eyes. "Gee, thanks."

"So what else can you do?"

Picking at the frayed edge on her shorts, she said, "Well, there's the healing ability, and the energy, light-shooting-out-of-my-hands part. Other than that, I've occasionally had some moments of what I suppose you could call 'sight'—but it's been a long time since anything like that happened." Looking over at him again, she said, "As the energy thing's become more powerful, it's like it's eclipsed everything else."

He glanced her way, then focused once more on the road. "So then what's the story with the gun that you pulled on me yesterday? I've seen your powers in action, and that was before they hit full throttle. So why not use them?"

"They're not something I use in front of humans if I can avoid it, so I carry the gun."

"That's understandable. But you could have used them on me."

"I could have," she admitted, momentarily caught up in watching the way he was holding the steering wheel with his left hand, his thumb stroking over the smooth leather in a way that struck her as incredibly erotic. Clearing her throat a little, she added, "But the gun was more…impersonal."

He grunted again, which seemed to be his standard response when she said something he didn't care for. They drifted back into another heavy silence for a few minutes, until her impatience finally got the better of her. Before she could stop herself or talk herself around in circles over whether it was the right move or the wrong one, Sayre tucked her left leg up under her, turned to face him and said, "So, I've been doing some thinking, and I need to talk to you about something."

The way his body seemed to brace itself, his muscles tightening beneath his skin, told her that he'd picked up on her nervousness. "Go on," he said in a low voice, sliding her another shuttered glance before looking back at the road.

"I'm, um, still coming to terms with how to handle this, but I don't…I don't want the time we're together to be spent fighting. I want to call a truce. One where we don't keep arguing about what happened before. All I ask is that you're honest with me, even if it's painful."

"Sayre," he rasped, so softly she almost couldn't hear him. His chest lifted with a deep breath, and she could literally *feel* the heat pouring off his big, powerful body, his jaw hard as he probably tried to work out where she was going with this.

"I don't know what you want from me, Cian. I don't even know what I'm willing to give you. But I know that I feel better when I'm with you than I've felt in a long time. Maybe, if we work together, then just *maybe* we can somehow find a way to be…friends."

He swiped his tongue over his lower lip, his face and throat flushed with a heat that she wanted to feel under her mouth and against her tongue. "There's just one problem with that, lass." His voice was rougher than she'd ever heard it before, husky and deliciously thick. "I want to do things to you that I wouldn't want to do to any of my friends, if I had any these days. Things I've wanted to do for *years*, Sayre."

Trying not to let herself get carried away with excitement over hearing him say he wanted her again, she pointed out the obvious. "You never seemed all that attracted to me before. Just possessive."

"Because I fought it with everything I had," he growled, the tendons in his neck straining in a way that made her want to nip them with her teeth.

Knowing this was make-or-break time, she clutched on to every ounce of courage she could find and went for it. "I don't want to argue about the past anymore. What's done is done, and there's nothing you could ever do to make it right. But I...I want things from you, too."

His head turned sharply to the side. "What are you talking about?"

Her confession came in a soft, breathless rush of words. "I want to know what all the fuss is about when it comes to pleasure and the man who was meant to be mine. I want to enjoy my time with you, the time that we're together, however short it is."

Slowing the car, he veered onto the grassy shoulder, then slammed the brakes so hard she had to brace her hands against the dashboard. "Say that again, Sayre."

"I think you heard me just fine," she whispered.

The way he was looking at her made it difficult to breathe—her body all ramped up on hunger for the things she'd been missing out on. For a split second, she froze, wondering if she were doing this because it was the logical, mature decision, or if she were simply being steered by her hormones. Then she exhaled a shaky puff of air, watched his eyes darken as she licked her lips again...and realized that she just didn't care about the reasons and justifications. She was doing it, to hell with what was stupid or dangerous or unwise for her future. The future was never going to be what she'd once hoped for, so she needed to take her happiness when and where she could find it. And that was here. *Now.* Right that very second…and as many seconds as she could have afterward.

"Let me get this straight," he said in a low rumble. "Are you saying I can touch you now?"

"I'm not saying you *can't.* I'm still figuring things out, and it's not easy when you're still not answering my questions."

"Christ, Sayre." He sounded equal parts frustrated and turned on, which made her want to grin…maybe even laugh, which wasn't something she'd done much of in a long time. She knew there weren't many people who surprised him, and it felt good to be one of them. "Are you…are you *blackmailing* me with your body?"

Instead of outright denying it, she gave him a look of open curiosity. "Could I do that?"

The look he gave her in return was so freaking hot she could have melted right there in the sumptuous leather seat. Quietly, he said, "You're playing games, lass, that you're not prepared to lose."

"Not really," she murmured, determined not to let him rattle her. "Because I think you're making a bigger deal out of this than it actually is. All I'm interested in is scratching an itch that should have been dealt with a long time ago. So long as you don't bite me and make a bond, why not indulge while we can?"

Because of the life-mate connection they shared, Cian held the ability to create a permanent blood bond between them if he ever sank his teeth into her throat—and that was something she intended to avoid at all costs. She couldn't think of anything worse than being stuck forever with a man who didn't want the same things as her. Not that she even wanted a bond with him anymore. She would have to trust him…and love him first, and those were two things that this particular male would *never* have from her.

He turned his head away from her, staring out the front windshield, his profile so stark he looked like he'd been carved from stone. "It's not that simple," he eventually said, sounding as if he'd had to force the gritty words from his throat.

Sayre sighed. "Fine. If you don't want me, then just say so."

"Not want you?" he muttered with a harsh, humorless laugh, shaking his head again. "I want the touch and taste of your body so badly it's all I can do not to just *take* it."

"Then look at me, Cian."

He did as she said, the heat and hunger in those smoldering gray eyes making her feel stripped down to her bare flesh, despite the clothes chafing against her warm skin. In that moment, she could have been wearing freaking Eskimo furs and she still would have felt completely exposed. It was a heady feeling, being the center of such intense focus, and the answering part of her soul gloried in it. Soaked it up like a freaking leaf with sunshine, even though her heart was screaming to be careful…cautious.

"I'm not playing a game," she told him, working hard to keep her voice even. "Yes, I want answers to my questions, and I'm hoping you'll eventually give them to me. But I want more than that, and I don't want to wait for it."

His eyes narrowed, the gray glinting like piercing

chips of silver. "Then spell it out for me. In *exact* terms, Sayre."

She took a deep breath, refusing to let herself break eye contact as she put it all out there. "I don't want either of our emotions involved. And I don't even know if I want the full sex act. But I...I want everything that leads up to it."

"No emotions, huh?" It was clear from his tone that he didn't like hearing that any more than he'd liked some of the other things she'd said to him since he'd suddenly burst back into her life. "Can you honestly tell me that you feel nothing where I'm concerned?"

She couldn't hold back the sharp burst of laughter that rushed up from her chest, her lips twisting with chagrin. "Oh, I *feel* plenty, Cian. Anger being first and foremost the majority of the time, along with a lot of other nasty things like pain and humiliation. But there's also hunger, and I'm tired of aching for something I can't find anywhere else. My powers have been keeping me prisoner for years, but here I am, sitting beside you, and I'm okay. Maybe...maybe if I work you out of my system, things will be different when you leave again. Maybe *I'll* be different."

She could tell he hated that idea, as well, but didn't have an argument for it. And, really, what could he possibly say? That he planned on sticking around this time? That he wanted her in a forever kind of way, just like her girlish heart had once hoped he would? Even if he tried to sell her on the idea, they both knew it would be a lie.

Without a single word, he tore that heated stare from her face and looked over his shoulder, checking for other cars before he pulled back out onto the road and floored the gas. Disappointment settled heavily in her gut, but she refused to beg. "Is this your answer then?"

"No," he growled, squeezing the steering wheel so hard she was surprised it didn't crack. "You want my hands on you, then they're going to be on you. But that wasn't the time or place."

Sayre was half convinced he was simply trying to buy himself some time to think of a way to let her down gently—until she noticed something that made her ridiculously happy.

The hand he'd just shoved back through his hair was actually shaking, and she couldn't help the small smile that crept its way into the corner of her mouth.

Yeah, this was bound to end badly. And yep, she was most definitely playing with fire. Hell, she had the matches lit and was dancing in the middle of a sea of gasoline, splashing through it like a kid in a puddle. But maybe that was okay.

Maybe—just *maybe*—it was about time she stopped playing it safe, and actually got a little burned.

Chapter 6

By the time they'd crossed into Maryland, Cian was in a world of pain unlike anything he'd ever known. He took shallow breaths and tried not to draw too much of Sayre's mouthwatering scent into his lungs, but it was a wasted effort. Now that she'd admitted she still wanted him, there wasn't any point in trying to keep his hands off her. He was locked on to every single detail of her, his hunger increasing with each second that ticked by, coiling tightly through his insides. Like a physical thing, it prowled beneath his hot skin, keeping perfect company with his beast.

To make matters worse, the more time he spent with her, the more it became increasingly clear that he genuinely *liked* her. Yeah, he lusted after the little witch to the point that it was going to damn near kill him to walk away from her. To leave without claiming her in *all* the ways that he craved. But he liked the woman beneath that beautiful surface to an equally dangerous degree. She was funny and spirited and fascinating. Different from the girl he'd known, and yet, the same.

Sweet, smart, beautiful Sayre. If he'd been a different man, with a different past...and a different future, he would have claimed her in a heartbeat. Even with that smart-ass mouth and attitude that could so easily rile him.

Finally reaching his breaking point, he sent up a silent word of thanks to whomever might be out there listening when he saw the sign for a small rest area a mile up the road. They were in a remote part of the mountains and hadn't passed another car for the last twenty minutes, so when they reached the turnoff, he took it and followed the dirt path into the trees, parking at the back of a small clearing that sat at the edge of a cliff. Restrooms and a few empty picnic tables were the only amenities, but the view out over the mountains was incredible.

"Is there any particular reason that you've parked here?" she asked, staring out at the view as she undid her seat belt.

He cut the engine, the air leaving his lungs in a rough exhalation. "You know damn well why I brought us here."

With a feminine little snort that he found entirely too adorable, she turned her head and gave him a cocky grin. "You're too old to drive for long periods of time without getting out to stretch your legs?"

Arching his right eyebrow, he said, "You've developed quite a gift for sarcasm, haven't you?"

Her next breath released on a sigh. "Sometimes life will do that to a girl. Does it turn you off?"

"There isn't a damn thing you could do to turn me off, Sayre."

She blinked at him with wide eyes. "Wow, you're not holding back, are you?"

"Why the hell should I hold back about wanting you? I wanted you when you were too young for me to even think about. Wanted you so badly it nearly drove me out of my goddamn mind. I want you even more now."

"Good," she breathed. "Because I want you, too."

"Then come on," he rumbled, reaching for his door handle. "I'm not kissing you for the first time in this small-ass car."

With a low, kind of nervous laugh, she opened her door and started to climb out. "This is a beautiful car, you know. You're just too big for it."

Did she just call us big? his wolf growled, sounding smug as hell. *She's got that right.*

Shaking his head at the arrogant idiot, Cian climbed out and slammed his door shut. His stupid hands were still trembling like a boy's, and he couldn't help but shake his head at himself, as well. So much for his legendary reputation and control. All it took was a single heated look from this girl, like the one she was giving him as he came around the front of the Audi, and he was undone. Damn near knocked back on his ass like someone who'd had their legs swept out from under them.

"I don't understand," he said when he was standing right in front of her and staring into those big, beautiful eyes, a shimmering ring of gold beginning to gleam around the smoky blue. It was like she'd been shocked wide open, her desire laid bare for him to witness, and it humbled him just as much as it scared the ever-loving hell out of him. "How can you do this, Sayre? How can you look at me like that? Don't you blame me for what's happening? For the fact that your life's in danger?"

She pulled in a deep breath as she stared up at him, and then slowly let it out. Voice thick with emotion, she said, "I actually blame you for a lot of things, Cian. If that bothers you, then don't touch me. It's your choice.

I'm simply being as honest as I can be with you about what I want."

"You were never this bold before."

"True," she agreed, keeping her gaze locked tight with his as she leaned back against the passenger's-side door. "But a person can change a lot in five years."

"And some things don't change at all."

"Are you talking about yourself?" she asked, some of the light in her eyes fading, and he knew she was thinking about the women. About the ones he'd gone through faster than packs of cigarettes.

"I was. But it's not what you think, Sayre. I was thinking about the way you affect me."

The frown between her slender brows smoothed out. "Oh."

A slow, crooked smile tugged at his lips. "Yeah, *oh*."

"Tell me," she said, the words soft and husky with need. "I mean, I know it's really just the connection, but I'm curious if it's as strong for you as it is for me."

"You want me to speak plainly?" he asked, his throat so tight with lust he could barely voice the question.

She nodded. "Please."

Cian stepped closer and allowed himself to touch his fingertips to the pink flush on her cheek, her skin so smooth and soft it was unreal. She'd left her hair down, and the wind was playing havoc with the wavy strands, silky tendrils brushing against his forearm and across the back of his wrist. "I'll tell you what I want, Sayre. I want you open and bare beneath me, your beautiful little body *mine* to do with as I please," he confessed, the lilting burr of his accent thickening with each word. "I want you wet and desperate and begging for me, lass. I want to make you feel so bloody good you can't do anything but scream when you come for me, your nails digging into my back and your body writhing. I want to get inside you, any way I can, and bring you off so many times you won't even be able to remember what it was like without my hands and mouth on your skin, laying claim to every part of you."

She shivered, and he loved the way he could feel the warmth of her blush surge beneath his fingertips, her temperature spiking with the fiery energy of her power, tiny sparks of light beginning to glitter in the air around them. Her eyes were glassy with desire, storm-dark and eager, those slim rings of gold at the outer edge of her irises starting to burn even brighter.

"I'm, um, good with all that," she whispered, her little tongue swiping across that succulent lower lip that he wanted to catch between his teeth and suck on, *hard*. It was juicy and pink, the sweet rush of her blood lying just beneath the tender surface, and Cian quickly shoved that dangerous thought behind thick iron gates in his mind, determined not to let it take hold of him and ruin this unexpected moment.

Given their past, he'd never once believed that she would let him get close to her like this. And there was always the chance that she would change her mind. Which meant he needed to get the hell on with it, enjoying it while it lasted, and pray to whatever higher power might be listening that he didn't blow it by losing control.

Lowering his head, he gently swept his lips across hers, using every ounce of strength he possessed to hold himself back, still terrified he'd scare her off. The wolf inside him shuddered with pleasure to finally have the taste of her, and their breaths blended together, the tips of her breasts pressing against his chest as he made a low, thick sound of hunger in the back of his throat. When he pulled his head back to check her reaction, making sure she was still with him, she frowned up at him. "What's wrong?" he rasped, curving his hand around her nape.

"Is there some kind of problem? Because despite what you keep saying, you seem pretty reluctant."

You fucking idiot, his wolf snarled, seething beneath his skin. *We've finally got her and you're blowing it!*

"Not reluctant, Sayre. Just trying to figure out if I'm dreaming."

Another soft burst of laughter seemed to catch her by surprise as it fell past her lips, and she smirked up at him. "Oh, man. That was a smooth line."

"I wish it was a line," he groaned, caging her in with his arms as he pressed his palms flat against the sun-warmed side of the car, her breaths coming in little pants of excitement that he couldn't get enough of. Then he leaned down and brushed his mouth over hers again, unable to believe how impossibly sweet her lips were. "This would be so much easier if it was," he growled against that tender mouth, flicking the center of her bottom lip with his tongue.

When she moaned and rubbed her tongue against his, he lost it and thrust past her lips, the kiss turning deep and deliciously wet. It was terrifying as hell, how damn perfect she tasted, the tender recesses of her mouth and that kittenish tongue that kept tempting him to take more on the cusp of landing her in some serious trouble. His gums burned with the weight of his fangs, every dark, dangerous part of him shocked into awareness by the feel and scent and taste of her.

Unable to keep his hands off her, Cian reached down

and grasped her hips in a hard, possessive hold, preparing to pull her into his lower body, against the part of him that was getting harder by the second, when she gasped against his mouth in a way that almost sounded like fear. Breaking away from the kiss, he pressed his forehead against hers, his body shaking with the effort it took to stop and wait for her to tell him that she was okay.

"Sorry," she whispered unsteadily. "I didn't want you to stop. I'm just…I'm not used to people touching me."

He knew she meant in a casual way, seeing as how she'd been living on her own for so long. But he also sensed that she was talking about physical intimacy. Whatever the little witch had done with other men after he'd left, there was still a part of her that was somewhat shy when it came to sex, and he both loved and hated it with equal ferocity. Yeah, he was relieved that she hadn't gone out and banged every guy she could find just to get back at him for being a jackass. But on the other hand, he didn't quite know what to do with someone who didn't share his level of sexual experience. That was something he hadn't messed around with for decades, and, for a moment, he was worried he'd do this all wrong. Go in for too much, too soon, and end up pushing her to call a halt to the whole thing.

He couldn't let that happen. Not when the taste of her had just hit his system like a shot of pure whiskey. She was even more addictive than he'd feared, and now he was hooked. Walking away from her at this point, before he'd gotten his fill, might damn well finish him off. And while he might not care all that much about dying, he wasn't going anywhere until he'd dealt with Aedan. No way in hell was he leaving this world until his brother had been taken care of, once and for all, and Sayre was safe.

The touch of her hands curling over his shoulders jerked him from his troubled thoughts, and he couldn't stop himself from lifting his head to ask, "Why are you really doing this, Sayre? With me of all people?"

Holding his gaze, she said, "I don't have to tell you my reasons, Cian. You're either game or you're not. No pressure. But if we do this, I want it to be worth it."

"And what, in your mind, makes it worth it?"

"In all honesty? Lots of things. But the pleasure is a part of it. Until this problem with your brother is over, I want you to make me feel good. I want you to rock my freaking world." Her beautiful eyes gleamed with challenge. "So are you up for it?"

Despite her mention of Aedan, which should have turned his blood cold, his shoulders shook with a silent laugh. "Poor choice of words, lass. I'm always *up* for it with you."

"Wow," she murmured with a smirk. "Look at the old man playing the comedian."

"I'm not that old," he grunted as he dipped his head and nipped the delicate edge of her jaw with his teeth.

"Sure you aren't, baby."

He rubbed his nose against hers, a smile on his lips that he couldn't have gotten rid of to save his life. "You're riling me on purpose, aren't you, you little witch?"

"Either way," she quipped, "you'll never know."

"Ah, lass. I told you that you shouldn't play with me," he growled, holding her head still with his hands as he brought his mouth down over hers again, claiming that damp, succulent part of her like he owned it. The kiss was nothing but pure, unadulterated craving, raw and aggressive and dirty as hell. His tongue pushed into her mouth, stroking against her own in a way that was suggestive of how he wanted to lick at that sweet flesh between her thighs, and he knew that she got it. That she understood what he was trying to tell her with the greedy, explicit demands of his lips and tongue and teeth. His hands burrowed deeper into the silken mass of her hair, turning her head at the angle he needed so that he could get to even more of that hot little mouth, the breathless sounds that she made and the way she clutched at his shoulders as she kissed him back driving him out of his goddamn mind.

Needing to learn more of her, he lowered his arms and pushed his hands under the hem of her shirt, touching her soft, smooth skin. His heart was hammering so hard he was surprised it hadn't torn free of his chest, his pulse roaring in his ears, the thumping beat keeping perfect time with the guttural howls of his beast. Loving the way she felt, he trailed two fingertips across her soft skin, his path leading to the shallow indentation of her navel. But just as he started to trace his fingertips over the sexy tattoo he knew was inked there, something dark and savage burst inside his head like an explosion, slamming into him with the force of a racehorse at full tilt. He cursed against her mouth, burning with the predatory need to take her down to the ground and bury every inch of his brutal erection deep inside her, at the same time he drove his fangs into the tender column of her throat and bit the holy living hell out of her.

What. The. Fuck?

Was it the force of her own desires suddenly pushing him to take the hot, rich spill of her blood into his mouth and drink her down, marking her as his? The draw of her power? Their connection? Or did the violent craving for complete possession have something to do with *him*? With what he was? With that part of him that he struggled so hard to keep contained?

Cian wished that he knew the answer, but he was at a loss. All he really knew was that touching her like this, being with her like this, was more incredible than anything he'd ever had before. Even better than he'd imagined it would be, and he'd played out this scenario in his head so many excruciating times it was permanently etched into his memory. Had hungered for it until he'd felt hollowed out inside, bled dry with need.

But if he didn't stop now, he understood what would happen.

There would be a damn good chance he wouldn't stop at all.

Sayre wanted to scream with frustration when Cian suddenly pulled away from her. One second she was lost in the dark, velvety heat of his mouth, his tongue rubbing against hers so wickedly it made her ache for more, and in the next she was staring up at his cold-as-stone expression as he took a step back from her, wondering what on earth had happened.

"Cian?"

He gave one sharp, curt shake of his head, then jerked his chin toward the car. "Get in," he said in a voice so low it sounded more predator than man. "We need to go."

She blinked, feeling like he'd just tossed a glass of ice water in her face. "You're kidding, right?"

His response punched from his lips with so much

force it made her flinch. "You want to get down and dirty in a goddamn rest area, Sayre?"

"No," she returned, though her voice wasn't nearly as strong as she wanted it to be, her system still reeling from the way he'd kissed her. "I made it clear that I don't plan on having sex with you. But I thought we could… that we could at least do *other* things."

"We could," he muttered, shoving one of his big hands back through the windblown strands of his hair, "but I need to think."

"Does this mean you've changed your mind?" she demanded, wanting to know *now*, so that she didn't make even more of a fool of herself later on.

The look he gave her said he thought she was crazy for even asking such a ridiculous question. For a moment, a warm, sensual buzz of pleasure swept through her, until her next thought quickly sobered her up. Of course he wanted her, at least in a sexual way. The laws of nature wouldn't have connected them if they weren't primed for intense attraction to one another. But even though he was finally admitting his need, it didn't mean that he had to like it. Or accept it. Or embrace it.

From the dark expression on his face, he didn't plan on doing *any* of those things. Not a single damn one of them.

As if he could read her mind, he growled, "You don't need to doubt my desire for you, Sayre. I'm harder than I've ever been right now, and it's because of you."

She couldn't help but look down, the sight of his thick erection trapped behind that denim fly making her heart leap into her throat. She gave a hard swallow, embarrassingly aware of the heat burning in her face. Damn it, she wanted to be sophisticated about this, but that just so wasn't her. All she could do was stand there and gape, wanting to know what the weight of him would feel like in her palm. If he would be smooth or ridged with veins, and how hot his flesh would be to the touch. If she could make him shout with pleasure, and how he would taste and feel on her tongue.

But as she watched him make his way back around the front of the Audi, his tension like a physical force blasting against her in the late-afternoon sunshine, she knew her curiosity wasn't going to be appeased today. Heck, maybe not ever, if he didn't manage to let go a little and relax.

She opened her door and climbed inside, her thoughts snagging on something that she couldn't quite put her finger on. She could understand Cian being worried about taking things too far, seeing as how the life-mate connection they shared naturally drew them together, even though there was only so far they were willing to go, neither of them wanting to be permanently stuck with the other. And if they had sex, that connection would no doubt compel him to bite her and mark her in a way that would be damn difficult to resist.

But she couldn't help thinking that there was more to it than that. That something darker than the magnetic, fate-driven "pull" between them was behind his reticence. And her gut told her it had something to do with the man who was trying to hurt her to get to him. She had so many questions about Aedan Hennessey that she didn't even know where to start. And she didn't even bother, knowing Cian wouldn't answer them.

After pulling her door shut, she latched her seat belt and then turned to look at him, surprised to find him just sitting there, watching her, his troubled gaze dark and endlessly deep, filled with so much confusion... as well as frustration. "Does it bother you at all to be around me?" he asked her.

"You mean with my power or just in general?"

His nostrils flared as he pulled in a deep breath, and he muttered, "Your power."

"So far? No," she said, giving him an honest answer.

He nodded, then looked away from her and started the engine. As they pulled back out onto the winding mountain road, he seemed to get lost in his thoughts, but the silence didn't bother her. Her emotions were too raw at the moment to make casual conversation.

Pulling the backpack she'd left on the floorboard into her lap, Sayre took out the iPod Jillian had given her for Christmas and her headphones, then scrolled through her playlists until she found the one titled *Free*. She'd paid for every track on the list, the meaning of the name going deeper than her measly bank account. It was an eclectic mix of songs that embodied what she wanted most out of life: freedom from her past and the things that held her back.

But as she listened to the first song, she realized that it wasn't quite fitting for her current set of circumstances, and she wondered if maybe she should put a new list together and call it *Strength*.

After everything that she'd been through, the last thing that Sayre considered herself was weak. But she was also realistic enough to know that there were times when even the strongest of people needed a little more.

And if she were going to make it through this thing with Cian without any permanent damage to her heart, she had a feeling she was one of them.

Chapter 7

As he steered the powerful sports car into the Alley, Cian couldn't help but recall the night Eli Drake had returned to the mountains he'd grown up in after an absence of three years. Was this how the mercenary had felt that night? Like he was walking into a dream? One that was both calming and familiar, and yet, oddly terrifying?

Had he felt as out of place as Cian did in that moment, like a stranger in his own home?

Shaking off the uncomfortable thoughts, he put the car into Park, turned off the engine and twisted toward Sayre. She was worrying her lush lower lip with her teeth, her gaze shadowed with something that seemed remarkably close to fear. It made his insides tighten, as if he physically rejected the idea of her feeling that sour emotion when it was his job to protect her.

He might fail disastrously when it came to upholding most of his duties as her mate, but ensuring she felt safe was one that he had every intention of carrying out.

For the moment, his wolf muttered. *Some hero you are.*

Ignoring the sarcastic jibe—leave it to him to have an inner wolf that constantly sported an attitude—he studied her as she slipped off the headphones she'd been wearing for the past hour and dropped them back into her pack. "You feeling okay?"

She pulled in a slow breath. "So far, so good."

"If it gets to be too much, let me know. We can have as much privacy as you want."

"Privacy didn't help before."

Knowing exactly what he was doing, he shot her a heated look, and let a slow smile lift the corner of his mouth. "If you need me to, I think I can find a way to get your mind focused on something besides your powers."

She narrowed her eyes at him. "*Now* you decide to flirt with me? God, you have some seriously craptastic timing."

He didn't know how she managed to make him laugh in the middle of some of the tensest situations in his life, but she did. "Craptastic? Is that even a real word?"

Shrugging a slender shoulder, she sighed. "I don't know. I just…" Confusion clouded her gaze. "You mess with my head, Cian."

Since that didn't necessarily sound like a good thing, he let it go as he opened his door and climbed out into the warm, slightly humid evening. Pulling in a deep breath of the forest-scented air, he almost felt light-headed from the way it hit his system. Not as potent as Sayre, but still meaningful, like he was pulling in a deep breath of home. There was no other place in the world that smelled like this to him, and it made his heart hurt to think that he was going to lose it again when all was said and done.

Only because you're too stubborn and pigheaded, his beast grumbled.

Mentally flipping off the wolf, he closed his door,

shooting Sayre a look over the top of the car as she did the same. Worry for her punched him low in the gut, and even though he knew this was the safest place she could be once Aedan made his appearance, he also knew that he wouldn't force her to stay if it became too much for her. With a nod of encouragement, he turned and faced the small group that was making their way toward them. Jeremy must have decided to come back to be there for Jillian, because he was walking right beside her, while Mic and Brody followed just behind them.

The mercs who worked with Eli Drake were there, as well, and he found a frown tugging at his mouth. He could have done without them, seeing as how Sayre had been pretty close to a few of them before he'd left, but he knew they were permanent residents in the Alley now. Single ones, from the looks of it, since the four of them—Lev Slivkoff, Kyle Maddox, Sam Harmon and James Bennett—were still without wedding rings. But that was hardly surprising. They were even bigger womanizers than he'd once been, though that seemed like a lifetime ago.

Keeping a wary eye on the group, Cian moved to stand at the back of the car, his muscles tightening with awareness as Sayre came to stand beside him. The wind was tossing her wild mane of curls against his arm, the silky caresses striking him as oddly sensual, considering it was simply the touch of her hair. But it seemed that his mind equated everything to do with the little witch with sex, from that devastatingly sensual scent that he wanted to draw into his mouth and bite down on, to the way she chewed on her bottom lip when she was deep in thought. If he didn't know how much she resented being linked to him, he would have thought she'd put

some kind of spell on him. One that made him crave
the scent and touch and taste of her.

I'll never *forget that hot little mouth of hers,* his wolf
snarled, baring its fangs at him. *Could gladly kill you
for pushing her away today.*

Yeah, he had to agree with the jackass on that one.
But he hadn't had any other choice. If he hadn't pulled
away from her, he'd have ended up screwing her beautiful little brains out in the middle of a rest area while he
marked the shit out of her throat, and then everything
would have gone to hell so fast it left his head spinning.
And the results would be just as bad for her, seeing as
how she would have been stuck with him. No matter
how badly he wanted her in his bed, he wasn't so much
of a bastard that he would ruin her life that way just for
the sake of his dick.

Not that the idea wasn't tempting, because, *hell*, it
was Sayre, and he wanted her in ways he still didn't even
fully understand. Ways he refused to look at too closely,
convinced he wouldn't like what he found.

Jillian was the first to reach them as she hurried away
from Jeremy's side and grabbed her little sister up in
a crushing embrace. "Ohmygod, I've missed you so
much," she said in a broken rush, while Sayre hugged
her back.

"Me, too," she whispered, and he could hear the tears
she was holding back in those quiet words. Sayre raised
up on her tiptoes and hugged her sister even tighter, and
while it no doubt made him a perv, he couldn't help but
notice the way her shorts had hiked up with the action,
revealing even more of her smooth, sleek thighs.

And he wasn't the only one who'd noticed.

Turning his head back toward the group, he caught

the way the mercs, as well as Max and Elliot, were checking her out, and had to choke back the sudden urge to snap at them with his jaws. But while he hated it, he couldn't fault them for their primitive interest, given that they were hot-blooded males and she was the embodiment of lush, guileless femininity. A sensual feast to each and every single one of a man's senses, and he couldn't help but wonder which of them had knowledge of that firsthand. Given his reputation, it made him a complete and total bastard, but he wanted to know which ones had stroked and tasted her and made her come. Which ones had touched what was *his*, and enjoyed her in the ways he'd never been able to allow himself to do before.

Damn it, he'd barely managed to get through kissing her today without seriously screwing it up, and he knew he needed to get a white-knuckled grip on himself before the next time. And there would *definitely* be a next time. No way in hell could he keep his hands off her now.

"It's good to have you back, scamp," Jeremy drawled, pulling Sayre into a hug when Jillian had finally released her, the healer's eyes damp with tears as she smiled at them.

While Sayre spoke with Jeremy, Cian stepped back to give them some space, and the others obviously took that as their cue to move in closer.

"That's an awfully nice ride you've got there," Lev murmured, grinning like a jackass. "One might think you were trying to impress someone with it."

Kyle laughed. "I doubt a guy with Hennessey's reputation needs a fancy car to impress a girl."

"Yeah, that's right," the blond merc drawled, with a

certain edge to his voice that spelled trouble. "He was the tomcat of the wolves, wasn't he?"

Max muttered for them both to shut up, shooting Cian a cautious glance. The kid was worried he'd lose his cool with the mercs, but he wasn't going to get into an argument over his reputation in front of Sayre. He didn't need to have that tossed in her face, and he knew exactly why the cocky mercenary had started in on him. Slivkoff had been close to Sayre before Cian had left, and from the way he kept stealing looks at her, he was interested in getting even closer. And that didn't sit well with him. Especially given how the guy's golden good looks and unusual blue-green eyes, not to mention his shit ton of muscles, never failed to make him popular with the ladies. Hell, he could have given Cian's rep a run for its money, and he was just about to pull the merc aside and explain why it would be in Lev's best interest to stay away from Sayre, when Jeremy slapped him on the shoulder, a little harder than a friendly clap, and told him they were all heading over to Brody and Mic's place for some dinner.

Given that it would mean spending an hour or two with a group of guys who were clearly lusting after his woman, along with two of his former friends who were pissed at him for the way he'd walked out on them, dinner was the last thing that Cian wanted to suffer through. But Sayre was already walking away with her sister, and there wasn't a chance he was letting her go without him. So he sucked it up, gave Jeremy a tight smile and followed after her, figuring this was going to be about as much fun as having a tooth pulled.

But it actually didn't turn out that bad. The steak and baked potatoes were better than anything he'd had in a long while, aside from Sayre's stir-fry, and even though things were strained with Brody and Jeremy, they didn't spend the entire time telling him to go screw himself. He ended up taking a seat off in a corner of the room, and let himself simply enjoy watching Sayre interact with her family and friends in a way he knew she hadn't been able to do in years. He watched her carefully, looking for any signs of pain or distress, but she seemed to be doing fine so far. She maybe looked a little overwhelmed by all the noise and conversation, seeing as how she'd been on her own for so long. But he was relieved she was holding up all right, even if it did make him a little uneasy.

It wasn't that he wanted her to suffer. That was the last damn thing that he wanted. But he couldn't get rid of the unsettling feeling that something wasn't quite right. That there had to be an explanation for why she was handling things so well, and the knot in his gut hinted that it might not be one that he liked.

As the others finished off the meal with coffee and cake, she stood by the empty fireplace, talking with Max, Lev and Sam. He still needed to warn the males to watch themselves where she was concerned, but figured it would have to wait. They'd had a hell of a day, and he'd noticed Sayre trying to hide a few yawns, which meant it was time to call it a night and get his woman out of there.

He shook his head at himself for still thinking of her as *his*, seeing as how he'd never done anything but push her away. But the wolf in him couldn't think of her as anything but something that belonged to him.

And the man in him just wanted... *Hell*, he didn't know what he thought or felt or wanted anymore, other than to keep her safe, no matter the cost.

He crossed the room, caught her eye and motioned for her to join him. She said something to the guys, then came over to him, her expression difficult to read, which didn't make him feel any better. Was she angry? Tired? Irritated that he'd taken her away from her friends? He didn't know, and that just made him feel even edgier, as if he were already losing control of the situation.

"What's up?" she asked.

"I think it's time to call it a night. You've had a long day and should get some rest."

"You're probably right," she agreed with a soft, easy smile that should have warned him she was up to something. "I'll go with Jilly and see you in the morning."

She'd already started to turn away from him, but he stopped her by taking hold of her arm. "What the hell, Sayre? I thought you understood that you're staying with me."

She blinked up at him, that pink, sin-inspiring mouth suddenly pressed flat with irritation. "Not if you're staying in your cabin, I'm not."

His brows knitted with frustration. "What do you have against my cabin?"

Michaela's dry voice cut into their quiet argument, making it clear that she'd been eavesdropping from her nearby spot on the sofa, while Brody sprawled at her side with his arm draped over her shoulders. "Use your head, Cian. I doubt Sayre wants to bunk down in the place where you did most of your *entertaining*. That's asking a bit much, isn't it?"

He stiffened, the urge to argue and defend himself instantly building. But what could he say? The beautiful Cajun had spoken nothing more than the truth, and he made a silent vow to thank her for making him look like a prick. He knew Mic cared about him as a friend, and was grateful for the way she'd helped him find Sayre. But she also loved her husband beyond anything, and was no doubt angry as hell with him for cutting off Brody like he had.

Giving Mic his back, he focused completely on Sayre. "If not my cabin, then where are we meant to stay?"

Jeremy came over and clapped him on the shoulder again, not quite as hard as the last time, but still enough to jar his teeth. "Mic's just razzing you. I mean, yeah, we all agree with what she said. But your cabin isn't exactly how you left it."

Cian scowled, not liking where this was headed. "What the hell does *that* mean?"

Though Jeremy tried to play it cool, Cian could tell something was up. The sparkle in the guy's hazel eyes was making him worry, and he gritted his teeth as Jeremy told him, "When we didn't hear from you for an entire year, we tossed your things into storage up in town and redid the place. We've used it as a guesthouse for the past four years."

Irritation shot through him like the searing slice of a blade. "You turned my cabin into a damn bed-and-breakfast?"

Ignoring him, Jeremy looked at Sayre. "I swear the place has been stripped and repainted. Even the furniture is new."

"Son of a bitch," Cian snarled, but no one was paying him any attention.

They were too busy heading out the front door, and taking his woman with them.

* * *

Cian was still cursing under his breath about meddlesome assholes as they walked across the grass-covered Alley, and Sayre had to bite her lip to keep from laughing. Without saying a word, she climbed up the front porch steps of his cabin, caught between embarrassment that everyone knew what had been bothering her about staying there with him, and relief that they weren't going to have to bunk down with her sister and brother-in-law. She loved Jilly and Jeremy like crazy, but she wasn't sure how much interaction with others she could take before needing some space. She was doing fine for the moment, but was still cautious and didn't want to push her luck.

The others left her and Cian to make their way inside on their own, and she could have sworn she heard Jeremy snickering under his breath as he and Jillian headed back to their place after hugging her good-night. She wondered just how bad it could be as Cian used his old key to unlock the door and walked in. Moving to his side, she heard his swift intake of breath as he flicked on a light, and she swept the room with a glance, then looked over at him. The expression of horror on his face was so hilarious she had to spin away, using the excuse of shutting the front door as she tried not to burst into choked gales of laughter.

Gone were the rustic furnishings, cream walls and gleaming hardwood floors. Everything had been redone in a brilliant shade of shamrock green, from the upholstery on the furniture to the carpet and the paint on the walls. It looked like some kind of psychotic nightmare—one where a demented leprechaun had thrown up all over the room—and she had to silently commend the creative nature of their revenge.

As if he'd been listening in on her thoughts, he shoved both hands back through his hair and said, "I can't believe they were so angry at me that they actually spent money on all this shit. Jesus."

"It's, um, interesting, I'll give them that. But maybe they thought you'd like it."

He sent her a *get-real* look. "They knew damn well that I'd hate it, Sayre. You know that as well as I do."

"If you don't like Ireland," she murmured, pushing her hands in her pockets, "then why do you live there?"

"This isn't Ireland," he growled, running his tongue over the edge of his teeth as he looked from one eyesore to another. "This is the seventh circle of Hell."

"So then you do like Ireland? Is that where your family lives? Is that why you moved to Dublin?"

He grunted in response, then rolled one of those muscular shoulders. Apparently, that was the only answer he was going to give her, and she held back a frustrated laugh. He took stubborn to a whole new level when it came to being closemouthed about his past, but she was willing to cut him some slack, since there were things she didn't want to tell him, either.

When a soft knock came on the front door, he muttered something under his breath as he stalked down the hallway, leaving her to see who it was. She smiled when she found Jillian standing on the front porch, and stepped outside to join her, leaving the door open so that she could see when Cian came back down the hall. Judging by his reaction to the living room, he was probably searching the rest of the cabin to see what else they'd done to it. It was either that, or he'd scented Jillian on the other side of the door and decided to give them some privacy.

"First off," Jillian said with concern, keeping her voice low enough that they couldn't be overheard, "how are you feeling?"

Sayre crossed her arms over her chest to ward off the slight chill in the air. "So far, so good. There's…I don't know how to describe it. I'm tuned in to everyone's energy, but it's not overwhelming me. At least not yet."

As a wave of relief spread across her beautiful face, Jillian nodded. "That's good. Maybe you're learning to control it."

A slight shrug lifted her shoulders. "Or it could be that there simply aren't that many people here at the moment."

"Maybe," Jillian murmured, tucking a long strand of blond hair behind her ear. "But promise you'll let me know the moment you start to feel that it's too much. Please don't keep it to yourself."

"Stop worrying, Jilly. I'm a big girl."

"I know that. But…God, Sayre. What are you doing?"

Not really wanting to have this conversation, she deliberately misinterpreted the question. "Um, I'm pretty beat, so I was planning on getting ready for bed."

Her sister didn't look amused. "You know I meant with Cian."

Softly, knowing her sister was only looking out for her because she cared, she asked, "Is that really any of your business? You know I love you. But there are some things that should be private, don't you think?"

"If he was committed to you, then yes. But that's not the feeling that I'm getting from the two of you."

With a lopsided grin on her lips, she said, "Can't a girl just be in it for a good time?"

Jillian didn't so much as crack a smile. "Some girls, yes. But...that's never been you. And with the male who's your life mate? This is a recipe for disaster, Sayre. You *know* that."

"Maybe. Probably." She tilted her head a bit to the side, willing her sister to understand. "But what's my other choice, Jillian? Go through life never knowing how incredible it is to experience what the rest of you enjoy on a daily basis?"

Shaking her head, Jillian argued, "Sex without love is different than being with the person who holds your heart, Sayre."

"And you know this how?" she asked with an arched brow, fully aware that her sister had never been with anyone but Jeremy.

But Jillian wasn't going to concede her point so easily. "I know from watching others."

"Well, even if you're right, you don't need to worry about me." Trying to look strong, she lifted her chin and straightened her spine. "I know what I'm doing."

"I just don't want to see you get hurt. Either physically *or* emotionally. You've been hurt enough by all this." Jillian blinked, and Sayre hoped like hell she wasn't about to cry, because then she'd cry right along with her. "I can't help but feel like I've lost you."

"Maybe this will help me," she said gently. "Maybe I can actually get to the point where I can function normally. Then I could come home, and maybe even start a life with someone else." But they would have to be human. She wouldn't risk depriving another Lycan of their life mate.

Though she'd tried to be convincing, she could tell
by her sister's expression that Jillian wasn't buying it.
"I'm worried for you."

"I know," she whispered. "But you don't need to be.
Really, Jillian. Just trust me, okay?"

"I'm afraid that's easier said than done. And not because I don't think you're equipped to handle whatever
life throws at you. I just… I don't trust Cian not to break
your heart."

She shot a quick look through the open front door
to make sure they were still alone, then gave her sister a solemn smile. "He doesn't have my heart. At one
time, that might have been a possibility, if he'd…if he'd
wanted the same thing. But he didn't, and what's done
is done."

"And what of the danger he's brought down on you?
Something we still don't know anything about!"

"I don't think that was on purpose, Jillian. I *know* it
wasn't. So as much as I'd like to, I can't blame him for
it." Not that he'd bothered to share any of the details
with her, either. She could only hope that now that they
were in the Alley, he'd open up and tell them exactly
what was going on.

Jillian's next breath released on a heavy sigh. "I know
that Cian wouldn't put you in danger on purpose. It's
just…I'm worried and I'm angry, and right now blam-
ing him sounds like a really stellar idea. And it doesn't
help that I've missed you so much. You hardly ever even
email me, Sayre, much less call."

"I know," she said, feeling incredibly guilty, "and I'm
sorry. It's just…staying in touch makes it harder. But I
think about you guys all the time."

"Just please promise me that you won't shut me out again."

"I promise," she murmured, giving her sister another hug.

Before she left, Jillian warned her that their mother was going to flip when she found out she was back, but assured her that she would try to buy her a little time before Constance Murphy descended on the Alley like a force of nature. As Jillian headed back to her cabin, Sayre walked inside and locked the front door, hoping they were done with visitors for the night. She went in search of Cian, and instead found her things sitting on the foot of the bed in the master bedroom, which had been decorated as hideously as the living room. He must have gone out the back door and brought everything back from the Audi while she'd been talking to Jillian, and she hoped like hell that he hadn't overheard any of their conversation.

Stepping back into the hallway, she saw that the cabin's back door had been left slightly ajar, and she could smell cigarette smoke, which meant he was probably out on the back porch polluting his lungs. Deciding to get ready for bed while he enjoyed his vice, she changed into a small tank-and-short set, then went into the horrendously green bathroom to brush her teeth. When she came back into the bedroom, a magnificently barechested and barefoot Cian was sitting on the bed with his back resting against the gaudy headboard, his long legs stretched out in front of him and crossed at the ankles.

"You look exhausted," he said the moment she walked into the room.

She snuffled a soft snort under her breath. "Thanks. Lines like that must get you laid *all* the time."

Instead of laughing, he gave her a hard, steady stare that brought a rush of heat to the sensitive surface of her skin. "You could look dead on your feet and you'd still be the most beautiful woman in the world, Sayre. I was just trying to say that I'm worried about you."

"Oh. Um, thanks."

"Come on," he said, jerking his chin toward the empty side of the bed.

"Are we both sleeping in here?" she asked, unable to hide the surprise in her voice. After the way he'd pulled away from her today, she hadn't thought he'd want to get near her again so soon.

She watched his strong throat work as he swallowed. "Yeah, we are. I…I don't want to take any chances being away from you. Especially at night. And the bed is big."

She didn't say anything more as she put her toothbrush back in her bag, then made her way over to the bed. Trying like crazy not to drool at the mouthwatering sight of him sprawled on top of the far side of the mattress, his lean, muscular body the most mesmerizing thing she'd ever seen, she pulled back the blankets and climbed in. There was a hole in the left leg of the faded jeans he'd thrown on, and she could see a glimpse of the dark hair that was sprinkled over his strong, powerful thigh. Given how hot that little glimpse of his leg was making her, she knew better than to let her gaze drift higher, taking in his ripped abs, rugged chest and those broad, sink-your-nails-into-them shoulders. And then there were his big, round biceps, corded forearms and thick wrists that led to large, beautiful hands.

God. Her body temperature was rising, her heart pounding like a freaking jackhammer, and she knew her power was on the verge of breaking free in an embarrassing display of sparks any second now. Doing the only thing she could, she squeezed her eyes shut, praying he would turn off the bedside light as she started to roll over, giving him her back. But he stopped her with the touch of his big, warm hand on her arm.

"Don't," he groaned, pulling on her arm until she'd rolled onto her back and found herself staring up into his breathtaking face, his lips slightly parted for his uneven breaths. He lifted his hand and gently tucked a strand of her hair behind her ear, a slight smile tugging at the corner of his mouth. The look in his molten, heavy-lidded gaze made her shiver, and she licked her lips, so nervous and excited she thought she might come out of her skin.

Then he completely blew her mind as he said, "You forgot to let me kiss you good-night, lass."

Cian didn't know where those words had come from, but he couldn't take them back. Didn't *want* to take them back. He didn't want anything but the feel of her mouth under his again, slick and hot and opened wide for the ravenous demands of his lips and tongue, and so that's what he took. With his weight braced on his elbow, he leaned over her and ran his tongue over her juicy lower lip, then sank it deep inside that sweet-as-hell hollow of flesh. And, Christ, it was perfect. Soft and wet and impossibly addictive, making him crave even more of her—*all of her*—in a way that was even deeper than the visceral hunger for this woman he'd been carrying with him for years.

"I want *more*," she moaned, curving her feminine hands around the back of his neck, his skin hot and damp beneath the softness of her palms.

With his right hand cupping the side of her face, he tilted her head back at a deeper angle with his thumb under the delicate edge of her jaw. "More of what, baby?"

"Of this. Of you."

"Sayre," he groaned, rubbing her name into those cushiony, kiss-swollen lips, fighting the instinctive urge to reach down and cup one of her perfect breasts in his hand, her nipples tight and thick as they pressed against the thin cotton of her top in a way that was guaranteed to drive him insane. "Damn it, you little witch," he panted, his blood pounding in his ears. "You're going to be the death of me."

She broke away from the kiss and pulled on the back of his hair to get him to lift his head until she could see his face. "Don't say that," she whispered, stroking her fingertips across the stubble that covered the lower half of his face, reminding him that he still needed to shave. There were too many tender, intimate places on her body that he *needed* to put his mouth on, and he didn't want to be worrying about scratching her when he explored every single one of them. "With everything that's happening," she added, "I don't want to hear you talk that way."

He ran his tongue over his lower lip, loving how he could taste her there. "And I can't hear you say you want me without wanting to do things to you that should have me drawn and quartered."

Her lips twisted with a rueful grin, some of the fiery heat in her gaze dimming. "I'm sure it's nothing you haven't heard a thousand times before."

"It doesn't matter, Sayre." They were gruff, husky

words that were thick with his need for her. "None of it matters, because you're different."

"Good," she murmured, looking relieved, if not entirely convinced. "I should be different for you, considering what's between us."

"No," he argued with a snarl, unable to soften the frustration scalding him from the inside out. "It's not good. I'm not talking about the life-mate connection. I wanted you *too much* before I even realized it was between us."

Surprise filtered through her smoldering look of need. "You did?"

"You're damned right I did," he growled, clawing on to his crumbling self-control with everything that he had. "As wrong as it was, I wanted you even when you were practically jailbait. I wanted to get you naked and under me, Sayre. I wanted to keep you trapped there, at my mercy, taking every inch of me until I was buried so far inside you there wasn't any chance I was ever coming back out."

"Cian," she moaned, just as her power started to break free in a shower of tiny, golden sparks that glittered around them like fireflies. Pulling away from her, he forced himself to sit up, needing to give himself a moment to think, to get his head on straight, since he was about two seconds away from completely losing it. But she followed after him, bringing that breathtaking body of hers up right beside him. He opened his mouth, ready to tell her that he wasn't leaving, that they just needed to be careful and take things slow—not because he wanted to, but because it was the only way he could keep his shit together—when she reached down,

grabbed the hem of her tank top and ripped it over her crazy little head.

Holy mother of God, someone whispered inside his head, but he wasn't sure if the choked words belonged to him or to his wolf. His head jerked back so quickly it was like she'd smacked him, his lips parting as his eyes narrowed to piercing, focused slits. Her nipples were very small, and very pink, the way they topped her firm breasts making his mouth water and his blood burn.

Somehow, she was even more perfect than he'd imagined, and now he was seriously in trouble, his hunger like a living thing inside his body, foaming at the mouth, champing at the bit to get closer to her. "What the fuck, Sayre?"

"I want this," she said in a voice that was soft but steady, her long hair streaming over her freckled shoulders, framing her mouthwatering breasts so perfectly she looked like a centerfold. Only he'd never seen a centerfold who even came close to looking as devastatingly gorgeous as Sayre Murphy. She was...damn it, there weren't even words, and he couldn't have torn his gaze away from her to save his bloody life.

Blushing so hard she looked sunburned, that adorable mix of shy and bold the sexiest damn thing he'd ever encountered, she added, "They're not as big as you usually went for, but—"

"Shut up," he growled, quickly finding his voice so he could cut her off. He'd walk over jagged shards of glass before he sat there and listened to her say shit like that. "Your breasts are beautiful, Sayre. *You're* beautiful. Every addictive little inch of you is perfect."

And then he was done talking, because he couldn't wait another goddamn minute to get his mouth on her.

Gripping her upper arms, he pushed her back into the god-awful green pillows that had tiny pink shamrocks all over them, and came down over her. Everything else faded away, and he lost himself in the girl he wished like hell he could be the right man for. Holding her blistering gaze, he touched just the very tip of his tongue to one of those swollen nipples, the taste and texture so damn good he groaned. She was exquisite, and he shuddered with a hard jolt of lust as he lapped at her and rubbed the flat of his tongue over the pebbled, succulent pink flesh. She was exceptionally sensitive, her skin flushing with color, those tiny sparks of light still pinging around them. It was like being caught in the center of a star, surrounded by the surreal bursts of color and heat, while waves of sensation crashed into him again and again.

Keeping his heavy-lidded gaze locked tight with hers, he loved watching the emotions flash through those hazy blue-gray eyes. Excitement. Hunger. *Want.* Unable to stop himself, he scraped his teeth over the tender flesh of her nipple, a choked curse rumbling through his mind when she arched into the sharp caress. She might be the softest thing he'd ever gotten his hands on, but she liked a bit of bite with her pleasure, and his head went dizzy with the possibilities. It was like she'd been friggin' made for him.

She was. Jackass.

"God, Cian." She clutched handfuls of his hair as she held him to her, a husky cry slipping from her lips as he took the tip of her breast in his hot mouth and started to hungrily suck on her. "No wonder all the women made fools of themselves over you."

He flinched as if she'd suddenly poked him with something sharp, letting her nipple pop free of his mouth as he pulled his head back. "Don't," he ordered, forcing the word through his gritted teeth.

"Don't what?" she asked, as he put his face directly over hers, a scowl wedged deep between his brows.

"Don't talk about other women. They don't have any place in bed with us."

She stared up at him, rosy and damp with desire, those tiny sparks of light still glittering around her. But she was being careful to keep her expression neutral, even as she pulled that succulent lower lip through her teeth. "If you don't want me obsessing about your past and not being enough for you, then tell me what you want me to do. Tell me what you like, and I'll do it."

God...damn...it. Though he wanted her so badly it hurt, he knew he needed to stop. He was too close to losing control, and too irritated by the way she was coming at this thing between them to keep it together. He knew why she kept bringing up other women, using the reminder to help her keep things from getting too emotional, and it was bugging the hell out of him.

That was...bad, because he was too aware of how easily that frustration could get the upper hand on him, his need for possession overshadowing his common sense as what he wanted battled against what he could take without being a total asshole.

Closing his eyes, he rolled away from her and threw his legs over the far side of the bed as he sat up. "It's been a long day, Sayre. You should go on and get some sleep."

"Wait, what?" He could easily hear the disbelief in those breathless words. "Where are you going?"

"I need another smoke." He sounded like he'd swallowed a mouthful of gravel, and got the hell out of there before she could say anything more. Once he was out on the back porch, he propped his shoulders against the cabin's rough cedar planks and tilted his head back, pulling in deep breaths of the crisp mountain air, trying to make sense of what was happening to him.

Every time he touched her, he could feel his need for the little witch ramming against the defenses he'd built inside himself, stone by stone. Shields that made it possible for him to get through each day without her…and without doing something stupid.

There were things behind those walls in his head that he did his best to avoid. Pain lay there. As well as despair and disappointment. Failure and regret and guilt. So much that it made his insides feel like a festering wasteland. They'd driven him away from her before, and he honestly didn't know what would happen this time around, now that Aedan had already learned the truth about her. Yeah, he knew what he *wanted.* But how badly did he want it? What was he willing to do for it? How much was he willing to reveal? To lay out on the line?

Before, he hadn't been willing to dig any deeper for the answers, because he'd known he wasn't right for her. And he still wasn't. But that didn't mean he had any of this shit figured out.

The only thing Cian knew with absolute, unchanging certainty was that he would never be what she needed.

Or even close to what she deserved.

Chapter 8

It was time to come clean.

Cian wasn't looking forward to it, but he knew he couldn't put it off any longer. After a shitty night's sleep on the green velvet love seat that sat beneath the window in his bedroom—since he hadn't trusted himself to sleep beside Sayre in the bed—he'd awakened at dawn. Standing on his back porch with a steaming cup of coffee in his hand, he'd watched the sun rise above the line of trees, struggling to find the right words for the explanations he would soon be making. He'd told Brody the night before that he wanted to talk to everyone today, and the Runner had told him to be at his cabin at nine.

Since he didn't want Sayre around when he was admitting all his ugly secrets, they'd decided that Max and Elliot could keep her busy, and then the two youngest Runners could be brought up to speed later. It wasn't an ideal solution, seeing as how she'd be spending time with the young men without him there, but he would deal with it because he had to. Anything was better than her sitting in Brody's living room and listening to his confessions.

While the sun continued its steady rise into an azure blue sky, he was careful to be quiet so that he didn't wake

Sayre, who was damn near cocooned in the ugly shamrock sheets, only her glorious hair and the cute little tip of her nose visible. He grabbed a shower, then dressed in jeans, his black boots and one of his favorite old gray T-shirts that he'd filched off Brody years ago. It was sappy and sentimental, but it made him feel better to wear it, knowing damn well that the meeting could go one of two ways, and he wasn't entirely certain of the outcome.

As he put his empty cup in the sink, he glanced out the kitchen window and spotted Jeremy working on a children's swing set at the edge of the glade. In that moment, it really hit him, how drastically his friends' lives had changed since he'd left, and he lifted his hand to rub at the center of his chest, where there was a sharp pang. He could see it so clearly it was like he was replaying a memory, all those big, badass warriors out there playing with their kids, making them laugh and squeal as they tossed them up into the air and blew raspberries on their little bellies, while the women looked on with heartwarming smiles.

You could have had that with Sayre, his wolf pointed out quietly, its tone more solemn than he'd ever heard it. *We could have had it, if you hadn't left.*

That was true, but at what price? Five years ago, Cian could have convinced himself that the danger wasn't as real as he'd feared—that Aedan would let go of their feud and never mark her as a target—just so he could have her. But it wouldn't have been fair to her. Would have just been one more sin to add to his many, and she hadn't deserved that.

So you left. And look where we are. Right here, dealing with the same things you were trying to avoid.

He grimaced, hating that the beast was right. And, yeah, if he'd known this would happen—that his past would find her anyway—he probably would have never found the strength to leave in the first place. He would have claimed her, despite knowing he wasn't good enough for her...that he could never love her the way she deserved, and they would probably have at least three kids by now.

Did you honestly just say that? his wolf roared, seething with sharp-edged, visceral fury. The beast had been against leaving her from the moment the idea had first come to him, never wavering in its conviction. In its primal world, a male didn't walk away from what belonged to him. He conquered and claimed and worshipped, devoting his entire life to ensuring the happiness and protection of his female, while doing everything in his power to plant his seed in her womb and create life.

"I didn't say I wanted kids," he muttered quietly to the animal. "I was simply stating a fact. If I'd stayed, I have no doubt the two of us would have kept her knocked up. We'd have done everything we could to make that happen."

And that was the truth. All of it. But it would have been wrong.

You call her living out in that cabin on her own, with no family and friends, a better outcome?

He cursed under his breath, unwilling to concede that the animal had a point. But then, his wolf had never bought in to his feelings about his bloodline...or the guilt he carried over his past. In its world, when mistakes were made, you moved on and didn't let them hold you back. It was a simple, primitive view, and one he was jealous as hell of. Because he would have given anything to be that way, too. To say to hell with his concerns over what Sayre deserved, and simply take her because it was his goddamn right to do so.

Unfortunately, his humanity was too much a part of him, his guilt woven into the very fabric of his character.

And now he had to go and unload his darkest, ugliest secrets to the people he cared about most in this entire world, aside from Sayre, and it sucked.

He took a moment to compose himself, shoved his hair back from his face, then turned and headed over to Brody's. They were all there before him, including the mercs, the curiosity in the air thick enough to cut with a knife. While coffee was being handed out in the kitchen, he kept himself occupied studying the framed photographs that covered the mantel. Most of them were of holidays they'd had there in the Alley, when everyone had been together. A few at Christmas, and then Easter, and what looked like the Fourth of July.

There were more kids in the photos than he'd expected, though he shouldn't have been surprised, given how his friends hadn't been able to keep their hands off their mates before he'd left. But what he really couldn't get over was how happy the Runners looked in the photographs, as if everything they could have ever wanted or needed was right there with them.

If it were possible for people to be blessed or rewarded for their hard work and sacrifice, then Cian knew that's what he was looking at. These families were a blessing, plain and simple, and he finally had to turn away before he started getting all maudlin about it. As everyone came back into the room and took their seats, he pulled in a shaky breath, ready to confess every shameful, appalling part of his story.

"So, yeah. There's something important that I never told you—any of you," he forced past his tight throat as he leaned back against the mantel, his hands shoved deep in the front pockets of his jeans so that no one could see them shaking. Forcing himself to look around the room, instead of staring at the floor like a coward, he went on. "It's something I hoped like hell you would never learn. That I'm not proud of. Not for the reasons you're going to assume, but because…because of the choices I made."

"Cian, just tell us," Brody urged, his elbows braced on his parted knees as he sat beside Mic on one of the leather sofas. "If you'd just trust us, we'd be here for you. You know that."

"I'm… I have… Shit, this isn't easy."

Brody gave him a supportive nod. "Just go for it, man."

"Right. Okay." He sucked in a deep breath, then quickly blurted, "My, uh, father is a vampire."

Silence immediately followed those six little words. Dead, heart-thudding silence. The kind where you couldn't even hear anyone breathing. And then a pale-faced Jeremy kind of coughed to clear his throat, and managed to croak, "What?"

Before Cian could respond, everyone started talking at once as they grappled to understand his shocking revelation.

He understood their confusion. In the Lycan world, vampires were a reclusive, seldom-encountered species. They were coldly calculating, elitist and basically assholes. Immoral, amoral and arrogant as hell.

Huh. When he put it like that, Cian thought it was

kind of hard to believe they'd never figured it out for themselves.

When Brody finally got tired of the noise, he yelled for everyone to calm down, then turned his attention back to Cian. "We can't scent it on you," the Runner said in a low voice that surprisingly held more curiosity than it did anger. Aside from Sayre, it was Brody's reaction he'd been the most worried about, and he couldn't help but be relieved by how things had gone so far.

Exhaling a slow breath of air, Cian said, "You can't detect it because my father is also part human, which means my blood is too diluted for scent recognition."

"So then you're a combination of three different species," Sam murmured. "Human, Lycan and vampire?"

Cian nodded, then reached over for the mug of coffee Mic had set on the mantel for him earlier, wishing it had a hefty dose of Irish whiskey in it. He took a large swallow, then set down the mug and tried to explain to them how it worked. How his vampire instincts weren't a voice in his head, like the wolf part of his nature, but more of a…a *hunger*. A greedy, chilling, twisted craving for blood and gratification, like a powerful internal drive that was continually focused on consuming more…and more. And one he was only able to control thanks to the dominance of his beast.

When he was done, he had to wipe the sheen of sweat off his face with his sleeve, his insides knotting as he waited to see how they would react. After a few moments, it was Jeremy who spoke first again. "So if vamps can halt the aging process by feeding on blood as their main food source, then…Jesus, man. How old *are* you?"

A rusty laugh rumbled up from his chest. "Of all the things you need to ask me, *that's* your first question?"

"I've just always assumed you were around my age," Jeremy went on, looking him up and down with a critical eye.

"Close," Cian murmured.

"How close?" Jeremy persisted, obviously unwilling to let this one go.

A heavy sigh slipped past his lips. "I'm roughly ten years older than you are, because I spent a decade at the age of sixteen. Then I came here to visit my mother's family—I met you and the others—and I decided to change the way I'd been living. I stopped feeding from the vein, and allowed myself to begin aging again. All because I wanted to be one of you. To make my home here."

Everyone took a moment to digest what he'd just told them, and then Lev spoke up for the first time, scratching his jaw as he said, "You know, that actually makes a lot of sense."

Cian raised his brows, wondering where the guy was going with that statement. "It does?"

Lev smirked. "Hell, yeah. You spent damn near close to twenty years being a know-it-all, smart-ass teenager. No wonder you turned out to be such an asshole."

It was Brody who tilted his head back and laughed the hardest, while the others either snorted or smiled. And even though Cian started off scowling, he soon found himself shaking his head and joining in. "Nice one, jackass."

Mic was the one who commented next, her blue eyes bright with emotion as she stared up at him from her place beside Brody. "I have so many questions, I don't even know where to start. I mean, I could sometimes sense that you carried a tremendous burden inside you. But I honestly never realized that it was this, Cian. I wish you had told us. You have to know that we would have never judged you for it."

Sliding her a grim smile, he said, "I know that, Mic."

But he also knew that he hadn't even gotten to the bad part yet.

Stalling for a bit more time before he dropped that final bit of "craptastic" news on them, as Sayre would say, he looked at Jillian. She'd been sitting beside Jeremy the entire time, her blank expression completely at odds with the flurry of emotions he could see rushing through her wide-eyed gaze. "Didn't you ever pick up on it, Jilly?" he asked her gently, searching for the truth in those velvety brown eyes. "Every time you had to heal one of my injuries, I thought for sure that you would see—"

She cut him off, saying, "Never. I…I tried not to pry. I *always* try not to pry."

"You honestly never suspected?" he asked, surprised that she'd never seen the truth when helping him, since a witch's power enabled her to often see into the mind of the person she was healing.

"I didn't," she told him, shaking her head. "I thought…I mean, I *sensed* that there was something different about you. I guess I just figured that you were part of some powerful, unique bloodline, or…I don't know. That you'd inherited *something* on your father's side. But I sure as hell never suspected vampire."

"What about you?" he asked, looking at Brody.

"I don't know what I thought, man. Maybe that you'd… Hell, I don't know. I figured you'd been scratched by something, or fed on something you shouldn't have, and it'd affected you in some way. But I never suspected it was something that was as much a part of you as your wolf."

"Huh." He looked around the room. "With all those comments you all used to make about the damnation of my immortal soul, I sometimes wondered if you didn't already know."

"Naw," Jeremy drawled with a wry, lopsided grin. "That was just because you're an ass."

Everyone laughed, releasing some of the lingering tension in the air. As if they suddenly felt more comfortable, the questions started coming more quickly, one after another, and Cian did his best to answer each one as honestly as possible, even though he hated talking about that part of his life.

But he did it. For them. Because they deserved to know everything, seeing as how he'd brought this nightmare with Aedan directly onto their doorsteps.

Breaking out in a cold sweat, he eventually explained how the "black" or "dark" blood that created a vampire came in different strains: old lines and new lines. Somewhat sane ones...and ones so evil the creatures shouldn't even be allowed to exist. As if he sensed where Cian was going with the information, Jeremy suddenly gave him a sharp look of concern and asked, "What does this all have to do with Sayre being in danger?"

He pretty much flung out the answer, needing to get the words off his chest. "I have a brother. A half brother named Aedan who is a year younger than me. We share the same father, but his mother was also a vampire, which means that the vamp part of him is dominant, overshadowing the human part. He's the reason I came back to protect Sayre, and he—"

"Wait a minute. You have a goddamn *brother*," Brody cut in, looking ready to bolt to his feet. Cian figured the only thing holding his former partner back was the touch of his wife's hand on his arm.

"Brody, calm down," she murmured.

"No, that's not gonna happen. Because it's one thing not to tell us about the vamp blood," the Runner growled, his scarred face ruddy with anger as he glared up at him. "I don't like it, but I get it. But why the hell did you need to keep your family a secret? What the fuck is that about, Cian? I didn't think we kept shit like that from each other."

"We didn't," he said, hating the hurt he could see that was fueling Brody's anger. "But Aedan is a twisted son of a bitch and there wasn't any way to tell you about him without telling you about the other."

"How about 'Hey Brody, I have a brother. He's a jackass, so I don't like to talk about him. But I just thought you should know'?"

"Christ, Brody. He's not a jackass." He couldn't stop his voice from rising, each word torn out of him like a bleeding chunk of flesh. "Aedan's an evil piece of shit, and I spent ten years of my life acting just like him! *That's* why I didn't want you to know!"

The Runner's face paled so quickly it was like he'd been gutted.

Dropping his head forward in defeat, Cian screwed his eyes shut, hating that look of shock that had just spread across his friend's face. Voice weary and thick with disgust, he forced himself to explain as much as he could stomach to reveal. "He's a hundred times more powerful than a rogue wolf. Their drive and their frenzy—that's Aedan on a mellow day. I heard he once took out an entire Lycan family of eight on his own, within a mere matter of minutes. He's *that* strong. That screwed up in the head, and I spent an entire decade with him when he was a boy. At the age of sixteen, I traveled the world at Aedan's side, doing more shit than I could ever possibly name that I'm not proud of. But Aedan always took things even further. I tried to get him to… hell, I don't know. To tone it down, I guess, and I made excuses for him for a long time, like he was someone I needed to look out for and stand by because he was my brother." Lifting his head, he forced himself to look Brody right in the eye before he went on. "Then, one day, I ran dry. He'd done something that I couldn't make any more excuses for, and I got out. But not before I'd made a lifelong enemy of him."

Jeremy's deep voice cut into the heavy moment of silence that followed. "And now he wants to hurt Sayre because of you? Because she's yours, and he holds a grudge against you for something that happened all those years ago?"

Before he could respond, Brody shot to his feet and paced away to the far side of the room, then turned around to face him with a dark, vicious scowl. "That's why you left," the Runner snarled, his thick chest rising and falling with the harsh force of his breaths. "God-damn it, Cian! When you realized what she was to you, you took off to protect her. You didn't even ask for our help. You just left!"

Hardening his jaw, he managed a curt nod, feeling sick to his stomach. In that moment, standing there in the face of his best friend's pain, he hated himself…

and he hated his old man more than ever for not ending Aedan when he'd had the chance.

Though their father's vampire strain was one of cunning and strength, the "dark" blood from Aedan's mother was as evil as it came. Their father had always claimed that she'd used that ancient power to enthrall him, leading him to her bed against his will. But Cian knew better. Colin Hennessey was nothing more than a self-serving son of a bitch who thought of nothing but himself, and he always would be.

When his father should have destroyed Aedan, once they'd realized just how far he was slipping away from them, he'd refused. Because of power. The fool had seen Aedan as a weapon that could be used to defend his position in Ireland, not understanding until too late that *no one* controlled Aedan, including the man himself. Aedan had been lost to the darkness inside him from the moment his vampire instincts had gained the upper hand, and there was nothing anyone could do that would ever bring him back.

"Jesus," Kyle rumbled, locking his fingers behind his head as he leaned back in his chair, while Brody completely turned his back on the room, his hands braced on his hips. "I knew you had some serious shit going on under the surface that none of us knew about, Hennessey. But I never guessed it would be this messed up."

He didn't know what to say to that, so he didn't say anything at all.

"I wish you'd talked to us," Jeremy said with a tired sigh, his blond hair falling into his eyes as he shot a worried look over at Brody. "That you... Shit, man, I just wish that you had trusted us."

He swallowed so hard that it hurt, knowing there

wasn't anything he could say at this point that would make things better. This wasn't one of those times when *sorry* was going to cut it. Not unless he wanted to sound like an even bigger dick than he already did.

It was Jillian who finally cut to the heart of the matter. "How does this affect Sayre? Does she even know?"

He braced himself, knowing exactly where this was headed. "She doesn't know specifics about the threat, but she knows that Aedan is my brother."

"And the vampire part?"

Locking his jaw, he shook his head.

Perched on the edge of her seat, she gave him a look that would have brought a lesser man to his knees, the love she held for her sister making her fierce. "You have to tell her, Cian."

"I know." He swallowed, then wet his lips, each thudding beat of his heart making him feel like he was sinking deeper into a pit of quicksand. "I just...I don't want her to be afraid of me." *Or disgusted by who I was...*

Damn it, he didn't want to lose what little part of her he had!

"I can understand that," Jillian offered with a husky note of sympathy. "But it doesn't mean you get a pass, Cian. The only choice you have is to *trust* her."

Scrubbing his hands down his face, he muttered, "It's not that simple, Jilly."

"It's *exactly* that simple. You're going to have to man up and tell her everything. All of it." Her dark eyes burned with conviction. "Even those parts that are the... hardest."

In other words, the secrets he was holding closest to

his chest. The ones that would cause him to lose her, and not for a handful of months, or years.

But forever.

Chapter 9

Cian spent another hour with the group, questioning them about how things had been since he'd left. Not long after his strained exchange with Jillian, Brody had cursed something guttural under his breath and stormed out of the room, his office door slamming shut behind him a moment later. Mic excused herself and followed after Brody with a worried expression on her face, but the others were willing to let Cian turn the tables and ask some questions of his own.

Even Slivkoff managed to offer some helpful information without sounding like a jackass, and Jillian spoke up a time or two, though it was apparent her thoughts were a million miles away, undoubtedly with her sister. But, together, the group filled him in on the problems they'd had to deal with during his absence, as well as the challenges they'd taken on. It was clear that the Silvercrest were now thriving, and that the pack had the Bloodrunners to thank for their success. Relations between the Alley and the pack's mountaintop town of Shadow Peak had never been better, and he was glad that his friends were enjoying the recognition they deserved.

The only part that sucked was that he hadn't been there with them. That he'd missed each of the milestones that had marked the passage of time in their lives. Hell, the simple fact that all the Runners, with the exception of Max and Elliot, had kids now would be something that took time for him to wrap his head around. Before Mason had found Torrance nearly six years ago, Cian had never imagined the group would all be settled down and doing their best to add to the pack's growing population.

Before they ended the meeting, they talked over the Alley's security issues, and Jeremy assured him that extra patrols were already in progress. If Aedan wanted to get to Sayre, it wouldn't be easy for the vampire, and that was what Cian needed. A way to slow down the bastard so that he could deal with him one-on-one, while the others got Sayre the hell away from him.

When Kyle asked if he wanted a tour of the security procedures they had in place, Cian took him up on it, and he said a somewhat awkward goodbye to the others before heading out. There wasn't any sign of Sayre as he walked across the sunlit glade, and it worried him, how desperately he wanted even the tiniest glimpse of her— so he told himself it was good that he was getting away for a bit and putting some space between them. He and Kyle left the Alley in the merc's Jeep, and headed for Shadow Peak, to the security headquarters that the Runners ran there. They grabbed lunch while up in town, his presence at the diner drawing more than a few curious stares, and he knew that news of his return would have spread like wildfire before the end of the day. Not that he cared. The few remaining relatives he'd had in the town had moved away years ago, and there was no one else he would have wanted to catch up with, aside from some of the Runners' parents. But he figured he could

pay them visits after this shit with Aedan was over, before he took off again.

After lunch, he and Kyle headed back down the
mountain, leaving the Jeep at one of the new security
outposts that had been built out in the forest. From there,
they spent hours walking most of the security routes on
foot, then grabbed the Jeep and made their way back.

By the time he and Kyle, who had been surprisingly
easy to get along with, were parting ways, the evening
sun was already setting behind the trees, and Cian was
bordering on desperate to see Sayre again. He wasn't so
naive that he thought she wouldn't have heard about the
meeting that had taken place that morning, and didn't
doubt that she'd demand to know what he and the others had talked about. And when he refused to tell her,
she would definitely be pissed at him. But it didn't matter. He still wanted—and maybe even *needed*—to be
close to her. To see her. Breathe her in. Soak her into his
memory so that he'd have a full reservoir to pull from
when this nightmare was over and he was no longer a
part of her life.

Jesus. He had to stop on the way up his front porch
steps and brace his right hand against the railing, as
that last thought slammed into him like a high-powered
kick to his sternum. Whatever his frame of mind had
been when he'd come after her, he was man enough to
admit that things were…*changing* on him. His need
for her was taking on a new face and shape, until it was
something he no longer even recognized. Something
that seemed to be shifting on him with each second that
ticked by, becoming stronger…sharper, like a reflection
in the fogged surface of a mirror as it slowly cleared.

Which meant he'd just have to claw on to every bit

of control he could find. And when he reached the bottom of the well, dig even deeper.

When he didn't find her in the cabin, his teeth snapping together so hard at the sight of all that damn green that it made his jaw ache, he went back outside and ran into James. From the looks of it, the sweaty, bare-chested merc had spent the better part of the day cutting the plush green grass that covered the entire expanse of the glade, the crisp scent of the freshly cut blades thick in the air.

"You didn't happen to see Sayre out here, did you?" he asked, while James chugged back a bottle of water.

The tall, dark-haired merc wiped the back of his wrist over his mouth, then said, "She's playing poker with her boys."

He froze, hoping like hell that he'd heard him wrong. "Her *what*?"

James's brown eyes crinkled at the corners, the smirk on his face making it clear he thought Cian's jealous reaction was funny. "Her guys. You know, Max and Elliot and Lev. They always used to play together over at Lev's place, before she moved. Me, Sam and Kyle would sometimes join them, but it was always the four of them together."

Something hot and uncomfortable crept its way up his spine, then curled around the backs of his ears and settled sourly on his tongue. He'd never experienced the vile touch of jealousy before Sayre, but he'd felt it nearly every day since. Even in the years they were apart, it was a constant emotion weighing heavily in his gut, forever reminding him that she was somewhere out there in the world, enjoying her life…with someone who wasn't him.

Only, she hadn't been. Instead, she'd been living in

her own personal prison, isolated and alone, and that was on him. Not because he'd made it happen, but because he hadn't been there for her, in whatever way that she'd needed him.

Feeling like an even bigger jackass than he did before, he headed over to Lev's cabin.

Without even bothering to knock, he gripped the heavy metal handle that was still warm from the sun and opened the front door, the music and laughter he could hear coming from inside telling him that everyone was still there. After letting himself in, he saw that they were all gathered around a card table in the middle of the merc's living room, and he knew, before she even opened her mouth, that Sayre had been drinking. The alcohol had slipped into her scent, giving it a ticklish edge that would have been intriguing, if she weren't sitting there getting wasted with a table full of guys who looked as if they'd like nothing more than to put her in their laps and let her wriggle that sweet little ass of hers all over them.

The instant she looked up and saw him standing just inside the archway from the hall, a wide smile spread across her pink face and she flung her arms up in the air, throwing cards everywhere as she shouted, "I knew you'd find me!" Then she reached over and grabbed Max's beer, lifting it high and damn near spilling it all over the place.

Christ, she wasn't just a little tipsy. She was *hammered*.

"'N case you were wondering what I'm doing with this bottle, I'm toasting fate for being such a bitch," she said with a tiny hiccup, while Max tried to rescue his beer and Lev and Elliot just looked on with stupid grins on their faces.

Making his way around the table, Cian crouched down beside her, drawing her face toward him with the touch of his fingers on her chin. Sensing that there was something bothering her—and hoping like hell that she hadn't found out what was discussed at the meeting—he asked, "What's going on, Sayre? You were fine when I left this morning."

A bitter laugh slipped past those pink, velvety lips. "That's because you ran out while I was *asleep*. And then...then your *harem* started showing up!"

His harem? What was she talking about?

In a moment of clarity, she must have read the confusion on his face, because she leaned in closer so that she could explain, her breath smelling like peach schnapps. "There's been a steady stream of 'em all day. Blondes, brunettes, redheads. Slim, curvy, short, tall. Pale, dark, and everything in between. And every single one of them was beautiful." Her voice got soft, and she made the saddest little damn sound that he'd ever heard, whispering, "So freaking beautiful. And they've missed you."

He bit back a guttural curse, understanding now how Eli had felt when his past bed partners had tried to visit him in the Alley, after he'd returned. Carla hadn't reacted well, and neither was Sayre. Not that he blamed her, seeing as how that green-eyed monster was one he was only too familiar with these days.

"I didn't ask them to come here," he told her. "And I've no desire to see them, Sayre."

She rolled her eyes, or at least tried to, ending up a little cross-eyed instead. "Sure you don't. That's *exsh-*

mactly…I mean *expactly*…damn it, I mean *ezfactly* what I expected you to say!"

"God, you're cute when you're wasted," he rumbled, easily catching her in his arms as she lost her balance on the chair and slumped to the side, crashing right into him. Moving to his feet, he held her soft weight cuddled against his chest as he turned toward the table and the three guys who were watching them, their expressions almost tender as they glanced at Sayre, who had gone as limp as an overcooked noodle in his arms. It was clear that they'd been looking out for her, even while enjoying her drunken revelry.

"I'm taking her back to my place," he told them, hoping they were smart enough not to give him any grief about it.

Max and Elliot smirked, while Slivkoff gave a low laugh. "'Bout time, don't you think, Irish?"

Cian narrowed his eyes at the jackass. "You got something you'd like to say to me, *Russian*?"

"Oh, I have lots of things that I'll say eventually. When it's just the two of us." The merc cracked his knuckles. "That way I can make sure that you're listening. Real careful-like."

Cian flipped him off with the hand near Sayre's knees, then turned and headed back outside, unable to get enough of the way she felt in his arms, even when she was too drunk to lift her head. He could feel her lips moving against his chest, and was trying to make out the words as he carried her across the grassy glade. Then her voice got a little louder, and he thought he caught something about letting a wolf out of a closet.

"Hey, are you singing that Shakira song?" he asked, nuzzling the top of her head with his nose, her hair so silky that the animal in him wanted to feel it stroking over every inch of his body, the wolf more tactile than a human could ever be.

"What's wrong with that?" Her voice was a little sleepy, but not quite as slurred as before, the fresh air no doubt helping to clear her head a bit. "Shakira is *hawt*!" she added, and he could sense her smile. "If I were a dude, I would so tap that."

He gave a loud snort. "If you were a dude, seeing you drunk off your ass in those little shorts you're wearing wouldn't be nearly so much fun."

She pulled her head back, her pretty mouth hanging open in a way that was putting some seriously dirty thoughts in his head. Not that he didn't always have those around her. "Ohmygod," she gasped, blinking up at him. "Did you just crack a joke? I didn't think you even knew how to do that anymore."

His lips twitched, but he managed to choke back the laugh burning in his throat, not wanting to encourage her.

She snuggled back against his chest and shimmied in his arms until she could bury her nose in the crook of his shoulder, almost as if she were trying to breathe in more of his scent, and a sizzling spike of lust shot straight to his dick. "This is so weird," she said around a yawn, making him wonder if she'd sensed that he was getting hard.

"What's weird, lass?"

She danced her fingertips across his chest, her voice so soft it was nearly lost in the evening breeze. "Being here, in the Alley. In your arms. I mean, a girl spends years thinking she'll *never*—as in the freaking moon will turn into cheese and pigs will fly before it happens—never, ever, *ever* be in a certain place, and then *boom*, there she is."

"Huh. That was quite an emphatic never about ever being in my arms."

"Well, I might not be human, but I get a clue as quickly as the next girl. You leaving like you did didn't beed…um, bade…I mean *bode* well for ever seeing that gorgeous face of yours again."

He couldn't stop himself from pressing his nose back into her hair, the sweetness of having her close somehow making him feel better than he had in…hell, in *years*. With a cocky smile in his need-roughened voice, he asked, "You calling me gorgeous, baby?"

This time, she was the one who snorted. "Like you don't already know. You've seen a mirror, Hennessey."

His response was heartfelt and low. "Yeah, well, I don't have anything on you."

"Oh, get real. I'd rather you just be quiet than lie to me. I'm so, so, sooo sick of all the lies."

She was finding her words better now, but her voice still had that singsong quality to it that was a sure sign of someone who'd tossed back a bit too much. And from what he knew about Sayre when she was younger, she wasn't a drinker. Which meant it probably hadn't taken much to get her to this point.

Cian got her into the cabin and onto the bed with relative ease, surprised to find she was still awake when he came back from the kitchen with a cold bottle of water for her.

"So, I've been meaning to ask you about your tattoo," he murmured, after she'd finished taking a couple of sips and was snuggling down into the pillows while he sat beside her on the edge of the bed. He'd slipped her sandals off her cute feet, but left her in her shorts and tank top, knowing better than to tempt himself with the exposure of too much flesh.

"Hmm." Her eyes were closed, and he thought she might have passed out, when she suddenly asked, "Which one?"

His own eyes went a little wide—though she missed it because she wasn't looking at him. "You have more than one?"

"Yep. I've got three of them little puppies."

He laughed, which had her opening her eyes just enough to glare at him. Catching a pale strand of hair that was stuck to her flushed cheek and tucking it behind the delicate shell of her ear, he said, "Please don't tell me you have a puppy tattooed on your sweet little ass."

"What?" she gasped, smacking him in the shoulder. "No, you goober. No puppies."

Bracing his left arm over her body, he watched her try to keep her eyes open, thinking she was probably going to have his head for questioning her like this once she'd sobered up. But he wanted answers enough that he was willing to risk it. Apparently, he was that much of a *goober*. "So if you're not sporting a slew of killer puppy tats, then what are they?"

"Well, the one on my belly is Sanskrit. It's meant to help me find peace and to keep me centered. And then there's one between my shoulder blades. You haven't seen that one yet. It's a...mmm, you smell *really* good."

Christ, she was killing him with that hungry look on her face. Coughing to clear the lump of lust that had just lodged itself down near his voice box, he said, "I'm glad you think so, lass. But you were telling me about the ink on your back."

She blinked as if coming out of a daze, making him wonder where her thoughts had drifted. "Oh. Right. It's a pretty little owl in flight that's meant to help me be wise."

"And where's the third one?"

"The third what?" she mumbled, just as her eyes fluttered shut again, her pink lips parted just enough for her gentle breaths.

Knowing he had it bad when just watching the witch breathing made him so fucking hard that he hurt, he groaned, "Tattoo, remember?"

"Oh, that one's high on my inner thigh." She cracked one sleepy eye open. "And no, I'm not showing it to you. It's a secret," she told him, looking so incredibly young lying there on the shamrock-covered sheets, the spray of freckles over her cheeks and nose too damn adorable for words. He honestly didn't know what fate had been thinking to link her with someone like him, but it sure as hell wasn't what she deserved. In another world, where fairness ruled, she'd have been connected to a male who could be everything that she needed. Not only a protector and lover, but also a partner. A male who made seeing that she was happy his single most important mission in life.

Without even realizing he was going to do it, he heard himself ask, "What do you want, Sayre?"

Since he'd thought she'd finally dozed off, she caught him by surprise when she said, "You. I want to trust you, Cian, but I'm scared."

Though his heart had just lodged itself in his throat, he somehow managed to rasp, "Why? What are you afraid of?"

She turned onto her side so that she faced away from

him and wrapped her arms around her pillow, her voice so soft it was barely a whisper. "It's not your brother, because I know you'll deal with whatever's going on between the two of you. But I'm frightened by how badly I want you. Of not being enough for you. Of you walking away again, like you did last time. If I decide to trust you, and then you cheat or get bored or just move on, it's going to hurt so much. Worse than when you left me before, and I don't know how I would…" She pulled in a shaky breath, and with a catch in her voice, she finished the thought, saying, "I don't know what I would do, except hate you. And I don't want that to happen."

His gut cramped with a powerful shot of self-loathing, because he knew he would no doubt end up hurting her in the end. Not with another woman. Never like that. The last five years had clearly shown him that if he couldn't have Sayre, he apparently couldn't be satisfied with anyone else. But he couldn't stay with her. She was honestly the best person he'd ever known, and he cared for her more than he was comfortable admitting, even to himself. The most honorable thing he could do for her was to walk away once she was safe, if he managed to make it through this in one piece. To give her a chance to live her life without his shadow hanging over it, dragging her down with him.

So it's better for her to live alone than with us? his wolf snarled. *We're her mate. Hers. There is no other male out there who can make her as complete as we can. No one!*

"I don't expect you to understand," he quietly told the beast as he leaned down and pressed a kiss to Sayre's freckled shoulder. She didn't even twitch, her even breathing telling him that she'd drifted off. Being careful not to wake her, he headed out onto the back porch and lit a cigarette, needing the quiet so that he could think. But the animal wasn't ready to let him be.

Of course you don't expect me to understand. You just expect me to live with your choices and suck it up without complaint because of mistakes you made a bloody lifetime ago. Haven't we suffered enough?

"I won't do that to her," he growled, exhaling a sharp stream of smoke. "I can't."

What you can't do is live without her. And if you think it's only because of the mating connection, then you're an even bigger fool than I feared. I guess that vamp blood inside you really has screwed with your head.

"Piss off," he grunted, wishing he could get his hands on the beast and wring its bloody neck, not wanting to hear it. Any of it. "And learn how to shut up every once in a while!"

"What the hell, man?" someone drawled off to his right. "I didn't even say anything."

Twisting to the side, he found Jeremy standing at the bottom of his back porch steps, the guy's hip propped against the railing and his hands shoved in the front pockets of his board shorts. "I wasn't talking to you," he muttered, feeling like an idiot for getting caught arguing with his wolf.

Jeremy's hazel eyes glittered with humor. "Good to know. I mean, I get that I can be a pain in the ass. But that was a little harsh."

Fighting the urge to roll his eyes, he sighed. "What do you want, Burns?"

"Can't I just hang out with an old friend?"

His right eyebrow shot up as he took a deep drag on the cigarette, then slowly exhaled. "Are we still friends?"

"You really asking me that?" Jeremy demanded, sounding pissed.

"I haven't exactly been welcomed back with open arms," Cian pointed out, his tone dry.

Some of Jeremy's irritation softened. "Brody'll come around. Just give him some time. When you left, we all took it hard. But Brody—man, it really wrecked him. Thank God for Mic or I think he might've gotten so lost in his anger he couldn't find his way back from it."

He took another deep drag, needing the burn in his lungs so that he didn't have to think about what a bastard he was. "So that's just one more thing I get to feel shitty about, huh?"

Leaning his head back to stare up at the blanket of stars that were beginning to light the darkening night sky, Jeremy said, "You know, I fought my feelings for Jillian for a decade. An entire goddamn decade." A harsh laugh tripped over his lips and he lowered his head, locking that sharp gaze back on Cian. "It nearly killed me, and it was all because I was too stubborn for my own good."

"But you got her in the end because you deserve her."

"And you don't deserve Sayre?"

He couldn't hold back a grim bark of laughter. "I don't even deserve to breathe the same air as she does."

Jeremy whistled low under his breath. "That bad?"

"Yeah," he muttered, finishing off the cigarette, then stubbing it out in the ashtray he'd left sitting on the porch railing.

"I don't recall you ever feeling unworthy before when it came to women. You've always been one of the cockiest bastards I've ever known."

"That was screwing," he said flatly, avoiding the

Runner's gaze, "and it had its purpose. I didn't make promises, and I wasn't expected to."

"And Sayre expects promises?"

"She doesn't *expect* anything from me." He locked his hard gaze back on Jeremy's steady one. "But she deserves more than what I can offer."

"That seems like something she can decide for herself, without you doing it for her."

Narrowing his eyes, he made a sharp, bitter sound of frustration deep in his throat. "Isn't there some kind of unspoken Lycan law that says 'thou shalt not screw over the woman meant to be yours'? We're meant to cherish our mates, not use them."

"Well, maybe she's the one who wants to use you. And if that's the case, then what the hell is holding you back?"

"Christ, Jeremy." He scowled as he shook his head. "You really suck at playing the concerned brother-in-law, you know that?"

A gritty laugh rumbled up from the Runner's chest, and he lifted his right arm, then rubbed at the back of his neck. "If you don't think this is awkward for me, think again, Cian. I love that girl like she was my own blood. But this thing between the two of you, it's screwed up. Normal rules don't apply."

And with those insightful, irritating words, Jeremy headed back over to his own cabin, leaving Cian to his heavy thoughts and dwindling pack of Marlboros.

Staring up at the same expanse of starry sky that had held Jeremy's attention moments before, the glittering pinpricks of light reminding him of the beautiful witch passed out in his bed, he wondered if it was possible to live with this much regret and not lose one's mind. To find a way to make things right and change what seemed an unchangeable course.

He honestly didn't know. But as Cian sat down on the top porch step and pulled out another cigarette, he realized that for the first time in what felt like forever, he was ready to try for a little hope.

Chapter 10

After another uncomfortable night spent sleeping on the love seat in the bedroom, while Sayre sprawled across the bed, completely passed out, Cian found himself sitting on the edge of the cushions with his elbows braced on his knees, his damn eyes glued to the sight of her. He'd known better than to snuggle up beside her when she'd been so soft and warm and open. Without a doubt, he would have ended up taking things too far, and then he would have regretted the hell out of it. So he'd been a good boy and slept on the love seat.

And. It. Had. Sucked.

I blame you, his beast grumbled, its frustration like another living thing in his body, burning beneath his skin.

"Yeah, I blame me, too," he muttered quietly, shoving his hands back through his hair as he moved to his feet. He needed to make himself get a move on, or he'd still be sitting there staring at her like a skeevy perv when she finally woke up, and that was the last thing that he needed. The girl already thought he was a faithless ass-hat. No sense in dragging her opinion of him down any lower.

Then do something nice for her for a change.

With a low laugh, he headed out of the room and toward the kitchen, surprised that the wolf had actually offered a helpful suggestion.

I'm not the jackass in this partnership. Jackass.

Smirking, he opened the refrigerator door, scoping out his options. Twenty minutes later, he was carrying a tray back into the bedroom, complete with toast, bacon, eggs and a glass of orange juice.

"Holy cow, Cian. Is that for me?" She'd opened her eyes when he'd sat down on the side of the bed with the tray, her eyelids puffy from sleep. "I didn't even know you could cook."

Trying not to blush like an idiot, he set the tray over her lap as she sat up, her back propped up against the gaudy headboard. "Breakfast is about all I can manage. Thought you might need a little pick-me-up this morning."

"Thanks." She picked up a crispy piece of bacon and took a bite, her gaze sliding toward him as she chewed. "I'm almost afraid to ask what happened last night," she murmured, not quite looking him in the eye. "I know you carried me back from Lev's, but the details of our conversation are kind of sketchy. Did I make an idiot of myself?"

"Naw," he drawled, his lips twitching as he recalled her singing Shakira to him. "You're actually pretty cute when you're wasted."

"Hmm." She took another bite of bacon, then grinned. "I'm even cuter when I'm chocolate wasted."

"Chocolate wasted?"

She laughed as she reached for the toast. "Never mind. It's from a comedy. You wouldn't get it."

His immediate reaction was to stiffen a little, but he

tried to play it off like she hadn't just insulted him. Did she think he was too old to appreciate a funny movie? Jesus, did he seem like that much of an uptight asshole around her? Not that she was wrong, but that didn't mean he *wanted* her to see him that way.

"Hey," she said softly, leaning over to the side until she could catch his gaze. "I didn't mean anything by that, Cian. You just don't seem like a slapstick kind of guy. Your sense of humor is more...smart-ass."

"Thanks," he said drily, letting the conversation go so that she could finish eating.

He carried the tray back to the kitchen when she was done, planning on making a few calls into the security posts to check in on things while she took her shower. After seeing how tightly the security was being run around the Alley, he knew his brother was too sharp a hunter to simply charge right in without first evaluating the situation, searching for a weakness in the system. He figured they still had a day or two before Aedan made his next move, in the flesh this time, and he wanted to make sure that the scouts the Runners had posted were ready for him, knowing a single mistake could cost lives.

To Aedan, killing men and women was as inconsequential as crushing a bug under his boot. Hell, his brother didn't even discriminate when it came to age, killing children these days as willingly as he did adults. He seemed determined to live up to the monstrous expectations that their world had of the vampire species, and Cian had heard from more than one source that there were numerous bounties out on Aedan's head.

He put on a fresh pot of coffee as he made the first call, the Lycan in charge giving him an update on the routes they were currently running. Just as he was getting ready to call the security headquarters up in Shadow Peak, someone knocked on the front door. He found Brody standing out on the porch, massive arms crossed over his chest, his scarred face settled into an expression that fell somewhere between irritated and resigned. The guy definitely didn't look happy, but Cian figured this was better than the fury that had been blasting his way most of the time since he'd returned.

"Let Sayre know you're gonna be gone for a while," the Runner muttered. "Jillian will keep an eye on her so that she's not alone."

Mimicking his former partner's pose, he tried to keep his expression as stoic as Brody's, but it wasn't easy. He was relieved the guy was actually talking to him, and more than a little nervous about what Brody had in mind for their outing, hoping he wasn't about to get taken out to the woods and hunted. "Where are we going?"

"Just get your damn boots on so we can get moving."

Sayre was taking the longest shower in history, so he knocked on the bathroom door and shouted that he was heading out, his imagination working overtime at the thought of her tight little body turning rosy and slick beneath the hot spray of water. He'd have given his bloody right arm to open the door and climb in there with her, letting his tongue get up close and personal with every silky inch of flesh, licking away each meandering drop of water…working his way closer to that most private, intimate part of her that he wanted to lick and suck and fuck so hard it was killing him. Wanted to take her until she couldn't do anything but beg and claw and chant his name.

"What the hell, Hennessey? Do I need to drag your ass out of there?" Brody shouted impatiently from the porch, and he cursed under his breath, yelling through the door again to remind Sayre to be careful and stay near the cabins.

He met Brody outside, and they walked in weighted silence over to where a shiny new Chevy truck had been parked around the side of the Runner's cabin. As he climbed up into Brody's new ride, the two car seats in the back making him smile, Cian found himself thinking about the first time he'd met Mason's wife, Torrance. They'd all been gathered in Mase's kitchen, and he'd been ribbing Brody about being broody, like he always did, while flirting outrageously with Torry just to get a rise out of Mason. Even with all the chaos surrounding them at that time, with the hunt for a serial killer going on and all the crap that Eric, Eli and Elise's father had been involved in, life had been so much simpler then. It might have sounded corny, but it was true.

God, in so many ways, those days seemed like a million lifetimes ago. And now look at him. Sitting beside his former partner while they headed up the road that led to Shadow Peak, without a damn clue what to say. Back then, he'd have started singing Julio Iglesias or some shit like that just to mess with the guy, but now he was afraid to even speak.

Ah, to hell with it, he thought. He was just going to say something and if Brody didn't like it, he could kick him out or turn around and take him back to the Alley.

Clearing his throat, he looked over at the guy and said, "So what's going on? Is this the part where you take me out to the woods and break my neck for being such a jackass?"

"Tempting, but no. We're going up to my grandmother's place." Brody slid him a narrow look, then turned his attention back to the road before muttering, "Mic wants Cianna to meet you."

Oh…Christ. This was *big*. He knew, from talking to Kyle yesterday, that Cianna was Brody and Mic's three-year-old daughter.

Propping his elbow on the door, he rubbed his fingers along his unshaven jaw, and was unable to keep the grin off his face. "So Cianna, huh? Cute name."

Brody snorted loudly. "Mic's the one who insisted on it."

He swallowed against the lump in his throat, then shook his head, wondering when he'd become such an emotional pussy. "I know you don't care, but it…it means a lot to me, man."

Brody didn't bother to respond until they'd pulled into his grandmother's driveway and he'd cut the engine. Turning his head, he pinned Cian with a hard, don't-screw-with-me look of warning. "You make her love you and then leave again without a single damn good-bye, then I'm gonna kill you. Understood?"

"Yeah, got it," he rasped, wiping his damp palms on his jeans. He'd never spent much time around kids— hell, he'd never really spent *any* time around them—so he wasn't sure what to expect, and that made him…nervous. What if she took one look at him and ran screaming? What the hell did he do then?

They climbed out of the truck and were heading up the front walkway, when the front door burst open and a little ball of pink came flying out, crashing right into his legs. Cian reached down, careful to keep his hold gentle as he gripped the little girl's shoulders to stop her from falling over.

"Up!" she shouted, her little voice imperious as she craned her head back and lifted her arms.

Unsure what he should do, he glanced at Brody, who jerked his chin at him in a get-on-with-it gesture.

It's just a kid, his wolf snickered. *Hold her by the scruff of her neck and feed her when she bellows. How friggin' hard can it be?*

Choking back a laugh, he said, "Right then," and reached down and lifted her tiny body into his arms—holding her under her arms, instead of by the neck. She seemed to know exactly what to do, as she perched her little bottom on his right forearm and braced her hands against his chest. She was a beautiful child, with long black curls like her mother's and Brody's bottle-green eyes, the scent of fresh-baked sugar cookies and cinnamon clinging to her in a way that reminded him of Christmas. She blinked a few times, and stared at him so intently he felt like she was trying to read his mind. Then she leaned in a little closer, grabbed his cheeks with her chubby little hands and quickly kissed him right in the middle of his forehead. "That's how Mommy does it!" she said with a giggle, then pulled back and gave him an adorably dimpled smile.

"Thank you." He had to give a little cough to clear his throat before he could go on. "That was the sweetest kiss I've had in forever."

She giggled again and started rubbing her hands over the stubble on his cheeks. "Your face is all scratchy like Daddy's."

"It sure is."

"You's ticklish?" she asked, that dimpled grin of hers infectious.

"Nope," he said, smiling back at her. "But I bet *you* are."

She wiggled to get down, and he and Brody spent the next thirty minutes playing chase with her in the front garden, while Abigail, Brody's grandmother, looked on with a smile from the porch. When Brody looked at his watch and told the little munchkin they were going to have to go so he could get back to work, she threw herself around Cian's right leg, squeezing him with surprising strength while looking up at him and shouting, "Kisses! I wants more kisses!"

"Come on, you little flirt," Brody rumbled, a smirk on his face as he came over, pulled her off and lifted her up into his arms. With his face close to his daughter's pouty one, Brody said, "What did Daddy tell you about mauling people for kisses?"

"But I likes him!" she wailed, blinking like she was on the verge of tears. "I wants to *keep* him!"

Muffling a laugh under his breath, Brody gentled his voice. "Cianna, baby, he's not a toy for you to keep. Now stop it with the crocodile tears and give your old man some goodbye squishes."

"Yes, Daddy," she whispered, as she threw her arms around Brody's neck and hugged him tight.

"You gonna be a good girl and help take care of Nana?" he asked, nuzzling her curls.

She nodded as she lifted her head, but her lower lip started to tremble. "Whens you come back?"

"I'll come see you tomorrow, baby girl. And Mommy's going to be here to stay with you when she gets back from taking Jack over to visit with her friend Rachel. Okay?"

She nodded, and Brody lowered her back to the

ground. As soon as her little feet touched the grass, she ran over to Cian and hugged his leg again. He figured he knew exactly what the Grinch felt like at the end of that holiday movie, because his damn chest was feeling all mushy and big.

As soon as he and Brody were back in the truck and reversing out of the drive, he waved to Cianna one more time, and said, "She's adorable, man." His chest shook with a low laugh as he turned his head and looked at Brody. "You know you're gonna have your hands full when she's older, right? Boys'll be lining up from Shadow Peak all the way down to the Alley, wanting to ask her out."

"They can try," he muttered, flicking his signal on as they neared the next corner. "But if they're smart, they'll stay the hell away from her."

They had the windows down, letting in the fresh air, and Cian braced his arm along the top of the door. "How old is Jack?"

"Two months." Brody slid him a rueful grin, then looked back at the road. "Between the two of 'em, I'm already going gray. But Mic wants to have a few more, so I figure the more the merrier."

He shook his head and grinned. "It's crazy to think of you having a family, but I'm happy for you, man. I always knew you'd be great at it."

Brody grunted in response, and they sat in silence for a mile or so, until the Runner made a rough, frustrated sound in the back of his throat and smacked the top of the steering wheel with his hand. "I want to be able to forgive you, Cian. But you pissed me off." Keeping his narrowed eyes on the road, Brody went on. "I've spent years feeling guilty as hell for not realizing you were going to bail on Sayre and everyone else. But you blindsided me like you did the rest. Made me wonder if I ever knew you at all."

"You didn't," he said, the quiet words filled with regret. "I made that clear yesterday."

"I'm not talking about some damn strain of vampire blood. You think any of us give a shit about that?"

"You should. And you sure as hell would if you knew the way I'd lived all those years I traveled with Aedan."

"Bullshit," the Runner scoffed, while a muscle started to pulse at the rigid edge of his jaw. "You were a kid, Cian. What the hell did you know? Do we blame Elliot for the mistakes he made before we brought him into our group? Hell, no. We just found a way to help him move on. That's what friends and family are about."

Dropping his head back on the seat, he closed his eyes and let those words soak into his system, wishing he could believe them. Because if he could, it meant that at least one of the obstacles keeping him from what he wanted most would no longer be an issue. And what he wanted was a certain little strawberry-blonde witch. Even now, she was in his head, never far from his thoughts, his need just to be near her so intense he had no frame of reference for it. No idea what the hell he was doing, or how he was going to find the strength to walk away when all this was over.

"I know I screwed up," he heard himself say, "and I'm sorry, Brody. I was just so terrified of what he would do if he found out about her." He scrubbed his hands over his face, exhaled a ragged breath as he lifted his head and stared sightlessly out the windshield. "Leaving was the hardest damn thing I've ever had to do, after struggling to keep away from Sayre during those months before the war. But I believed it was the right choice, so I *forced* myself to do it. And it had to be the way it was. I knew if I tried to talk to you, I'd cave. If you'd said the things you just said to me right now, I never would have gone. And he would have found her even sooner than he did."

"I hate it," Brody grumbled with a rough sigh, "but I get why you did it. I'm not saying it was the right thing, but at least it makes some sense to me now."

"I feel like there is no right fucking answer anymore. As if this is all inevitable somehow, and no matter what I do, bad things are gonna happen." A hard laugh jerked from his throat, and he shook his head again. "Probably some twisted-as-shit karma coming back to kick my ass. I just wish Sayre didn't have to pay for my mistakes."

Turning onto the road that led to the Alley, the Runner said, "She's not going to pay for anything. You came back to protect her. That says a lot about how you feel about her right there, Cian."

He swallowed, wondering if the color was draining from his face as quickly as the blood. "It's not like that, Brody. I don't want her getting hurt, but I don't...I don't have those kinds of feelings for Sayre. She's an amazing woman, but what's between us is purely physical."

The jackass didn't argue. He just threw back his head and laughed, the deep sound gruff and full of humor. And he was pretty sure he could hear his wolf joining in right along with him.

Cian scowled. "Shut up, you ass." *Both of you!*

"Sorry." Brody's shoulders shook as he pretended to wipe away tears from his eyes. "You're just pretty damn funny."

"You know, I'm starting to wonder why I even wanted

you talking to me again," he muttered, sounding like an irritable jerk.

"Don't try to hide it, man. We both know you missed the hell out of me."

He grunted, but couldn't stop the corner of his mouth from twitching when the goofball winked at him.

Jesus. Broody Brody had just winked at him. And grinned!

Just like that, the five years that Cian had been gone suddenly felt like fifty. He'd known having a family would change the guy, but he'd never imagined Brody could be so...so friggin' happy. He was pleased as hell for him, but a part of him was also burning up with jealousy.

"And while we're having this gooey heart-to-heart," the Runner murmured, parking the truck beside his cabin, "I'll go ahead and apologize for losing my shit when you told us about Aedan." His auburn hair brushed his shoulders as he shrugged. "I don't know why that hit me so hard. I guess I just always thought of you as the closest thing to a brother I would ever have. It threw me to learn you already had one."

"Brody, man, you were more of a brother to me than Aedan ever was."

"Yeah, I kinda got that after I cooled down and thought about it," the guy rumbled, cutting the engine. He looked over at Cian as he opened his door. "Just don't forget that we're here to help. There's no need for you to handle this shit on your own."

He managed a jerky nod, but his damn throat was too tight to get any kind of verbal response out.

They climbed out, meeting around the back of the truck, both of them standing there with their hands shoved in their back pockets, no doubt looking awkward as hell. "If you and Sayre don't have plans later," Brody said, "why don't you come over to our place again? I know Mic would like to spend some time with the two of you."

Cian smiled. "That'd be great. I'll talk to Sayre and let you know."

Brody nodded, and Cian asked him to make sure the scouts posted at the bottom of the drive into the Alley didn't allow access to any more female visitors from town, seeing as how that was something he didn't want Sayre having to deal with. And he didn't want to deal with it, either—none of those women interesting him in the least. With a speculative glint in his green eyes, Brody said that he would, then turned and headed toward his cabin, while Cian made his way back over to his.

He took the porch steps with an eagerness that should have given him pause, but he was tired of trying to control every single damn emotion and desire that he felt where Sayre was concerned. He'd just started to reach for his keys so he could unlock the front door, when he heard a voice coming from inside the cabin that made ice sweep through his veins, the blood no doubt draining from his face for the second time in the past ten minutes.

"You're making the biggest mistake of your life!" Jillian and Sayre's mother, Constance Murphy, snapped, her sharp voice rising with each hard, slashing word.

In contrast, Sayre's tone was calm and controlled, though she definitely sounded tired. "Considering how you almost destroyed things for Jillian and Jeremy, you'll forgive me for not listening to any of your relationship advice, Mom."

"That's not fair, Sayre."

"Not fair?" Leaning a little closer to the door, Cian caught the sound of Sayre's soft, bitter laughter. "What wasn't fair was you lying to her all those years ago to keep them apart."

Though everyone in the Alley was aware of how Constance had tried to sabotage Jillian and Jeremy's relationship, he was surprised to hear Sayre calling her out on it. That took a lot of guts, considering her mother was one hell of an intimidating woman.

"I didn't want to see her hurt!" Constance argued, her tone making it clear that she still believed she'd been in the right.

Sayre obviously didn't agree. "But what you did hurt her more than anything. I won't let you do the same to me and Cian."

He sucked in a sharp breath, his heart hammering as Constance shouted, "Don't be so naive, Sayre. There is no you and Cian!"

"That might be," she conceded, her voice still coming through clear and strong. "But it doesn't give you the right to talk trash about him. I won't listen to it."

Cian slumped against the door, a little dizzy with shock, unable to believe what he was hearing. After the way he'd treated her, Sayre was the *last* person in the world he would have ever thought he'd hear defending him.

"You're making a mistake." Constance's clipped, harsh words vibrated with her anger. "He'll lie to get what he wants from you, promise you whatever you want to hear, and then where will you be?"

"He hasn't broken any promises, Mother. He's been

honest with me about what he's willing to give, and I've been honest about what I'm willing to take."

"You *slept* with him?" the older witch croaked, sounding *more* than horrified. She actually sounded afraid. "You know what that means. He'll know——"

Sayre cut her off, her tone firm but gentle as she said, "I love you, Mom. I really do. But what I do with Cian Hennessey isn't any of your business. It's between him and me and no one else."

"He's your life mate, Sayre," Constance said unsteadily. "You... God, you have no idea how dangerous this game is that you're playing."

"It's not a game."

"He doesn't deserve you! He's nothing more than an arrogant, no-good——"

"Stop!" Unlike the calm tone she'd used up to that point, this time Sayre's words cracked like a whip. "Just stop. I don't ever want to hear you talk that way about him. If he wanted me, I'd be damned lucky to have him."

"You just like his looks!" Constance cried. "It's lust, Sayre, and you're too innocent to realize it!"

"That's not true," she countered, her low voice thrumming with emotion. "Do I think he's quite likely the most badass, rugged, gorgeous male to ever walk the planet? Of course I do. Every woman with eyes in her head knows he's beautiful. But he's *more* than that, Mom, and you would know it if you had ever taken the time to talk to him. He's intelligent, witty and he can be incredibly kind. He's one of the most honorable men I've ever known. And believe it or not, I think he's trying to do the right thing by me."

"By leaving you broken and alone when he takes off again?" her mother scoffed, sounding surprisingly bitter.

Sayre's response was soft. "I didn't break the first time."

"Didn't you?" Constance questioned with a catch, as if she were on the verge of tears. "How is losing your home and the people who love you not breaking?"

With a swift intake of air, Sayre said, "I know you mean well, but you need to leave now."

"Sayre."

"I mean it, Mother. This is Cian's home and I won't have you coming in here and acting this way. He doesn't deserve it."

Angry footsteps neared the door, and Cian had only seconds to move back a few steps before Constance ripped it open, her dark eyes narrowing with fury the second she caught sight of him. Mouth pinched even tighter than before, she pulled the door closed behind her, then stepped toward him. "You're a bastard," she hissed, the loathing in her voice impossible to miss.

"Actually," he murmured, hoping like hell she wasn't about to turn him into a friggin' newt, "my parents were married. Much to my mother's misfortune."

She cursed under her breath and stalked past him, no doubt plotting some awful revenge against him for daring to come back into her daughter's life. Constance had never liked him before, and she obviously didn't like him any better now.

He smoked a cigarette while he waited for the woman to make her way over to her car and drive off, his thoughts churning with everything he'd overheard.

He didn't know what to make of her. Not Constance, but Sayre. He'd never known anyone so brave and strong and giving. *Forgiving.* He didn't deserve her concern or loyalty or any of what she was giving him.

But, Christ, he wished that he did. He'd have given anything in the world to go back and change those years he'd spent at Aedan's side. To undo his past and all the countless scores of women. To be a different person, with a different bloodline. To have a different emotional makeup.

This was, in all honesty, the worst sort of punishment he could be forced to endure. Being so close to what he would claim in a heartbeat if he could, but unable to have it. Thank God he was too damaged to love her, because he'd be relentless then, doing everything he could to make her love him back. And she'd be crazy to give her heart to him. Damn it, just having her loyalty was more than he'd ever expected.

Needing to see her, to be close to her, he quickly turned and opened the front door. The sight of her leaning back in the ugly green velvet chair that sat across from the equally ugly sofa, her eyes closed and her mouth soft and pink, made something in his chest flip over.

She smiled when she opened her eyes and saw him coming toward her, after he'd shut the door behind him. "Hey you. Where'd you end up going with Brody?"

With a grin tucked into the corner of his mouth so she wouldn't take him seriously, he said, "He took me up to town to meet a young lady."

She laughed, shaking her head, her expression making it clear she knew exactly who they'd gone to see.

"You're not even jealous?" he asked, lifting his brows with mock surprise. "I got a kiss and everything."

"I'll bet you did," she drawled. "I'm going to have to warn the little flirt that you're a heartbreaker."

"She's a cute kid." He took a few steps closer to where

she sat, loving the way the sun shining through the side window was setting her hair alight, the red strands looking like fire. Clearing the knot of lust forming in his throat, he said, "Brody, man, he's a great dad. It's obvious he adores her."

Her head tilted a bit to the side. "Why do you sound surprised?"

Pushing his hands in the front pockets of his jeans, he shrugged. "I'm not. I just…it's kinda strange, seeing the way things have changed."

She nodded, her gentle expression telling him that she understood.

Reaching up to rub at the knots of tension at the back of his neck, he said, "I, uh, heard you talking to your mom."

Her eyes went wide, and she turned an interesting shade of pink as she shot to her feet, then quickly took a few steps away, as if she needed to put more space between them. "Wow…that's, uh, really embarrassing."

"Sayre…the things you said. I just wanted to thank you. It's been a long time since anyone has said anything like that about me."

Avoiding his gaze, she snorted under her breath. "Then you should be keeping better company."

"To be honest," he rasped, "I haven't had much company since I left."

Her eyes immediately cut back to his, narrow and wary. "Now that I'll *never* believe."

"Before you get your claws out," he said, taking a step toward her, "and we get off track, I was just about to get to the good part."

"And what's the good part?"

His voice got lower. "Me showing you how much I appreciate it."

Both her eyebrows shot up with surprise. "And just how were you planning on doing that?"

Knowing he was about to shock the hell out of her, Cian moved with the speed his father's "dark" blood afforded him as he picked her up and carried her into the bedroom. Her back hit the mattress with his body braced above hers before she'd even managed to draw in a breath to scream, and he said, "I want to show you by making you feel good, Sayre. I want to make you cry out my name until everyone in the Alley can hear it."

"Why?" She studied him through her long, gold-tipped lashes, her provocative scent rising with the heat of her body and making him feel like the animal he was. "Because you're trying to prove a point?"

"No, baby." He lowered his head, burying his face against the slender curve of her throat, her skin tender and infinitely sweet beneath his open mouth. "Because I need to know what you look and feel and sound like when you come. And I don't want you holding back when it happens."

He knew the exact moment she chose to surrender— her hands fluttered against his shoulders as a shiver coursed through her strong, feminine little body. Then her head shot back as she arched up into him, her beautiful breasts pressing against his chest, while her scent became something so lush and thick it was like being drenched in her.

And that was it. He friggin' lost it.

Chapter 11

Chanting under his breath in a low, husky stream of words, Cian told her how incredible she was, how beautiful and sensual and how goddamn hard she made him, while he sat up, straddling her hips, and stripped off his shirt. Then he reached for hers. Seconds later, her bra had joined their shirts on the floor, he'd forced a knee between her legs and his hand was pushing into her unbuttoned shorts. His fingers slipped beneath the elastic waistband of her white panties, while his hot, heavy-lidded gaze devoured every inch of her, from her flushed cheeks to that sexy little tat circling her navel.

Breathing so hard and fast he was damn near panting, he lowered his head and took one of those plump, candy-pink nipples between his lips, sucking hard and then rubbing it with his tongue, his hand in heaven between her legs. She felt insanely perfect, her breasts firm and ripe, the folds between her legs deliciously wet and as soft as satin. Swollen and slippery with slick, warm juices that had his mouth watering with the visceral need to taste her. To lap at her like a cat with cream… or a *wolf* with something that it couldn't get enough of.

And then there was that darker, chilling part of him that was painfully aware of each hard, pounding beat of her heart…the enthralling rush of her pulse. But he fought that bastard back with everything he had, refusing to let his fangs drop from his burning gums.

"God, Sayre. I've waited forever for this," he growled against her wet nipple, as he slipped a blunt fingertip through that hot, slick cream, stroking between the silken folds of her sex, every part of him focused with predatory precision on how good she felt. How right. Keeping his eyes locked hard on hers, he moved his mouth to her other breast, tonguing that delectable nipple while he watched the hunger and excitement spill through her as he circled the tender, puffy entrance between her legs, then pushed just his fingertip inside. She gasped, her beautiful eyes darkening as he pushed in another inch, the plush sheath so soft and tight he was only managing to hold himself together by a bloody miracle.

"I like it," she breathed out, each throaty word slipping over his skin like a physical touch, as she pulsed her hips, taking him deeper. They were both breathing loud and harsh by the time he'd buried his finger in her up to the knuckle, their skin damp with sweat and burning with a heat that the gentle breeze blowing in through the window did little to cool.

Her eyes slid closed as he found the tight knot of her clit with his thumb, rotating the callused pad with firm pressure against the sensitive bundle of nerves, and he let her plump nipple pop free from his mouth. Rising up over her, he put his face above hers and said, "Eyes open, baby. Let me watch you."

Her lashes fluttered, then lifted, and… *Oh, Christ*, there she was. It was like looking directly into the heart of her, as if he could literally see every sensation pulsing through her, rushing through her system. Hot, violent, wild. She was coming undone right before his eyes, and he'd never seen anything so painfully perfect in his entire life. Never felt anything like thrusting his finger in and out of her plush, slick sex, the tight hold making him shudder.

"Don't stop," she gasped, her nails biting into his skin as she squeezed his shoulders. "Please."

"Stop? Jesus, Sayre. I couldn't stop even if the bloody roof was coming down on our heads," he groaned, covering that succulent mouth with his, his tongue sliding between her parted lips, mimicking the primal, penetrating rhythm of his finger. She was so tight, he had to work to get a second finger inside her, forced to break away from the kiss and suck in air, his blood roaring in his ears as the lush sheath gave a hard pulse, his hand soaked all the way to his wrist. She was close, pink-faced and damp, those glittering sparks that he loved so much breaking free, skittering in the air around them, making her shine.

"God, I love this!" she cried, breathless with need, her lashes fluttering as her gaze went hazy and dark. "Your fingers feel so big. I can...I can feel them stretching me."

In that moment, Cian wanted nothing more than to strip her goddamn shorts and panties down her beautiful legs, spread her firm thighs as wide as they'd go and devour every glistening inch of her with his hungry gaze...then devour her even harder with his mouth. But the tremors coursing through his tensed muscles and the savage clawing of his beast to be set free—so that it could mark and bite and claim—told him he wasn't there yet. That his control wouldn't last if he pushed it that far. So he shoved his own needs down deep enough that they couldn't screw this up for him, ignoring the fire in his gums and the raw, throbbing ache in his steel-hard cock, and focused on making her come.

Moving his mouth to her ear, he nipped the tender lobe with his teeth, his low voice rough with emotion as he said, "One day soon, when I have more control, I'm going to give you three fingers, Sayre. You won't be able to take them at first, baby, but I'll put my head between your legs and suck this tiny clit that's under my thumb into my mouth. I'll lick it with my tongue. Sip on it. Nibble it. Suck it so hard you're gonna claw at my shoulders until you draw blood. And you'll be so greedy for me that this sweet little sex will suck those three fingers right in. It'll be tight as hell, but will feel *so...fucking...good*, and you'll come so hard you scream my name, over and over, until that sexy-as-hell voice of yours just gives out."

"Oh, God," she moaned, gasping for each breath. "Cian!"

He ran his parted lips over her feverish, delicate skin, the muscles in his wrist flexing as he shoved his fingers deeper inside her, stroking the tips against the front wall of her sheath, until he found what he was looking for. He knew he had it when her nails dug into his rock-hard biceps and she gave a breathless, keening cry, her beautiful body writhing as he aggressively stroked that cushiony spot while his thumb worked hard on her clit. "You're getting so wet that you're soaking me, Sayre." His voice was dark and raw and deep, too guttural to belong to anything other than a Lycan male in the throes of lust.

As if his words and the sound of his voice were what she needed to push her over the edge, her head went back, she sank her nails into his bare shoulders and screamed like a little banshee. Crashing over that dark edge and into oblivion, she came so hard and hot and wild, her scent rising, getting richer...deeper...sinking into his system like a goddamn narcotic. And all the while, her tight sex was throbbing against his hand, convulsing around his fingers so perfectly it was like a dream, while these throaty whimpers kept spilling past her rosy lips.

"Sayre, Christ, no more," he choked out, shaking so hard it was making the bed rattle. "Shh, baby, shh. I can't take it."

"Wh-what?" she gasped, blinking her eyes open, the look in them so hazy and sweet, he had to lower his gaze. But it didn't help. The sight of her bare breasts and trembling belly, her shorts wrenched open, his big hand shoved down the front of her panties, was the most provocative thing he'd ever seen. So beautiful it was burned into his mind, carved into his flesh like a scar.

"I'm barely holding myself together here," he growled, feeling his wolf punch against his insides, desperate to get out, while that savage, aggressive pull that he'd felt the first time they'd kissed started blaring in his head again, roaring for him to take and mark and possess. "If you make one of those little sounds again, I won't be able to...to keep...to keep from *nailing* you to this goddamn mattress."

"Mmm. If it feels anything like *that* did," she moaned, grinning up at him, completely oblivious to the fact that she needed to be...careful, "I doubt I'll complain. Heck, I might even beg you."

Sayre quickly squeezed her eyes shut again. The way Cian had just stiffened, as if he couldn't believe what she'd said to him, made her wonder if she'd lost her mind.

Honestly, when was she going to learn?

"Sayre," he growled, his voice even grittier as he pressed closer against her, his cock a hard, thick ridge shoved against her hip. "*What* did you just say?"

She forced her eyes back open, and as if listening through a fog, she heard herself tell him, "I want you, Cian. I...I don't think that should come as a surprise."

His heavy gaze was savage and hot, full of molten, primitive need. "How? *How* do you want me?"

Her breath came in short, sharp pants, and she licked her lips. "All of you. Every part. But I can't do it with so many secrets between us. Are you...I mean, will you tell me about Aedan now?"

He froze, not even breathing...then cursed so viciously it made her blink. And before she even knew what was happening, he'd pulled his fingers from her body and was rolling away from her in one smooth, effortless move. One moment she'd been surrounded by his heat, and in the next, she was lying on the cold sheets, staring at the sleek, powerful length of his back, his shoulders tight with tension. His head hung forward, the dark fall of his hair shielding his profile, but she knew that firm jaw would be locked, that telling tic pulsing beneath his tanned skin.

Sounding as if the stark words were being ripped out of him, he said, "I'm going outside for a smoke."

She would have laughed, but wasn't sure it wouldn't come out as a sob. "Sure, whatever. Like I haven't seen you do *that* before."

"I don't want to." The confession seemed to punch its way free from his chest, his biceps so hard they looked like boulders. Shoving one of his big hands back through his hair, he said, "But I *have* to, Sayre. I can't…I don't have any other choice right now."

"It's fine, Cian. Go."

Without another word, he shot off the bed, grabbed his shirt and got the hell out of there. She knew it would be useless to wait for him and hope he'd come back to her, ready to open up and let her in, finally answering her questions. This, his leaving the room, *was* her answer. And while there was a part of her that felt like a fool for defending him earlier, she couldn't regret it. She just…she needed to be smart where her emotions were concerned, and not lose sight of what was happening between them. Needed to remember that with the life-mate connection, there was some powerful mojo working to draw them together. So while they wanted each other, it didn't necessarily mean that they wanted the same things…or in the same ways.

Yes, she knew that he cared enough about her to want to see her safe and protected. He was just *that* kind of guy. But he was also the "other" kind of guy, and while he wanted her now, she knew she couldn't let herself think in terms of him wanting her forever.

But when he made her feel the way he had just moments before, touching and kissing her as if she were something…*God*, as if she were something *vital* to him, it was difficult to keep those rational threads of reason woven into the framework of her thoughts. To remember, and not forget. Not dream. Because dreaming could be fatal to her heart, and that particular organ had already taken too many hits. Each time she'd seen him with another woman, it had been like a physical strike. Like a blade stabbed into the middle of her chest.

It was up to her to protect that part of her that could be too easily broken for good this time. In a way that never healed. And that could never be forgiven.

Feeling decades older than she was, she forced herself to get up and get a move on. She sorted her clothing, pulled her hair up into a ponytail, put on the hiking boots that she gardened in and decided working outside was a better use of her time than sitting in Cian's cabin and brooding over him.

But, hey, at least he hadn't walked away and left her hanging again. Her body was still buzzing with a warm, sensual burn of pleasure from the mind-blowing orgasm he'd given her, her muscles deliciously loose, and she no doubt had some kick-ass color in her cheeks. And it was a beautiful day, the sun shining in a cloudless sky, which meant she needed to get her butt outside and enjoy it. She figured she could hunt down some gardening tools and do some maintenance work on the colorful flower beds that had been planted between the cabins. Maybe she'd even try to find Kyle, since she'd missed the way he teased her and that soft-edged Southern accent of his, and see if he wanted to help her.

And seeing as how he'd spent the better part of yesterday with Cian, she was hopeful the merc might have some useful information for her. But as it turned out, she never ran into Kyle. She spent the day out in the summer sunshine, working on various projects, and enjoyed herself, for the most part. Although...she couldn't quite shake the feeling that something was, well, *off.* Yeah, she knew everyone was on edge because Cian's psycho brother was apparently out there somewhere, preparing to make a move against her. And since she wasn't a fool, she was freaked out about it, too. But there was more going on than she knew about. It didn't matter who she was talking to, they all seemed to be looking at her in an expectant way, as if there were something they wanted to ask her, but weren't sure if they should.

As the day wore on, it became increasingly clear that something was definitely going on. And that something was seriously pissing her off.

Not only had Cian not shown his face again and gone off to God only knew where, but it was like everyone had suddenly learned a secret she didn't know about, and now they didn't know how to act around her. She knew it must have something to do with the meeting Cian had held with the others the day before—the one she hadn't been invited to. And when she finally bit the bullet and just asked her sister for details, point-blank, Jillian wouldn't tell her a damn thing.

It was obvious she felt bad about that. But Jilly clearly thought she should be talking to Cian. Which was easier said than done, since the man was doing a damn good job of avoiding her. She'd even tried texting him, but he wasn't responding.

"Fine," she huffed to herself as she opened the front door of his cabin and headed back outside. She'd gone back to the cabin an hour earlier, after bombing out on getting some answers from her sister, and was tired of wearing down the floorboards with her pacing. "I'll find something else to do to keep busy," she muttered, heading down the porch steps again. She was trying to decide if she wanted to go back to gardening, or if she should just find a cool place in the shade and read a book on her smartphone, when someone called her name.

She turned and saw Max jogging over to her, a wide smile on his handsome face. "Hey, Max. What's up?"

"I was wondering if you wanted to hang out tonight," he said as he came to a stop right in front of her, the wind playing havoc with his dark curls. "I haven't got to spend much chill time with you since you came home."

Her lips twitched as she tilted her head back to stare up at him. "Drunken poker games don't count?"

He laughed as he pushed his hands in the front pockets of his jeans and lifted his brows. "Not that it wasn't fun watching you get obliterated, but I was hoping you might come over and have dinner. I think Elliot was planning on stopping by, so it'll be just like old times."

She almost winced, but somehow managed to hold it back. Old times for her hadn't necessarily been happy times, though she'd always been grateful for Max's friendship. He had a mellow, natural cool that made it impossible not to like him, and she'd always found him easy to be around. Despite what she'd insinuated to Cian the night he'd left the Runners, she never would have gone to Max or Elliot for sex. Their friendship had always been too close for that, and she never would have jeopardized it just to make a point.

Not that she ever planned on confessing any of that to Cian. The guy was already cocky enough when it came to his appeal. God knew he didn't need any encouragement.

She accepted Max's invitation, glad that Elliot could join them, and spent the rest of the evening trying to shake off her funk and simply enjoy spending time with two of her best friends. She'd missed these guys like crazy. Max was still the easygoing, nowhere-near-ready-to-settle-down guy that he'd always been. And Elliot was still kind of quiet, but funny as hell. He didn't talk about having a woman in his life, and it made her heart hurt that he was still so wary of trusting himself, after going through a horrific ordeal five years ago. One that had resulted in the deaths of two innocent young women, and had nearly turned Elliot into a rogue wolf. The Runners had saved him, but she knew he still carried the scars of that experience on the inside, and hoped he'd one day be able to leave it in the past.

When she finally headed back over to Cian's around nine, she was surprised to find him sitting in the velvet chair in the living room all alone, as if he'd been waiting for her, the only light a soft glow filtering in from the kitchen.

"What's up with all the plants out on the porch?" was the first thing she said to him, having seen them as she'd come in. Small ones, big ones, some with colorful flowers and others with big, waxy green leaves that looked so beautiful it stole her breath, like something from the tropics. There was a fortune in plants sitting out on his front porch, and it made her a little giddy to think he might have gotten them just for her.

Leaning forward, he braced his elbows on his parted knees and answered her question. "I spent most of the day running patrols out in the woods, but I did a quick run up to town with James to check in with the security headquarters there, and we passed the new garden center just as they were getting a delivery. So I asked him to stop so I could grab you a few things. I figured you might want something to keep you busy while we're here, and I know it's something you enjoy."

She blinked, no idea what to say in response. This guy…he seemed to do nothing but put her off balance. Pull her close; push her away. An ebb and flow that went against everything inside her, every part of her, because fate wanted nothing more than to pull them so close they became one and remained that way. A unit. Unbreakable and unstoppable.

But fate wasn't life. It wasn't what would protect her heart. Keep her from shattering into so many pieces she couldn't ever be put back together again.

"Have a good time tonight with Max and Elliot?" he finally asked her, breaking the awkward silence.

A little surprised that he'd even bothered to find out where she'd been, she said, "Yeah, it was great to catch up. I've missed them."

"I'm sure they've missed you, too." He moved to his feet and hooked his thumbs in his front pockets, his shuttered gaze impossible to read. "Brody and Mic invited us over for dinner, but I told them you were busy."

"Oh. You didn't mention it before."

Voice a little too tight for her not to pick up on his tension, he said, "I didn't realize you were going to stay out."

"Yeah, well, I didn't realize you were coming back," she replied just as tightly, a fresh wave of irritation spiking through her at the way he'd avoided her for almost the entire damn day.

He frowned as he rubbed a big hand over his mouth, and she realized this conversation was going nowhere fast. Getting it back on track, she exhaled a rough breath and added, "You know, you should probably give Max a big ol' thank-you."

His dark brows started to draw together. "And why's that?"

"Because I tried to get him to tell me the big secret," she explained, crossing her arms over her chest, "but he held firm and wouldn't budge."

Agitation spilled over the quick spark of surprise she'd spotted in his sharp gaze, veiling its light like clouds over the gleaming heat of the sun. "You questioned Max about me?"

She gave a soft snort. "Cian, I'm not stupid. I know something went down at the 'briefing' you held with the others yesterday. It's obvious that everyone knows something big that I don't. Not even Jillian would tell me, and that *hurt*. She just kept saying to ask you about it."

He lifted his powerful arms and gripped the back of his neck, then ran his hands up the back of his head, his body so tense and hard he seemed even larger, when his presence was already so overwhelming it blotted out everything else around him. He constantly burned like a pulsing star in the center of her existence, blindingly white-hot and elusive, always too far away to touch, even when he was right the hell in front of her.

She couldn't help but wonder if she would still feel that way if he were buried deep inside her. Would she stare up into that beautifully masculine, fallen-angel face and finally feel at home? Or would it be like staring into the eyes of a stranger, cold and lonely and empty?

Swallowing her grief like it was a bitter pill she'd been forced to take, she choked out, "Is it another woman?"

Slowly lowering his arms to his sides, he shot her a startled look. "What?"

"If it's about your brother, I can't understand why you wouldn't tell me. So is there someone else? Up in town? Or somewhere else? Did you learn you have a child with someone? Is that what everyone's hiding from me?"

His shoulders dropped as if the weight of the world had just landed on them. "Sayre, stop," he said, shaking his head. "There are no kids, and there's sure as hell no other woman. I don't want anyone but you." Scrubbing his hands over his gorgeous face, he muttered, "God, life would be a whole lot simpler right now if I did."

She flinched, hating that he noticed, those molten eyes darkening to stormy gray.

Giving her a piercing look, he took a step closer to where she stood. "Let me finish, lass."

"What more is there to say? You want me—I believe that. But it's the connection. You can't help it. And you don't *want* it, Cian. You don't want to feel that way. *That's* why you keep pulling away from me."

"You're wrong," he said, softly but with an unmistakable vein of anger. Or maybe it was…hopelessness. Something lost and filled with pain. "Despite everything, how wrong and completely shit this is for you, the truth is that I *wouldn't* change it. I know that's unfair as hell to say, but I wouldn't want this connection with anyone *but* you."

She blinked, more than a little undone, and thought *God. Just God.* They were pretty words from a pretty mouth on a pretty face. Hard, rugged, masculine—but undeniably beautiful. And yet, it was what was beneath his skin that had her tied in knots. Ever since they'd returned to the Alley, the pieces had been coming back to her. Fragments and memories and emotions. The ones that had drawn her to him all those years ago. That had made her fall for him so hard she was still crashing through space, waiting for the landing. Terrified it would be unforgivably brutal and break her, but secretly hoping, like a fool, that he would be there to catch her in the end. That when she crashed, it would be *into* him, into the private, most intimate part of him, and she'd be safe. Rather than against the hard, jagged edges he kept trying so hard to hide behind.

Drawing in a slow, steadying breath, she asked, "If not another woman, then what?"

Frustration scored his words. "Why, Sayre? Why do you keep pushing this?"

"Because everyone knows but *me*. And I deserve to not be left out in the dark, because it's my life that this brother of yours supposedly wants. *Mine*, not theirs. And after everything that's happened, that's happening *now*, you owe me this. The truth. What are you so afraid of?"

The skin around his eyes pulled tight, that muscle pulsing like a heartbeat in his hard jaw. "If I tell you, it will…change things."

"What things?"

"Sayre." He sounded like a man being forced over the edge from a terrible height, but she knew if she backed down now, he might never tell her. Not until it was too late and she was being faced with a cold, hard reality in the middle of Hell.

If Aedan were coming for her, she wanted to know what she and everyone else here was up against.

Thoughts spinning, she studied him, using everything she had to understand him…read him and pick the clues out in not just what he was saying, but what he wasn't. "Is it me, Cian? You think whatever you confess is going to change *me*?"

He scowled, turned away from her and stalked to the window, then braced his hands on either side of its dark, reflective surface. His posture was rigid, his powerful muscles bulging beneath the tight stretch of his skin, making him look exactly like the hard, dangerous creature she knew he could be. He squeezed the sides of the window frame so tightly she was surprised the wood hadn't cracked, sensing a deep-seated anger and pain seething inside him, and in a dizzying moment of clarity, she suddenly understood what had been holding him back.

"You think it will change this. *Us*. The way that I feel about you."

He smacked his open hands against the window frame so hard it made the glass shake. "I know I don't *have* you. I *know* that. But I don't want to lose you, either. I don't want to lose the small part of you that I *do* have."

"Then you're just going to have to trust me."

A low, humorless laugh jerked from his chest. But he remained silent, his shoulders heaving with the harshness of his breaths.

"It isn't that hard, is it? I've trusted you. With my life. With my body."

He groaned as he leaned forward, pressing his forehead against the glass. "Don't want to lose that."

"Then trust me when I say that you won't," she told him, taking a few cautious steps closer, wanting so badly to reach out and run a soothing touch over the rigid length of his spine, his broad shoulders stretching the cotton of his T-shirt until she was surprised it hadn't shredded. "So long as you're honest with me, you won't lose anything."

Quietly, he said. "No, Sayre. I'm going to lose everything. I don't see any other way."

"Just tell me. *Now*."

He turned then, the look in his beautiful eyes so dark and pained, it made her gasp. Voice little more than a choked thread of sound, he rasped, "I'm…a…vampire."

She blinked, thinking she must have heard him wrong. "Um, say that again, please."

"My father is part vampire, and he passed the bloodline onto me. It's not as dominant as my wolf or my human sides, but it's there. A part of me."

"Ohmygod," she breathed, her thoughts flying so fast she couldn't keep up with them. So many things were crashing together in her mind, mysteries that suddenly made sense, holes filled with an answer that she'd never, *ever* expected.

He drew an unsteady breath. "God didn't have anything to do with it, lass. It's pure evil."

She straightened, glaring daggers at him. "Bullshit."

Cian figured it was his turn to look surprised, because she'd just shocked the hell out of him.

"Don't look so stunned," she snapped. "You're a lot of things, Cian Hennessey, but evil isn't one of them."

He laughed low and rough, the bitter sound making him cringe. "I wish that were true. But you don't know the things I've done."

Her gaze glittered with challenge. "Then tell me. If this is part of the reason you left me, then I deserve to know."

"Sayre," he said with a tired, wrecked sigh.

"*Tell me*, Cian."

Almost as if he had no control over himself, he could hear the graveled words bursting from his throat. "At the age of fifteen, we're fully matured, at least physically. At that point, if we consume blood as one of our main food sources, we can halt the aging process."

Her eyes went wide. "Have you ever done that?"

He gave a jerky nod, and stared at the pulse rushing

at the delicate base of her throat, unable to meet her eyes as he said, "I spent a decade by Aedan's side at the age of sixteen. I…I was angry, at my parents, because of… well, because of *him*."

He turned, braced his shoulder against the wall beside the window and explained it all. Everything. How he hadn't learned of Aedan's existence until he was fifteen. Aedan's mother had been killed, and the boy had come to live with them at his father's estate in Ireland. He'd been…God, he'd been so angry, when he'd realized what it all meant for his family. That his father had betrayed their mother, their vows, their so-called love, and taken another woman. He'd felt as if everything he'd ever believed had been turned upside down, torn apart and destroyed, his rage toward his father so consuming he'd burned with it. A raw, seething rage toward everyone and everything, except strangely enough, for the boy.

The connection between him and Aedan had been… impossible to resist. They'd bonded over their shared hatred of their father, and that bond had grown fast and furious, until they were nearly inseparable. Though his arrival had changed the way Cian looked at his family, destroying everything he'd believed about honor and loyalty and the kind of man his father had taught him to be, he'd never blamed Aedan. He'd seen Aedan as the innocent. The one without blame, and it'd been obvious that the boy's life with his mother had been nothing like the supposedly perfect childhood Cian had been given. One that, it turned out, had actually been built on nothing more than lies. Unable to let it go, with Aedan by his side, Cian had searched and investigated, uncovering more and more of his father's infidelities, each new discovery making his hatred for the man grow.

And his mother…*Christ*. That had been the straw that broke the camel's back as they say. The one that had driven him away, setting him on a path of destruction.

Voice graveled and raw, he told Sayre of how he left home, and began his life as an angry sixteen-year-old with Aedan at his side, as if it were the two of them against the world. "I seduced innocents," he growled, the guttural words stark with disgust. "Got them in my bed, or against a wall, or over a table, and used them. Fed on them, whether they were willing to give me their blood or not. Killed the dregs of society for sport. Because I *could*. I was angry at everyone and everything, other than Aedan, and I took it out on whoever was unlucky enough to catch my eye." A quiet, painful laugh fell past his lips, and he squeezed his eyes shut, as if that could somehow shield him from what was happening. "I thought I could take what I had finally started to see that my father glorified—a vampire's power and strength and ruthlessness—and shove it in his face. Show him what a bastard he was. But the joke was on me, because he didn't give a shit what kind of destruction I caused."

Softly, she asked, "And what about your mother?"

"I don't know," he whispered, the words halting and low. "The last thing I said to her was how pathetic I thought she was for continuing to stay with him, for not leaving him, after what he'd done to her. I told her she embarrassed me for being weak, and then…"

"Then what?" she persisted, when his voice had trailed off.

He opened his eyes and turned his head to look at her, his breaths coming hard and fast, his throat burning. "She died before I ever made it back to see her again."

"Oh, Cian," she whispered, her gentle voice cracking. "I'm so sorry."

He flinched, but buried the pain beneath the rage that had been his constant companion for so many years. Even when he'd been playing it up as the womanizing jackass, trying to act as if he didn't have a care in the world. "Don't be sorry," he snarled. "It was *her* choice. I begged her to leave him, to go back to her pack and start a new life. But she refused."

With an impossibly sad look in her eyes, she said, "You sound so angry with her."

"I am. I always will be. She didn't fight for herself."

She nodded, her dark eyes soft with understanding. "And she refused to let you fight *for* her, didn't she?"

He blinked, feeling just as lost as he had all those years ago, and stunned that Sayre had read him so perfectly. Swallowing, he managed to say, "She forbid it."

She took another step toward him, close enough now that he could feel the delicious heat of her body against his arm. "Did you ever think that maybe she was protecting you?"

His brows pulled into an even deeper scowl. "From what?"

Almost afraid of how easily she could seduce him—*intoxicate* him—he watched as she lifted one smooth, perfectly freckled shoulder. "I don't know. But if you're anything like she was, then I think it's a possibility that you need to look at."

"Christ," he groaned, closing his eyes as he dropped his head back on his shoulders. It was barely past nine, but he was exhausted. Tired down to his very bones, the revelations of his sins draining him in a way that physical exertion could never do. When she prompted him with the gentle touch of her hand against his bare forearm, he said, "I will, Sayre. I will. Just…not now."

"Will you tell me the rest?" she asked, her other hand softly stroking his spine, her position at his side cocooning him in warmth. He knew she was asking for the rest of the story with Aedan, but he simply didn't have it in him to unearth any more skeletons that night.

"I'll give you the long version tomorrow, if you want it. The short version is that I finally got my head on straight, and realized what I was doing. What I had become. I…I went against Aedan because of it, righting one of his wrongs, and he took it as the ultimate betrayal, swearing to take his revenge against me one day."

"And then?"

He lowered his head, and could no more stop himself from looking at her beautiful face than he could stop needing air. "Then I tried to go home, but I couldn't stand to be near my father. So I bit the bullet and decided to visit my mother's family. After she'd married my father and became pregnant with me, she'd never returned, knowing they would never accept us as vampires. She never even told them the truth about my father's bloodline. They had no idea when I'd been born, or how old I was meant to be. I came to her relatives as her teenaged son, and that's when I met the Runners."

A soft smile touched her lips. "You found a home with them, and wanted to stay."

Nodding, he said, "I did. I stopped drinking blood as a main source, allowing myself to begin to age again, and when I was old enough to be a Runner, I moved here permanently. I became one of them, and I left that old life behind as best as I could."

With a slight catch in her voice, she asked, "So then you can grow old with your friends?"

"I can. I can grow old and die, if that's what I choose." A wry grin tugged at the corner of his mouth. "And I will, Sayre. There isn't a single goddamn part of me that wants to live forever."

Chapter 12

Sensing his exhaustion, Sayre took Cian's hand and led him back through the quiet rooms of the cabin, until they'd reached his bedroom. Trying not to blush like the virgin she was, she pulled his shirt over his head and tossed it to the floor, the sight of his broad shoulders and all those hard-edged muscles on his abdomen making her mouth water. The guy was just too freaking gorgeous for words. Taking his hand again, she pulled him with her until they were lying down in the middle of the bed, the open window allowing the wind and moonlight to filter in, their heads resting on the pillows as they lay on their sides and gazed at one another.

Keeping her voice soft, she asked him questions as they popped into her head, both serious and silly, and he answered each one in a deep, husky rumble that made her shiver with awareness, her body heavy and aching with desire. He explained that garlic didn't have any affect on him, and he could see his reflection in a mirror, as well as walk into a house uninvited. When she asked about sunlight, since it was rumored among the Lycans that they shared the night with vampires, he explained that he was naturally more nocturnal than a human, even more so than his fellow Runners, but that the sunlight didn't physically harm him.

She had no idea how much time had passed when his breathing deepened and his eyes fluttered closed, sleep overtaking him as his voice trailed off. She could sense him relaxing in a way that was whole and complete, as if he were resting easier now that he was no longer carrying the burden of so many secrets, and she had to bite her lip to stop herself from saying his name. If he needed sleep, then she would simply lie there and watch over him, while everything that he'd told her carefully worked its way through her mind.

There was still so much that she didn't know, or understand. But there was also so much that now made sense, like pieces of a puzzle slowly working themselves into place. The way that his arrogance had most likely been a cloak he'd used to hide his self-loathing for the things that he'd done when he was young. She'd also wondered, over the years, if his relentless womanizing was because he'd had his heart broken at some point. And now she knew that he had. Just not by a woman. By his family.

But he had a new family now. One that he could claim, if he would only stop running long enough and let it happen.

She just…she just didn't know if she could be a part of it.

But, *oh, God,* how she wanted to. She wanted to hold him and take him into her body and keep him forever, but didn't know if she could be that brave. If she could say to hell with the fear and simply follow her heart, knowing there was such a strong chance that he would break it.

Trusting his touch had hardly been an easy decision, but this, tearing down that last barrier and letting him in, now that she was seeing things in a clearer light… *this* was so much *more*. Infinitely more intimate, because she would be showing him more than just her outer layer. She would be letting him directly into her heart, and there would be no more secrets, then. Not even from herself. Because of her bloodline—because she was *witch*—everything would be out in the open if they had sex, her true feelings laid out before him like a sacrifice, his to do with as he pleased.

That was what her mother had feared. And now Sayre feared it, too. Not because of his bloodline or his tortured past, but because she could feel the walls between them breaking down, crumbling to dust. Could feel herself being drawn dangerously close to the emotional truths she wasn't yet ready to face.

But she wasn't going to let it pull her away from him. Instead, she shifted closer, put her face close to his on the pillow he was using, and lifted her arm, curling it over him, her fingers pressed against his broad, powerful back. They were still lying like that nearly a half hour later, when his eyelids quivered, then slowly opened. Neither of them said a word as their gazes locked together, the only sound that of their rough, quickening breaths, the air around them building with a crackling tension that was thick and rich and provocative.

It was like they'd slipped into another world where the two of them were the only inhabitants. His eyes narrowed, focusing on her mouth as she caught her lower lip in her teeth. It was the hunger, the *need*, she could see tightening his beautifully masculine face and darkening the tops of his cheekbones that gave her the courage to reach down and undo the top button on his jeans. Then she undid his zipper, biting her lip even harder when it became abundantly clear that he wasn't wearing any underwear, and she eagerly reached for him.

He grabbed her arm so quickly it made her blink, his low voice little more than a choked whisper. "What are you doing, Sayre?"

"Learning you." She flicked her wide-eyed gaze up from where she'd been watching her trembling fingers try to curl around his long, shockingly thick erection, and she smirked when she caught his stunned expression. "What's wrong, Cian? Did you expect me to run and hide when I finally got a good look at your goods?"

"Uh…"

She laughed softly, loving the way he felt against her palms, so hard and feverishly hot, the thick veins that pressed beneath his skin throbbing with the pounding beat of his heart. "I might not have your *extensive* experience in these matters, but I'm not afraid of you or the way you make me feel." She stroked him tightly with both hands. "I'm not afraid of *this*."

"That's good," he groaned, shuddering so hard that it shook the bed. "'Cause you're his favorite thing in the entire fucking world."

She smiled so big it made her face hurt. "That's awesome," she drawled with a wealth of satisfaction, unable to get enough of the way he was looking at her. His hooded gaze pierced her with its intensity, his every reaction telling her how much he loved the feel of her hands on that utterly magnificent part of his body. Her confidence built with each tremor of muscle and serrated moan, her touch becoming bolder as she gave herself the freedom to explore him like she'd always wanted to do. With her hot gaze focused on her actions, she gently tested the weight of that heavy, rounded part of him with one hand, while she stroked the other to the top of his shaft, studying the broad, flushed head. He was getting hot and slick there, and she used her thumb to rub the slippery moisture into his hot skin, encouraged by the way he hissed through his teeth, his nostrils flaring as he sucked in a harsh, ragged breath.

"Damn it," he growled, the rigid shaft getting even harder—and *bigger*—in her hands.

If it weren't obvious by her scent and the drunk-on-lust look on her face that she was thoroughly enjoying herself, the skittering sparks of light suddenly shooting off of her were an unmistakable sign.

"You gotta stop before this goes too far," he rasped, his hooded gaze burning with molten heat, as if his beautiful eyes had been lit from within.

"Not gonna happen," she responded, shaking her head.

He made a guttural sound deep in his throat, and pushed her onto her back. "You're so playing with fire, little witch."

She shot him a feisty smirk as she continued to stroke him, her power crackling in the air like an electrical storm, illuminating the room with glittering points of light. "Look around you, Cian. Fire doesn't exactly scare me."

His incredible silver eyes smoldered with craving as he lowered his face over hers, then lower, until their lips were softly touching. She shivered, loving the way he breathed her in, as if he couldn't get enough of her scent, or her taste, his tongue stroking against her bottom lip once…then again. He nipped it with his teeth,

his next breath a little harsher, tension coiled tight in
the long length of his body as he pressed harder against
her, his heavy erection throbbing in her grip. With a guttural curse on his lips, he shifted position, kneed her
legs apart and moved between them. Then he pulled her
hands off his cock and pinned them near her head as
he pressed that massive shaft right against the seam of
her shorts. She gasped, thinking it felt beyond wonder-
ful, until he pulsed his hips, grinding against the moist
cushion of her sex, and *that* felt so insanely amazing
that her eyes nearly rolled back in her head.

God, in that moment, she would have given *anything*
for there to be nothing between them. To feel him so deliciously hot and hard against her naked flesh.

"I want you so badly," he growled, the gritty words
vibrating with need as he braced himself on his elbows,
his forehead dropping against hers. "So badly, Sayre,
I think it could break me." He reached down with one
hand and shoved her shirt up under her breasts, his body
pressed so close she could feel the mouthwatering flexing of his abs. Then he lowered his hand again, curled
it behind her left knee and jerked it up against his hip,
his next rolling thrust rubbing against her in a way that
made her sob with pleasure, her nails digging into the
sleek, powerful muscles in his back.

"Cian," she moaned, unable to say more than his
name.

"I would sell my goddamn soul for the right to take
you," he panted. "Take you for fucking ever."

Her nails dug in a little harder, and she could tell by
the flare of heat in his eyes that he liked the bite of pain.
"It *is* your right."

He grimaced at her husky burst of words and stilled

at the end of a powerful stroke, his color fever-high as he started to pull his head back, his eyes wild. "God, I wish that were true."

Curving her hands behind his strong neck, she pulled his mouth to hers as she gasped, "It is." Then she kissed the hell out of him, hard and wet and aggressive, tangling her tongue with his…until he ripped the control right out of her hands, and took it for his own.

Claiming the sweet, sleek inner surfaces of her mouth with his tongue, Cian kissed Sayre so deep and explicitly, it was like he was trying to decode her. Lure out her unspoken emotions and secrets, craving the flavor of them. Needing anything of hers that was private and sacred, just so he could feel *close* to her. So he could hold a little part of her that no one else had ever held. Needing it to be his, and his alone.

He was thrusting against her with so much power now that the bed was slamming against the wall, and he wasn't even inside her. But that wasn't going to stop him from crashing over the edge so hard he damn near turned himself inside out. When it hit him a moment later, the force of his release was so intense it was like his heart had stopped, every muscle and tendon in his body straining and taut. He kept his mouth locked tight against hers, growling hoarse, broken curses into that sweet, honey-flavored space as his body shuddered and pulsed, his climax spilling him all over her soft stomach and that sexy-as-hell tattoo. He could only breathe out a huge groan of relief that she'd climaxed with him, her throaty cries echoing in his ears, while the rich, drugging scent of her pleasure hit his system so powerfully he gave another hard pulse, completely drained.

Collapsing onto his side, back in his original position, he couldn't stop himself from pulling her onto her side, as well. She lay facing him again, her flushed cheek pressed into the pillow, eyes closed, and he didn't even spare a second glance at the god-awful shamrocks. He was too lost in Sayre, his heavy-lidded gaze devouring the sight of her still flushed from her orgasm. Then she lifted those long, gold-tipped lashes and looked right at him, and the smile she gave him was so damn beautiful it made Cian feel as if he'd been knocked upside the head with a bat, his ability to think all but obliterated. So he simply let himself feel…and enjoy. They lay there for what felt like forever, faces close together, breathing the same air, completely lost in the moment. Unable to keep the words burning on his tongue inside, he eventually said, "I know it doesn't change anything, but I just…I want you to know that the women who came here to see me yesterday, they don't mean anything to me, Sayre. They never did."

She touched her fingertips to the stubble darkening his jaw, the tender caress making him tremble. "God, Cian. I don't know if that makes it better, or worse."

Understanding what she meant, he shifted forward until he could press his lips against the center of her forehead, trying to show her the tenderness she deserved as he cupped the side of her face in his hand and stroked her soft, warm cheek with his thumb. When her breathing became deep and slow, he gently pulled his head back, lost in the precious sight of her as she fell asleep against him, those beautiful lips curved in another soft, satisfied smile that made him feel like he'd conquered worlds. He wanted to stay there and watch her forever, but the gnawing feeling in his stomach reminded him that he hadn't eaten dinner. Forcing himself to get up, he changed his jeans for clean ones with hands that still weren't quite as steady as they should be, and headed into the kitchen to make himself a sandwich. A few minutes later, he went out onto the front porch for a cigarette, needing some more time to think in the quiet about everything that had happened...and how the little witch had surprised him, once again.

Instead of pushing him away after he'd unloaded about his bloodline and his past, she'd pulled him closer, and he didn't know what to make of it. How to wrap his head around it, when he'd been so sure she would run screaming and never want to set eyes on him again.

Not yet ready to go inside after he finished his smoke, and not wanting to spend any more time worrying about Aedan, he pulled out his phone, took a seat on the top porch step and spent a long time cruising her blog, watching videos of her with the sound low. It was probably kind of stalkerish, but damn it, he was drawn to every part of the woman, and he couldn't help feeling incredibly proud at what she'd achieved. Isolation would have broken most people, but Sayre had found a way to survive. And while he might be physically stronger, he didn't doubt for an instant that she was stronger than him where it counted.

He was still huddled over his phone minutes later, watching the way the sun turned her hair a fiery red-gold in another video, when Jillian's quiet voice came from just in front of him, at the bottom of the steps. "Did you tell her?"

Setting the phone down beside him on the porch, Cian lifted his head and nodded. "I told her tonight."

"And how did she take it?" she asked, just standing there with her hands pushed in her front pockets.

He gave a husky laugh. "Better than I would have, that's for damn sure. She's...she's friggin' amazing, Jilly."

She lowered her chin, her shoulders lifting as she pulled in a deep breath, and he suddenly picked up on her tension.

"What's going on?" he asked, moving to his feet, his worried gaze locking tight with hers as she lifted her head and glared up at him.

"I've been so worried about her," she said in a voice so low it was barely audible. "About how she would get on being back here, with so many of us around. But she's doing great."

He nodded again, the tension between them slowly building, making his insides churn. He knew something bad was coming, but he didn't know what. Had Jillian seen Sayre with one of the other men? Had Sayre told her that she'd had enough of his bullshit? None of that fit with how she'd been with him earlier—but damn it, he didn't know what to think.

When she didn't add anything more, he asked, "Is there something else you want to say, Jillian?"

Her head tilted a bit to the side. "I was just wondering if you've figured it out yet? I didn't get it until today, when I was spending time with her. So have you?"

He could feel a muscle begin to pulse in his jaw, his nostrils flaring as he pulled in a slow, deep breath. "Figured what out?"

Stepping up onto the bottom step, she said, "Before you left, I actually felt bad for you. I knew you were afraid of what was between you and Sayre, but I had faith that you would find your backbone and do the right thing. But you didn't. You ran like a coward, and we... we *lost* her. Because of you!"

"What the hell are you talking about?"

She climbed onto the step just beneath him, fuming with rage. "She went into that meltdown with her powers because you left her! It wasn't the war or the battle or her powers growing too quickly—it was *you*!" she hissed, shocking the hell out of him when she reached up and slapped the side of his face so hard it jerked his head to the side. "I sensed it, when it started, when you started feeling that pull for her. But I didn't panic, because I was so sure you were going to figure it out and do right by her. I'd seen the way you stared at her, the way you watched her...like a man who'd finally found the answer to every wish he'd ever had. And then you ran!" she shouted, tears spilling from her glistening eyes and rolling down her cheeks. "Did you ever stop for one second and think about what that would do to her? Did you, you selfish son of a bitch?"

"Jilly, come on," Jeremy murmured, seeming to come out of nowhere as he wrapped an arm around his wife's waist and pulled her back against him. A sob broke from her throat as she glared up at Cian, waiting for his answer, and he felt like the lowest pile of shit that had ever existed.

"Christ, Jillian. I'm...sorry," he choked out.

"You should be. Because when you bail on her again, guess what? It's going to happen *again*, Cian. And she'll run. We're going to lose her, because you're too much of an asshole to grow up and do what's right!"

"Jilly, baby, that's enough," Jeremy rumbled, as he lifted her up and cradled her against his chest. She wound her trembling arms around his neck, pressed her tear-soaked face against his shoulder and let him carry her away, her muffled sobs echoing softly on the wind until the Runner had taken her into their cabin.

Feeling as if he were moving through quicksand, Cian turned and climbed back up the steps, the side of his face still stinging as he reached down and picked up his phone, thumbing it off. Then he went back inside, locking up behind him. When he walked into the bedroom, he was surprised to find that Sayre was still asleep, cuddled up in the middle of the bed. He figured it was a miracle that Jillian's shouting hadn't woken her, but he was glad. He wanted nothing more than to crawl into bed and hold her in his arms, so after stripping off his jeans and slipping on a pair of boxers, that's what he did.

And then, with her body tucked up close to his, he finally let himself think about what had happened. About what Jillian had told him.

Yeah, he'd picked up on the fact that Sayre was handling being in the Alley better than any of them had hoped. And maybe he'd known, deep down, why that was. But he hadn't let himself admit it. Hadn't wanted it to be true. Hadn't wanted to be the cause of even more of her pain. More goddamn friggin' pain than he could ever atone for.

He knew he should walk away from her, but—

So she deserves to be alone? Forever? his wolf grumbled, cutting him off. *Because after what you learned tonight, you* know *that's what will happen!*

God, the beast was right. If he truly *were* the thing stabilizing her power, or buffering it, or whatever was going on between them, then what would happen when he left? It stood to reason that she would suffer the same problems as before, just like Jillian had said. That she would be forced back to her little cabin in West Virginia. Alone. Isolated. The most beautiful woman in the world, in his eyes, wasting away because of his screwups.

Not if we stay with her. Not if we claim *her.*

He gritted his teeth, hating how tempting that suggestion was. How deeply it called to him, the visceral need felt in every single cell of his body. One there was a damn good chance he would no longer be able to resist, whether it was best for her...or not.

But no matter what, he had to kill Aedan first. Had to destroy that threat. And if by some miracle he survived, well...there were things he would obviously have to figure out then. Sayre deserved more than a hollowed-out man who'd had the ability to love burned out of him, if he'd ever even had it to begin with. So he would have to figure out a way to...to somehow...

Shit! He didn't know. There was no goddamn magic answer in this twisted situation—but the one thing he vowed he wouldn't do was run. Not until he'd figured things out and knew, without any doubt, that she was all right. That she wouldn't have to go back to living in her own little world of seclusion.

But for tonight, he just wanted to hold the little witch in his arms...and find a moment of peace. As a man who'd never had many of them, he knew to hold on tight and grab them when he could. And none had ever been as perfect or as sweet as this one, which seemed fitting.

Because there was always the chance that it could be his last.

Chapter 13

Cian knew he was dreaming, but he couldn't stop. Couldn't make himself wake up. Like someone who'd been bound and gagged, he was forced to watch the horrific scene play out in his mind without any way to stop it. The nightmare was from the last night he'd spent with Aedan, in the fortress home they'd taken in Romania, after they'd killed the owners and acted like the dark lords of the castle. Well, acting on *his* part, because he'd already known at that point that he could no longer keep living at Aedan's side.

But his brother had believed. For Aedan, the monstrous reality of their lives had been no act.

On that particular night, Cian had come home earlier than planned, leaving Aedan in a nearby town, creating havoc at a local festival, drinking too much and fondling girls too young to be looked at with sexual intent, much less touched, plying them with liquor to make them forget their fears. His brother's fondness for fresh-faced innocents was why Cian had started to draw away, as well as Aedan's growing penchant for savagery and violence. The anger that Cian carried toward his father, and even his mother, was no longer driving him into the darkness, and as slivers of light began filtering their way into his consciousness, the way they lived simply became too much.

He'd slipped away from the festival without Aedan even noticing and wandered the halls in the ancient castle, restless and uneasy, knowing he would leave soon… and dreading the scene with Aedan when he did. Dreading even more the decisions he still needed to make regarding his brother's future.

Before he realized where his feet were taking him, he was down in the lower part of the castle, walking stone corridors that were cold and damp, his path illuminated by the flashlight he carried with him. At first, he attributed the low whimpers to nothing more than the groans of an old building. But the deeper he traveled, the clearer they became, until he started following the odd noises. His heart beat with dread the closer he got, the stench of fear thickening in the cold, dark tunnels.

Then he found her, locked inside a rotting cell, the padlocked wooden door easily breaking with his strength as he smashed his way inside. The human girl was a small, shivering lump on the floor, and she only shuddered harder when he asked if she was all right. Such a stupid question, when the girl was clearly anything but okay. Choking on the unspoken curses crowding into his throat, Cian kneeled on the filthy stone floor beside her and moved her to her back as carefully as possible. She groaned, trying to push him away, and blood spattered his face as she struggled. He blanched the instant he realized the sprays of blood were coming from her throat. She'd been bitten there many times, the wounds left open and bleeding so freely he was amazed she was still alive. He clutched her tight to his chest and prayed he could get her out before Aedan returned, sick with disgust at what his brother had done. The girl was no more than twelve, and it was obvious she'd been horribly abused.

She was too out of it with pain, weakened by blood loss, to protest when he stood with her in his arms, her frail body like a doll's, her short blond hair matted with blood and things he didn't want to identify. He sniffed at her temple, relieved that while Aedan had fed freely on her blood, he hadn't given her enough of his own to harm her. Then he hurried to get her out of the fortress, hiding in the nearby woods for several minutes, until he was finally able to get her name and address out of her. She lived in one of the local villages, and within half an hour, he had her home and in the care of her terrified, yet grateful parents.

There were tears, so many tears he felt as if he were drowning in them, and all the while, he kept thinking of the other mothers who had cried over the broken bodies of their children. Young men that Cian had killed over the years, simply because his anger had allowed Aedan to convince him it was their way. Their *right*.

"If you want her to live," he told them, "get her to a healer and then take her away from here and don't ever come back."

When they asked how, he looked around their small cottage, and knew they were doomed without his help. He went back home and quickly retrieved enough money that they could travel halfway around the world and live comfortably for the next twenty years without ever lifting a finger, and brought it back to them. Then he loaded them on a bus that would take them into a bus-tling city, where they could make their way to a healer whom Cian knew could be trusted not to go to the authorities, before taking a taxi to the airport and flying out. That night, never to return.

Then he burned down their cottage, and destroyed the bus they'd taken, making sure there were no clues for Aedan to follow.

And after that, he went back to the cell. And he waited for Aedan. Waited for the battle he knew was coming. For the blood and the accusations and—

Enough! a deep, guttural voice roared inside his head, and he jerked awake with a gasp, sitting up in the bed, drenched in sweat, while his wolf's rough voice echoed through his mind. Cian scrubbed his hands over his face and shoved his damp hair back from his brow, then sent a silent thank-you to the beast, grateful for its intervention. He'd had enough of that goddamn dream to last a lifetime.

Glancing around the sunlit room, he realized he was alone and a frown pulled at the edges of his mouth. "Sayre?" he called out, his voice still rough from sleep. She didn't answer, and as he pulled in a deep breath, he knew she'd already left, since he couldn't scent her presence in the cabin. Just that sweet, lingering trace of her that now filled every room. It was infused into his sheets and the very air. Clean and pure, while his own repulsive nature damaged everything he touched.

He showered until he'd damn near taken off a layer of skin, but still couldn't shake the vileness of his memory. Recognizing that he was too raw and wound up to face her right then, he pulled on some clothes and his boots, needing to get out and get his head focused on something else. But his beast wasn't happy about it.

She's ours, you idiot, and you're blowing it, the wolf

snarled, losing its patience with him and the entire situation.

He ground his jaw, understanding the wolf's anger. But he knew they needed more than a life-mate connection to make things work. Nature could only add so much to the equation, and the cold hard fact of the matter was that he was most likely missing too many elements that were needed to complete it. And, God, did that piss him off.

Shoving the infuriating thought from his mind, he went outside and sniffed the air as he searched for any sign of Aedan, same as he'd been doing for days now. He didn't think for an instant that his brother had given up. No, Aedan was simply biding his time, no doubt loving the way they were all walking around on pins and needles, looking over their shoulders at every sound, just waiting for him to make his appearance. The security patrols were running like clockwork, but it didn't ease his tension. If Aedan wanted in to the Alley, he would find a way. Cian just had to be ready for him when it happened.

Heading down his porch steps, he looked toward Jeremy and Jillian's place, figuring Sayre was over there. Trusting her to be smart and stay inside the borders of the Alley, he decided to head over to Sam's. The merc had told him he could stop by anytime if he wanted to talk over possible strategies for dealing with Aedan, and this was as good a time as any. Sam had apparently had some experience dealing with vampires in the past, and he was a good sounding board. Cian ended up spending the next few hours there, while they came up with a couple of extra security ideas that he planned to talk to

Brody about as soon as the Runner got back from checking on his wife and kids up in Shadow Peak.

Hoping that Sayre would be back at the cabin by then, Cian told Sam he'd catch him later and headed back over, calling out her name as he shut the front door behind him. She didn't respond, and he frowned, wondering if she were planning on avoiding him the entire day. Even though the idea irritated the hell out of him, he knew he'd been doing the same damn thing to her, and so he forced himself to give her the space that she needed. Using the time to check in with some of the informants he kept out in the field, hoping they might have heard of any sightings on Aedan, he didn't actually start to worry until lunchtime came and went, and she still hadn't made an appearance.

Standing at his front window, he stared out into the quiet glade, and wondered if Jillian had told her about the link between him and her loss of control over her powers. Was that why Sayre hadn't come back to the cabin...and to him?

Determined to talk to her about it, he'd just opened his front door and stepped back onto the porch when Jeremy came running up, his expression set in a fierce scowl that had Cian's heart pumping with dread. "What's going on?" he asked in a voice that was hoarse with fear, a thousand horrible scenarios running through his head. "Where's Sayre?"

Jeremy's scowl deepened. "She isn't with you?"

"Hell no, she isn't with me!" he snarled, his gums burning as his fangs prepared to drop, his beast roaring with fury.

"I don't know where Sayre is," Jeremy told him, talking fast. "She was with Jillian until a half hour ago, and we thought she'd come back here. But I just got word that one of our scouts has been found with his neck broken over on the east border."

"Shit!" he growled, spearing his fingers into his hair so hard that it stung, his mind racing. The only sure way to kill a Lycan was to either behead him, or sever his spinal column. And Aedan knew that.

Though he wanted to throw back his head and bellow with rage, Cian knew he didn't have the time. Lowering his arms, he told Jeremy to get everyone mobilized and searching for Sayre. "Make 'em spread out, but they need to go in pairs. Do not let anyone try to face him alone. And whatever the hell you do, don't underestimate him. He will cut you down without a second thought."

"What about you?" Jeremy grunted. "Who are *you* pairing up with?"

"I'm not," he muttered, moving too quickly for the Runner to stop him. Heading toward the east border, he caught Sayre's intoxicating scent not far from where the scout had been found, as well as the rancid odor that belonged to his brother. Moving with inhuman speed as he followed the scent trail, Cian was more terrified than he'd ever been in his life. He could recall moments as a child when he'd been frightened—the most memorable the night he'd learned about the vampire part of his nature, and realized he wasn't what he'd believed himself to be. But even that life-changing moment hadn't come close to this.

Though he followed a crazy trail through the woods that Aedan had clearly laid out to screw with him, the route like something a child would take while playing a game, Cian managed to find them within minutes of picking up her scent. The location was a small clearing the Runners had used for training purposes back before the war against the Whiteclaw, far enough from the Alley that no one would hear him if he howled. But he knew they would be able to follow the same trail that had brought him here—just not as quickly. Sayre sat straight-backed on a fallen tree trunk at the far edge of the clearing, while Aedan paced back and forth in front of her, his crimson eyes narrowing in hard and tight on Cian the instant he stepped out of the surrounding woods.

"See, Sayre," his brother drawled with a sickening smile. "I told you it wouldn't take him long to track us. It's that bestial nature of his. Like a dog with a bone, he could probably follow your mouthwatering scent straight into the depths of Hell."

Ignoring the asshole, Cian locked his worried gaze with hers. "Are you okay?"

She nodded stiffly in response, then immediately returned her attention to his brother, watching him the way someone never took their eyes off a snake that was preparing to strike. There was a nasty bruise forming beneath her right eye, and the corner of her lower lip had been busted, but he couldn't see any other marks on her. Not that the ones she had didn't matter. They made him want to rip the monster's heart out of his chest and then shove it down his throat, making him choke on it. But he was infinitely thankful that they weren't worse—that she was alive and breathing.

When he returned his full attention back to Aedan, his brother lifted his hands and showed him his raw, blistered palms. "I'm sure it will make you happy to know that the little witch gave me a hell of a jolt when I grabbed her."

"Too bad she didn't fry your psychotic ass to a crisp."

"Aw, I love you, too, big brother."

"Cut the bullshit, Aedan. What do you want?" he asked, studying his enemy as he came farther into the clearing. The boy who had been his brother, and was now a maniac, looked so familiar, and yet, different. It'd been years since Cian had seen him, and he knew he'd been right to warn the others not to confront him. They might be badass Lycans capable of ripping grown men in two if it were needed, but Aedan—Aedan was something else entirely.

His hair was still dark as pitch, so black it looked blue in the hazy afternoon sunlight, but instead of the longer cut he'd always worn it in, the thick mass was now shorn close to his scalp, making it easy to see the metal he wore in his eyebrows and ears. Though he was several inches shorter than Cian, only just reaching six-one, his whipcord-lean physique was more muscular than it'd been before. His once naturally pale skin was now ghostly white, most of it on display since he wore nothing but a low-slung pair of jeans that barely covered his lean hips. And those crimson eyes that burned with hatred would make it impossible for him to go out in public without dark glasses covering them. Not to mention the short, thick black talons that curved over the tips of his fingers, pointed and lethal.

But what was truly disturbing were the tattoos that covered every inch of skin on his arms and chest. They were horrific scenes of murder and sexual abuse, the victims' eyes shocked wide with fear and pain, their mouths hanging garishly open for their bloodcurdling screams.

"What do I want?" Aedan drawled, pulling Cian's attention back to those feral, blood-colored eyes. "I think that's obvious."

"If you wanted her dead," he grunted, "you would have already killed her."

"Oh, she'll die eventually. But…well, to be honest, this is more enjoyable than I expected it to be. Watching you worry and squirm. It would be a shame to end it too soon," he crooned as he stepped closer to Sayre and ran his hand down the gleaming fall of her hair. "So consider this visit a little gift to myself," he added, his thin lips spreading in a wide smile. "I got to spend some lovely *alone* time with your woman, and now you know how easily I can get to her whenever I want."

Hoping like hell that Sayre would keep her mouth shut and let him do the talking, he said, "She isn't my woman, Aedan."

Stepping away from Sayre, and closer to the place where Cian stood, his brother tsked. "Come now, Cian. Lying doesn't become you. It never did. Even when you were a sinner, you managed to be noble."

"There was nothing noble about the way we lived."

Aedan gave a snide rumble of laughter. "God, you're boring."

"And you're insane."

"At least I'll get the girl in the end, and not you. That's only fair, don't you think? Since you took my sweet little Elizabeth from my dungeon and stole her from me."

"Do you scent my mark on Sayre?" he growled. "No, you don't. Because I haven't claimed her, Aedan."

"Just because you haven't had the balls to make it official doesn't mean this beautiful little piece of ass isn't yours." Tilting his head back, he flicked his tongue out like a snake, then looked at Cian and laughed. "I can *taste* the possessiveness coming off you in the air. It's thick in your blood, brother."

"What does any of that matter if I have no intention of ever making her mine?" he countered. "You're wasting your time."

Aedan smirked. "I'm afraid I don't agree. I think you want her so badly it's *killing* you, Cian. Fucking ripping you to pieces."

His hands flexed at his sides, his claws beginning to prick his fingertips. "You're wrong, Aedan. I'll protect her because she's innocent in all this, the same way I've protected others from you in the past, like Elizabeth. But you're letting your madness cloud your judgment."

"You didn't protect Elizabeth from me. You stole her!" Aedan roared, his body rapidly changing, preparing for battle, as his temper got the better of him. The instant his fangs released, nearly two inches in length, his skin turned milk white, as if every ounce of blood had drained from his veins. Against that corpse-like background, the macabre tattoos looked even sharper, the violent scenes writhing as his muscles rippled. He was raw power, cut and lean and horrifically lethal, and Cian wondered how it'd taken him so long to see it when they'd been young. Had he been blinded by their joint hatred of their father? Or had it been the love he'd once held for Aedan that had made him such a fool?

He hated to admit it, but it was most likely the love. Despite what Aedan's birth had meant to his mother— a devastating sign of his father's betrayal—Cian hadn't been able to do anything but love the boy who had been nothing but scrawny limbs and shaggy hair. A familial love, which was the only type he'd ever been capable of feeling. And it's not like he could have blamed the boy for their father's infidelity. Aedan had had no one, and so Cian had taken over the role of protector.

Instead, he should have taken his head when he'd had the chance, but he'd been too weak, and he put the blame for that weakness where it belonged. On his love. If that right there wasn't a blinding endorsement for how that particular emotion was something he wanted no part of, he didn't know what was.

You know nothing, his beast muttered. *You never have.*

He wasn't surprised they disagreed on that particular point. Hell, most of the time they hardly agreed on anything. But the one thing they were both fully prepared to do was protect Sayre. At any cost.

Tired of letting this son of a bitch stand between him and his woman, Cian released his own lethal set of fangs, his long Lycan claws piercing through the tips of his fingers as he charged Aedan in a blur of speed. He managed to get in a solid strike across the bastard's ribs before Aedan backhanded him with so much power he was surprised his head hadn't snapped off, the hot rush of blood filling his mouth telling him that his lip had been smashed. Shaking it off, Cian rolled his head over his shoulders and narrowed his gaze, just as a deep, guttural growl surged up from his chest. Aedan might have the cold, calculating hatred of a vampire, but Cian had the scorching, primitive fury of his beast, and the ruthless animal was seriously pissed that their mate had been put in danger.

In the next second, Aedan flew at him in a flurry of strikes, his talons slicing across the front of Cian's shirt, shredding the cotton but only grazing his skin as he twisted to the side. He wasn't hurt badly—it was only a scratch—but Sayre reacted as if he'd been gutted. Surging to her feet, her face pale and her eyes wide with fear, she flung her arms forward, throwing up one of those crackling, blinding walls of energy between him and the vampire.

But Cian wasn't going to let it hold him back.

"Sayre, stay out of this!" he roared, gritting his teeth as he pushed into the light, his skin sizzling from the searing burn. But he didn't back down, determined to reach his brother and inflict as much damage as he could.

When he'd made it through the wall, stalking toward Aedan—who was watching the whole thing with another one of those chilling, maniacal smiles—Cian pulled off the tattered remnants of his shirt and tossed them on the ground. "Come on, you sick bastard. You want blood?" he snarled, knowing damn well that his eyes were turning the same haunting shade as his brother's, his rage fueling his bloodlust. "Then come and get it."

"Not today, I'm afraid," Aedan murmured, pushing his hands in his front pockets as if they weren't in the middle of a vicious fight to the death. "Like I said before, brother, this is proving so much more entertaining than I'd hoped. And I was already aiming high, after spying on your dreams these past few months."

He froze, unable to believe what he'd just heard. "What the hell are you talking about?"

Aedan laughed low in his throat, and took a step closer, though nearly ten yards still separated them. When Sayre had thrown up her light, his brother had scrambled away like a frightened cat. But now he was all cold, malevolent confidence. Lifting his brows, he said, "Think about it, Cian. How else do you think I learned about her after all this time?"

"You saw my dreams of her?" he growled, flexing his deadly claws at his sides.

Aedan smirked as he shook his head. "You're jealous I saw you thrusting like an animal between those silky thighs? That doesn't sound like you, brother. I can remember a time when you liked screwing your meals while others watched. It made you *hotter*."

He flinched and cut a quick look toward Sayre, who was still standing by the fallen trunk as she stared at his brother with complete focus, her expression impossible to read.

When Cian returned his attention to Aedan, he found the bastard staring right back at her. "You'd probably faint if I told you what my precious brother dreams about doing to you, little witch. Some of it was so depraved, I couldn't get enough of watching, just like a voyeur." His head cocked at an eerie angle, as if his neck wasn't attached correctly. "Though you've probably been having those dreams, too. It's because the two of you were quickening for one another. That happens when life mates spend too much time apart, at too great a distance."

"How the hell would you know?" Cian demanded, wanting to rip out the bastard's eyes so he couldn't look at her that way. As if he was seeing her like she'd been in so many of his dreams, passionate and wild and hungry for pleasure.

"I'm a hunter, brother, and hunters study their prey. I've been learning everything I could possibly need to know about your doglike nature for years." He finally tore his attention away from Sayre, and slid Cian a gloating look. "Although, it wasn't the sex dreams that truly caught my attention. They were just the cherry on the top of my *favorite* part. The thing that reached out across the world through our link and clasped on to me, digging its way into my mind."

He swallowed, knowing exactly what Aedan was talking about.

"You see, Sayre, Cian's been dreaming about more than just nailing you to every available surface he can find. He's been having bad, *bad* dreams. And it's funny, the things you can tell about a person's feelings, when they're afraid. You see what they care about most in those moments. What means the most to them. Like when a fire alarm goes off, who does the husband run to first, his wife or his kids?"

Cian bared his fangs. "Shut the fuck up," he snapped.

Ignoring him, Aedan went on. "And because Cian and I shared so many...meals together," he explained with an evil smile, "we formed a connection. One that bound us in a way others will never understand. I'm sure he would feel my fears, if I had any. But I can assure that I feel his. I feel them as if they were my own. And do you know what most people fear for the most? The things that they lo—"

"That's enough!" he roared, cutting the bastard off.

Aedan threw back his head and laughed. "Careful now," he chided. "You're giving yourself away, brother."

Catching the scent of the others in the air, he said, "My friends are almost here, Aedan. You're powerful, but you're also massively outnumbered."

"And you can't hide here with your animal pals forever. Our time is coming, Cian, whether you want it to or not."

"I'm an animal, too, Aedan."

The vampire's crimson eyes burned with madness. "Which is why I'll win. Vamp trumps your noble beast, brother. Always."

Voice thick with frustration, he asked, "Why can't you leave me be and get on with your own damn life?"

"Because I'm lonely? Because this is fun?" Aedan's eyes narrowed, a guttural tone to his own deep voice that sounded like tightly coiled rage. "Because you deserve it for betraying me? Do I really need a reason, *brother mine*?"

His jaw tightened. "You won't win this."

"You're suffering, Cian. You look as if you're living in the depths of Hell." A slow smile twisted his thin lips. "That means I'm already winning."

"It doesn't mean jack shit."

In a flash of movement, Aedan was suddenly at his side, his cold mouth pressed close to Cian's ear. "And just in case you were getting any ideas," he whispered, "killing yourself won't save her. It'll just mean I don't have to go through you to get to her. But she's still *mine*, even if you're rotting in the ground."

In the next moment, the Runners and the mercs, along with Jillian, caught up to them and burst into the clearing, and Aedan disappeared in a blur of speed that the others probably hadn't even caught.

"Where is he?" Brody demanded, his fangs gleaming beneath the curve of his upper lip. His massive body vibrated with rage, and Cian felt the sharp slice of guilt tear through him. He hated that he was putting his friends through this. Hated that he couldn't reach Aedan. Hated every part of it. Every miserable piece of this screwed-up situation.

And beneath it all, there was the sickening guilt that this was all *his* fault. For starting Aedan on this path. For not ending him when he'd first realized what his brother was capable of, after his father had refused to take action. For the niggling fear that he hadn't tried hard enough to find Aedan these past five years. The fear that there was a part of him that hadn't *wanted* to find Aedan badly enough, because he hadn't wanted to see his brother die. A part that had privately been relieved he couldn't go home to Sayre, knowing where that path would lead, too frightened of the things the little witch made him feel. Of how much stronger those feelings would be now that she was a young woman, and no longer untouchable.

Christ, had he ever wanted to touch anything as desperately as he wanted to touch Sayre Murphy? Ever needed anyone as badly, or simply craved their happiness?

The answer was as simple as it was obvious.

Not. Even. Close.

Chapter 14

Shoving away from Jillian, who had thrown her arms around her in relief, Sayre suddenly turned and took off, running as hard and as fast as she could back toward the Alley. Tears ran unchecked down her face, the enormity of the danger Cian had faced making it difficult to stand, much less move at this speed. But she made her way back to the cabin as quickly as possible. She was too raw to talk things over with anyone, including her sister, and she knew Jillian would try.

There'd been moments in her life when her "sight" had proven incredibly useful—but only for her loved ones. Never for herself. Never when she'd needed it, and God, could she have used it now. Being blindsided by an undeniable truth when she'd watched Cian fighting his brother had left her reeling. Left the ground shaking beneath her feet in a way that made it difficult to breathe…to think. All she could do was *feel*, seething in a maelstrom of emotion, the tears coming harder, faster, until she was sobbing with them, every part of her body trembling, breaking apart.

In that moment, when she'd thought he might actually die out there in that clearing, she'd realized that she didn't need to fear she was falling too hard and too fast for him, because it had already happened. Her heart was already his, irrevocably and completely, and *that* scared her in a way that Aedan Hennessey never could.

Had she known, when she'd agreed to come back to the Alley with Cian, that this was where her need would lead her? To loving him?

Whatever the answer, it no longer mattered. She was already at the point where it was too far to turn back, because he'd earned it. He'd *earned* her heart—every scared, agitated cell of it—when he'd faced off against that monster to protect her.

Now she just had to decide what she was going to do about it.

"You bastard!" she screamed only seconds later, when he shoved the bedroom door open, breaking the lock with ridiculous ease, apparently unwilling to let anything come between them—*except himself.* Fired with savage, visceral frustration, she picked up one of the heavy books from an ugly green bookshelf and hurled it at his head with surprising strength. "You son of a bitch!"

He'd ducked to avoid the book, but the breath whooshed out of him when she nailed him in the stomach with a wooden bookend. "I get that you're angry," he grunted, "but I need to know if you're all right. Are you okay?"

"You're damned right I'm angry," she snapped, her hair lifting slightly from her shoulders as the air between them began to crackle.

"You have every right to be. It's my fault he got near you."

She shuddered, recalling the sickening fear that had burst inside her the instant she'd set eyes on Aedan. But she wasn't going to let him distract her so easily. "I'm not angry about him coming after me. Yeah, it sucked. But that's not why I'm livid. I'm pissed *because of what you did*!"

His head jerked back as if her words had clipped him on the chin. "What?"

"Why would you do that? Why would you just…just try to throw your life away like that? You saw what he was like! How did you expect to fight him and come out alive? I could have watched you die out there!"

He sighed, his shoulders dropping as he took a step toward her. *"Sayre."*

The way he was suddenly looking at her, as if she were the most precious thing in the world, only made her cry harder. His bright, long-lashed eyes were still painfully beautiful, even when she'd seen them tinged with crimson. So unlike his brother's. Aedan's eyes had resonated with pure evil, especially when seen within a face that was so coldly devoid of emotion. She shuddered again as she relived the memory of Cian taunting that monster to fight him, and shouted, "No! Don't come any closer. I…I'm liable to punch you if you do."

He looked stricken to see her so upset, his breath leaving his lungs in an audible rush. "I wasn't trying to die out there, Sayre. I'll do whatever it takes to protect you, but I'm not going to throw myself on a fucking sword. If I thought it would help, then yeah, I'd be tempted. I'd be an asshole if I felt any differently, because *I'm* the one who got you into this mess. But it wouldn't stop him. It would just leave you alone to deal with him without me, and I can't let that happen."

Trembling, she said, "No matter how this ends, it will be bad for you, Cian."

"And that's what I *deserve*," he growled, his chest heaving as he fisted his hands at his sides, his claws and fangs already retracted.

But his chest and arms were still streaked with crimson smears of blood, and she knew, *she goddamn knew*, how close he could have come to dying out there.

"Why d-did you do this?" she sobbed, shaking so badly her teeth were chattering. "Why d-did you come back? I'm not yours. You haven't claimed m-me, and you never will. So why didn't you just k-keep screwing your way around the world and let him kill me?"

He took a harsh breath, his brow furrowing as he slid his gaze to the side. "I haven't."

"You haven't what?" she snapped, sniping at him like a child in a fit of temper.

He shoved a hand back through his hair and cursed under his breath. "I haven't…been…with anyone. Like that."

"What?"

He pulled in another deep breath, and slowly brought his hooded gaze back to hers. She jolted from the look burning in those molten eyes, feeling like she'd just been shoved hard in the chest, though no one had laid a hand on her. "I haven't been with another woman, Sayre. Not since I left you."

She swallowed so hard that it hurt. "Cian, that…that doesn't even make any sense."

"You think I don't know that? I mean, I know I can't have you. Not like that. And I don't want to go through the rest of my life like *this*. But from the moment I walked away from you, I haven't even *seen* other women. Hell, before I even left, it'd been…weeks since I'd taken anyone to my bed."

"You still slept with them," she said unsteadily, "after…after we realized what we were. What we are…"

"I know." He exhaled a ragged breath and grimaced like a man in physical pain. "I tried like hell to ignore it, Sayre. To prove I didn't need you. That I could keep going the way I always have, doing the same things to cope."

"To cope?"

He shook his head as he looked away. "Never mind."

"No! No more freaking secrets. Or I walk."

"Fine. It was how I coped with the bloodlust," he growled, pacing away from her. His heavy boots were loud against the bedroom's hardwood floor, his hard-edged muscles rippling with power beneath his blood-stained skin. "The constant fucking—it was either *that* or keep feeding the monster inside me and stop aging. And I didn't want that. I wanted to live here, with the others. So I screwed my way through the pack and kept that twisted part of me at bay as best as I could."

"And after you left?" she whispered, her thoughts reeling so rapidly she had to reach out and brace her hand against the bookshelf.

"I've been feeding on supplies of human blood that I purchase on the black market. It's why I don't look as though I've aged, because I haven't. Not since I came back for you."

"And the blood worked?"

"When I've needed it," he muttered as he lifted one of his powerful arms and rubbed the back of his neck, the position causing his beautiful biceps to bulge. "For the most part, I've been…I don't know. Dead inside. I've felt nothing." He flicked her a shuttered look from beneath his lashes. "Nothing but the need for you."

She wanted to ask how he dealt with that need without going crazy, then blushed as she figured she already knew the answer, considering how she'd had to take matters into her own hands over the years. Not that her self-made orgasms were anything to brag about, compared to how Cian could make her feel. As if he'd read her mind, he arched one of those dark brows as he looked at her, and the corner of his grim mouth actually twitched.

Needing to put the conversation onto a different subject, before she embarrassed herself, she blurted, "I'm sorry for what Jillian did last night. She finally fessed up before I snuck away today. I honestly wasn't running. I just…I needed some time to myself to think, and then I…well, I ran into your brother."

He stopped pacing and took a step closer to her. "Promise me you won't do that again, Sayre."

"Yes, of course. I understand now. I…I don't think I really did before," she admitted in a nervous rush, wetting her lips. "Aside from those humans you killed at the cabin, I guess the threat didn't feel as real to me as it should have. But it does now."

His brows lowered over his sharp, steely gaze, and he took another step closer to where she stood. "And the thing with Jillian? You're not angry…about your powers?"

"Cian, that's *my* problem, not yours. And, anyway, I have enough things to be pissed at you about without throwing *that* on there."

He grimaced, until he caught the way she was smirking at him. "Smart-ass."

"In all honesty, I already suspected you were the reason."

He looked surprised. "You did?"

Nodding, she said, "I started feeling different the morning after you left. And from that point on, each day got a little worse. I'd hoped I was wrong, but I think that deep down, I always knew the truth."

"Christ, Sayre. I'm so damn sorry," he groaned, and the next thing she knew, he was right in front of her. His hands pushed their way into her hair, and then he claimed her lips with his, ravaging her mouth like he was trying to brand her with his need. The carnal, devastating kiss was heated and hungry, demanding everything she had to give, his slick tongue rubbing against hers in a way that was guaranteed to melt her down. But no matter how tempting it was, she couldn't let him distract her from what was important.

"Why did you do what you did?" she gasped against his mouth. Her trembling hands curled around his strong wrists as he held the sides of her head in his hands, the masculine sprinkling of dark hair tickling her skin.

With a serrated groan, he broke away from the kiss and pressed his forehead to hers. "Because I can't lose you. Not like that. I can't let him hurt you. I'd rather die."

"If you really feel like that—if you would be willing to *die* for me, Cian—then why are you fighting this? Why not just claim me?"

"Because I'm bad for you, little witch."

She moved her hands to his broad, muscular shoulders and pushed until he finally relented and pulled his head back to look at her. "Do you really believe that?" she asked him, staring into those smoldering, tormented eyes.

A gritty, bitter laugh burst past his lips. "Ask anyone who knows me and they'll tell you the same thing."

"I'm not interested in what anyone else has to say,

Cian. I only care about what I feel and see. And I *see* the good in you. The more time I spend with you, the deeper I see it."

"You're seeing what you want," he muttered.

"No," she argued, willing him to believe her. "I want *you*. Not some fairy-tale prince. You're not perfect, and I don't care. I'm not perfect, either. But together, I think we might be. If you would just give it a chance," she finished softly, keenly aware that she'd just made herself incredibly vulnerable—but believing he was worth it. Worth fighting for.

"You deserve more than that," he grunted. "More than me."

She blinked up at him, giving him a shaky smile. "More than a life spent with the only man I'm meant to be with? More than the promise of a family with that man?"

His scowl deepened. "Use your head, Sayre. You know exactly what kind of family we would have."

She flinched, feeling as if he'd just slapped her, and pushed away from him. "If you think I wouldn't love and adore my children, no matter their breed, then it just goes to show that you really don't know me at all, Cian."

"Sayre," he sighed, "that's not what I meant."

"Isn't it?"

"No," he muttered, shoving his hand back through his hair again in a telling gesture of frustration. "I just...I don't want to screw things up for you."

"And what about you?"

"Lass, my life was screwed to hell and back a long time ago. And no one is to blame for that but *me*. You said so yourself, when I found you in West Virginia."

God, he frustrated her! "Cian, I was wrong. When I

said it was your fault that I was in trouble, I was angry. And I was *wrong*. It's not. You're not responsible for what your brother does."

"Like hell I'm not." They were raw, graveled words. "I should have ended him a long time ago, when I had the chance. But I chose not to—I chose *wrong*—and now his actions are a result of that choice. Of that mistake."

"You know what, Cian? It's time for you to shut up."

"Sayre."

She glared up at him as she stepped back into his body, then reached up and curved her hands back over those broad, rugged shoulders. "I'm serious. Your words are just pissing me off, and I'd rather kiss you than listen to you put yourself down." Then she tugged him down as she rose up on her toes, and kissed him like she was going to die without his taste in her mouth.

He shuddered, then wrapped those strong arms around her, jerking her even closer as he thrust his way past her lips and raked the inside of her mouth with his wicked tongue. She opened her mouth wider, wanting to take in even more of him, desperate for all of him, body and soul. She didn't even care that her busted lip was stinging like a bitch, her desire for him burning through her like a wild, rushing flame, her power breaking free in a shimmering burst of those tiny, flickering points of light.

"God, your mouth is so damn sweet," he groaned against her lips, and she could feel the emotions burning in those husky words, the hunger and need and craving that went deeper than the physical, and it made her want to shake him until she could get to the truth. But she was too busy trying to open his jeans so she could get to even more of him, while he literally tore her clothes off her body, her underwear shredding beneath his hands as he pushed her back onto the bed. Everything was moving hard and fast and furious, their harsh breaths filling the air as he shoved her to the middle of the bed and came down over her, that hot, slick tongue curling around one of her sensitive nipples, the sensation so intense it made her toes curl. He gave the same attention to the other breast, sucking on her nipple like it was a juicy piece of fruit, then turned her to her stomach, moved the fall of her hair to the side and latched that talented mouth on to the owl she had tattooed there.

She hadn't thought that particular patch of skin between her shoulder blades would be an erogenous zone, but boy, had she been wrong.

She trembled, gasping, her hands clawing on to the bedding, her blood pounding as he made a hard, thick sound deep in his throat and turned her over again, his mouth going straight for her belly this time.

"I need you in my mouth," he growled against her navel. He flicked the ink there with his tongue, then licked at a patch of skin just beneath it. "Need to taste you so fucking badly, Sayre. Can I?"

Instead of giving him a verbal response, she simply pushed hard on those mouthwatering shoulders and spread her thighs as wide as she could, holding her breath with anticipation of his tongue touching that most private part of her. But it didn't. Instead, she felt his soft, warm lips brush against the tiny symbol she had tattooed high on her inner thigh.

"A beautiful little Celtic cross. For Ireland," he murmured, and she knew that what he really meant was *for me*. And he was right. It had been for him. A way for her to carry him with her, even when she'd so badly wanted to hate him, but couldn't. Her dark, tortured Irishman. So eager for connection, though he would never admit it.

"It's fitting," he said huskily, "seeing as how this part of you is like my own personal holy ground."

She was still laughing softly when he turned his head and pressed his open mouth right over the hot, drenched center of her sex, her laughter choking off into a breathless gasp. *Oh...oh, wow.* That was seriously mind-blowing. Bone-melting. He pushed his face into her, his tongue and lips everywhere, going at her with an aggressive, unapologetic hunger that felt so freaking good she could have cried, the guttural groans that he gave making it sound like he was feasting on something lush and sweet. Something he couldn't get enough of, as if he'd been starved for the taste of her.

Though Sayre had fantasized about this moment an embarrassing number of times, she'd had no idea it would be like *this*. That he would spend so much time with his dark head buried between her thighs, pulling pleasure from her writhing body as if it were *his* to control. His shoulders kept her spread wide and his thumbs held her tender folds open as he did things that would have shocked the hell out of her, if she hadn't discovered a love of steamy romance novels. She'd thought, given her extensive reading, that she had a good handle on what this would feel like. But the heroes in her books didn't have anything on Cian.

It wasn't just his skill, though the man was clearly incredible at it, every part of him made for sin. But even more than that, it was the way he didn't try to hide how badly he needed it, letting her feel every bit of his hunger. A craving that was as visceral and primitive as the

animal that lived inside him. He moved his tongue inside her body like he might die if he didn't get *more* of
her, his mouth nothing less than voracious as he licked
and sucked at her slippery flesh, consuming her. Driving her out of her mind with pleasure. And then she was
coming in a hot, mind-shattering rush, hoarse cries spilling from her lips as she trembled and pulsed, melting
against his mouth in wave after wave of release, while he
growled dirty things against her sensitive flesh, telling
her how perfect she tasted. How he couldn't get enough
of her. How he wanted her to keep coming for him...
harder and deeper and wetter. And so she did. Over...
and over...until she was as boneless as a rag doll, arms
and legs flung wide, her head foggy, thoughts drifting
somewhere out there in a glittering, throbbing darkness.

She didn't know how many minutes had passed by
the time she finally came back to herself. He was still
nuzzling her with his open mouth, lapping at her with
his tongue, the sounds he made telling her how much
he was enjoying himself. And while it was incredibly
lovely, she was eager for her chance to return the favor,
her mouth watering at the thought of getting that thick,
beautiful part of him between her lips.

"What are you doing?" he growled, locking his gaze
with hers when she sat up and pushed against his shoulders, shoving him to his back. She quickly moved to kneel
between his thighs, wishing she'd gotten the jeans off him
as she flicked her gaze up. Her breath caught when she
found him watching her with a hot, heavy-lidded stare,
his mouth and chin glistening with her juices.

"Don't even think about stopping me," she told him,
tugging the waist of his jeans down enough that she
could curl her hands around that thick, steely shaft, the

head so ripe and succulent looking she couldn't wait to get her first taste. "This is *mine*."

Something hot and wicked flared in his eyes as she made that pronouncement, and she knew she had him.

"You want me in your mouth?" he asked in a graveled voice, licking his slick lower lip as he braced his upper body on his elbows, looking so freaking sexy it was unreal.

Desperate for him, she answered the question with actions instead of words, as she leaned down and covered the broad, wet tip of him with her mouth and swiped at his hot flesh with her tongue. Flicking her eyes up again, she caught him watching her from beneath the thick black fringe of his lashes, his color high, marking the sharp crests of his cheekbones, his sensual lips parted for his ragged breaths. In that instant, she realized that she could so easily get addicted to this. To the raw intimacy of the act, and how right it felt as she started to suck on him, taking him deeper while she stroked the bottom inches of his shaft with her hand, knowing she was making the most powerful male she'd ever known tremble with need. Her senses were in overdrive, her body vibrating with a fine tremor as she tried to soak in every part of him, from his warm, musky scent, to the salty, exquisite taste that sat on her tongue like that was where it belonged.

"Finish me," he growled, keeping his head lifted as he dropped down to his back, his eyes glowing like bright chips of molten silver.

"With my hands?" She whispered the words against the very tip of him, laving the moist flesh with her tongue. She knew exactly how much he liked it by the way he gasped, the muscles in his abdomen rippling as his fingers speared hard into her hair, clutching her to him. "Or with my mouth?"

"Christ," he hissed, his expression so intense it was almost a scowl. "Are you trying to make me crazed?"

"No. You just make me hungry."

He stilled, holding his breath. "For what?"

"Everything," she whispered, letting her lips rub against the hot, sensitive crown, the thick shaft throbbing in her hands. "All of it. I want to crawl inside your head and live in your thoughts. Taste your emotions. Feel your pleasure."

"You *are* my pleasure," he growled, the tendons in his strong, corded throat straining beneath his skin.

"Then *show* me," she told him, taking the succulent head between her lips again, ignoring the sting of pain from where Aedan had struck her when she'd tried to get away from him. Forcing that dark thought from her head, she focused on *her* male, making her mouth as hungry and as wet as she could for him, greedy for his release as her hands stroked the broad inches she couldn't reach. She loved his raw, gritty curses and the way he gripped her hair as he got close, but she was *crazy* for the way he shuddered and shouted when he came, his feet planted flat on the bed, hips pumping as she stayed with him, doing everything she could to make it good for him.

When she finally lifted her head, he grasped her by the arms and hauled her up over his chest, surprising her with the way he took her mouth, kissing her as if he would go mad without the touch of her tongue against his, their mouths moving together as they fought for a deeper angle, a deeper way to taste—until he suddenly made a sharp, guttural sound deep in his chest. Before she could react, he quickly rolled her onto her back, his big body caging hers in as he braced himself over her on all fours.

She started to ask him what the hell was wrong, only to break off with another gasp when she saw the fresh smear of blood on his mouth from her bleeding lip. It was clear from the way he'd reacted that the taste of her blood had been a shock to him, the way he was taking such deep, rough breaths and eyeing her mouth telling her he was still struggling to get himself under control.

Then he slid her a dark, glittering look from beneath his thick lashes, and there was a...a *precision* to the way he was watching her that told her he was up to something. That his clever mind had just come up with an idea...or a plan of some sort. One he had no intention of sharing, judging by the hard cast to his masculine features.

"Cian," she whispered, her eyes going wide as he moved his hand to her face and pressed the pad of his thumb to the cut on her lip. Then he trailed the crimson-stained pad down the front of her throat, over the hammering beat of her pulse at the base, and lower, trailing it between her quivering breasts. Wetting the pad with her blood again, he coated both her nipples, then traced his thumb around her navel, lower, down into the strawberry-blond curls on her mound.

When he was done, he snagged her heavy-lidded gaze and murmured, *"Trust me,"* as he leaned down and pressed his open mouth to her throat, his warm tongue lapping against her bloodstained skin.

"Oh, God," she moaned, shivering with poignant arousal. Watching his beautiful mouth follow the same path that his thumb had taken was the most erotic expe-

rience of her life, her power so charged it was literally arcing from her body in shimmering bolts of light. He took his time licking her sensitive skin, the thick sounds he made in the back of his throat telling her how much he loved it. Especially when he'd followed the crimson path right into her curls, and lower, his mouth just as ravenous as he'd been before, making her come twice before he suddenly lifted his head and jerked away from her, crouching on all fours at the foot of the bed.

"Cian?" she whispered, moving to her knees so that she could reach out to him, his tortured expression tearing at her heart. "What's wrong?"

"I don't care if you want to or not," he groaned between his harsh breaths, his hands fisting the bedding as he lowered his head, hiding from her gaze. "I just need you to listen to me, Sayre, and I need you to do as I say. Get dressed and get the hell out of this room. Then... run as fast as you can."

"What?"

"Go to Jillian and Jeremy's." He lifted his head, and she gasped when she saw that his eyes had turned completely crimson again. "Run, Sayre. Now!"

"No," she breathed out, unwilling to leave him.

"Goddamn it, woman! Get the fuck out of here!"

She shook her head, and he curled in on himself, shuddering so hard it looked painful, every hard, powerful muscle in his magnificent body coiled tight beneath his damp skin.

Careful not to make any sudden movements, Sayre shifted closer to him. "I'm not afraid of you, Cian. Please, let me help you."

He ground his forehead against the bed and groaned like a man in agony. "Christ, you're impossible."

"I don't mean to be," she said softly, carefully inching her way closer. "I simply care about you too much to run away from you when you need me."

He shivered like someone with a raging fever. "Even when the things I need aren't something I deserve?"

"I don't think you get to make that decision."

A raw, fractured sound tore from his throat, muffled against the bedding. "Damn it, lass, I'm trying to do right by you."

"Hmm. Have you ever thought that maybe you should just *do me* instead?"

"Don't!" he barked, breathing in rough, uneven bursts. "Christ, don't do that. Don't flirt with me right now. I can't take it."

"Then just let me comfort you," she murmured, reaching out and stroking his broad back with a gentle touch. They stayed like that for untold minutes, until his breathing had finally slowed and his body was no longer gripped in that terrible tension. He rolled to his side and let her put a pillow under his head, his expression still strained, though his eyes had returned to their natural silver.

When she laid down beside him and rested her cheek on her bent arm, he reached out and stroked his hand over her hair. Then he wrapped his arm around her and yanked her against him, tucking her head under his chin as he threw his long leg over hers. Burying his face against the top of her head, he spoke in a low, husky tone that was so solemn it made tears burn at the back of her throat. "No matter what happens, my biggest regret will always be that I wasn't able to claim you as *mine*."

Clutching on to him with desperate hands, Sayre had to fight back the urge to shout at him to open his damn eyes, look in a mirror and *see* the truth she could have sworn burned in that silver gaze every single time he looked at her. But what good would come of it? He wouldn't see the truth until he was ready. Until he finally allowed himself to move on from the past and was ready to fight for his future. To fight for *her*. Not in the way that he was fighting to protect her from Aedan, but for her heart. For the future she prayed they could have one day. That she so desperately wanted.

But there was no guarantee that he would ever reach that point—and she no longer knew if she could continue to play it safe. Doing so went against everything her instincts were telling her to do. She might have started out hiding behind her emotional armor, afraid of the damage he could leave behind—but she understood him better now. The damage was already done, which meant it was time to go all in or go home. And she didn't have a home without him.

She wanted Cian. The wolf, the vampire and whoever else he might have living inside of him. She didn't care, she simply wanted them all.

She wanted *her* man.

Chapter 15

Twenty-seven hours later...

Pure green, for as far as his eyes could see. That was what always caught Cian off guard when he came back to the land where he'd been born. The deep, vibrant green.

Would look incredible against Sayre's golden red hair, his beast murmured, its guttural voice as dejected as his own. He kept having to blink goddamn moisture out of his eyes, so what the hell was that about? He'd never cried in his life, and now *this*. He felt like he was in a sappy romance flick. And it didn't help that he'd spent the entire seven-hour flight across the Atlantic poring over all *The Green Witch* videos that he'd downloaded onto his phone before leaving, still marveling at what Sayre had achieved at such a young age, and completely on her own. He was so damn proud of her there weren't even words to express it.

And he missed her so much it was killing him, each moment that took him farther away from her cutting him like a blade.

Though it'd been the hardest thing he'd ever done, Cian had left her sleeping beneath the covers just after the sun had set, and gone to speak with Brody, pulling the Runner away from his dinner. Hating that he hadn't been able to tell her goodbye, he'd been in a grim, miserable state as he told Brody that he'd devised a plan for dealing with Aedan, and would need his promise to keep Sayre under heavy lockdown, whether she wanted it or not, as soon as he was gone.

Then he'd climbed in the Audi and left her. Again. Only this time had been a thousand times worse than before, because he damn well *knew* what he was leaving behind.

As he'd held the witch in his arms after she'd fallen asleep, Cian had finally started to understand what they'd been doing. How they'd both been navigating a minefield of emotion, both gut-wrenchingly terrified of getting hurt…and so determined to protect themselves, they were living in lies and half-truths.

At least he was. He had been for…God, for too many years to count.

And with that stunning realization came another one that would have taken his damn legs out from under him, if he hadn't already been lying down. One he still couldn't think about without feeling like the biggest idiot on the face of the planet. All these years since he'd discovered the truth about his old man, he'd always been convinced he *couldn't* love because he was too much like him. Because he carried his blood in his veins, and had done so many wrongs. But the truth was that he was too afraid of being vulnerable, just like his mother. Of giving his love to someone who didn't love him in return, and ending up completely destroyed.

He'd wanted to stay there in that bed with Sayre, and keep working these stunning revelations through his mind, feeling like a man who'd always been blind suddenly discovering the gift of sight. But as always, the timing hadn't been right. He'd been forced to leave her, and yeah, he knew how she must be feeling about that. No doubt cursing him to hell and back for walking away from her all over again.

That seemed to be another constant, the way that doing the right thing always made him a massive dick. Maybe that's what he should ask them to put on his tombstone. Then again, maybe not. He could just imagine the questionable array of "objects" that would be left on his grave as mementos.

Though that last thought made him snicker, the quiet burst of laughter quickly died as he steered his Range Rover onto the winding country road that would take him to Killian's Mount, the seaside estate where he'd grown up. Despite the fact that the sun was still shining, he was nothing but a cold, aching shell, every cell of his body suffering from withdrawal.

But nothing about the way he was feeling changed anything. In fact, it only made him more determined to follow his current course of action.

An alive and kicking Aedan Hennessey meant that Sayre would never be safe.

So Aedan had to die. As soon as possible. By *whatever* means necessary.

It was as simple as that.

Stopping at his first destination, an overgrown-with-ivy cottage that sat on the edge of his father's land, Cian went inside and set his plan in motion. Within minutes, he was back in the Range Rover and driving toward the main house, the salty scent of the sea crashing against the nearby craggy cliffs clinging to his hair and clothes.

More cottages had been added to the estate since he'd last visited, but it didn't surprise him. His old man had never managed the art of self-control when he'd been younger, and he obviously wasn't any closer now. God only knew how many half siblings Cian had within the borders of the estate. Aedan might have been the first of his father's illegitimate children, but he was hardly the last.

He was also the only one that Cian had claimed. A mistake he wished more than anything he could go back and change.

By the time he was climbing the stone steps leading up to the front door of his father's palatial home, he had his teeth clenched so hard he was surprised they hadn't cracked. He didn't bother to knock—simply let himself in, and hoped like hell that the bastard took offence at it. Pissing off his old man was one of his favorite pastimes—though it didn't come anywhere close to spending time with Sayre, or kissing Sayre, or making the beautiful little witch come so hard she screamed. Hell, *anything* that involved Sayre topped his list of favorites. Even when she was frustrating him to the point of tears, his life was better than it had ever been without her. And he knew, without any doubt, that particular little fact wasn't ever going to change.

For the first time ever, Cian was actually letting himself be happy about it. Was embracing the hell out of it, and holding on as tightly as he could, ready to fight for it with everything that he had.

As he made his way through the sunlit halls, it didn't take him long to track down the object of his visit. He found his father in the library, sitting in a heavy leather chair by the far wall of windows, a book on his lap.

Colin Hennessey was a big, robust man who looked no more than fifty, and Cian had definitely inherited his father's height and his broad shoulders. Everything else, thank God, he'd taken from his mother. Her coloring. Her eyes. He was grateful for each and every trait that she'd passed on to him, wanting to see as little of this jackass as he had to when he looked in a mirror.

"Father," he murmured, crossing his arms over his chest as he propped his shoulder against the door frame. "I wish I could say it's good to see you, but we both know that would be a lie."

Colin sighed heavily as he set aside the book he'd been reading, and it was clear that he was unsurprised to see Cian standing there. But then, he knew one of his father's security detail had no doubt notified him the instant he'd driven onto the property. Steepling his fingers together as he rested his elbows on the padded arms of the chair, Colin said, "Still angry, I see."

Cian slowly lifted his brows. "Did you honestly expect a hug?"

Exhaling a tired breath, Colin replied with a question of his own. "How long are you going to make me pay for a sin that you know I'm sorry for?"

"I don't care if you're sorry," he said tightly. "I could have forgiven you for anything but breaking her. Betraying her. So your answer is forever. Any love or respect or care I held for you died the day I realized what a miserable excuse of a man you are."

"You hold me to your standards, but I'm not a Lycan, Cian. I'm part man, part darkness, and you don't know how impossible Alice was to resist."

"Don't. I know exactly how easily you fell into bed

with Aedan's mother. And she was simply the first of many."

Colin frowned. "I'm not like you," he repeated.

"If you'd loved your wife, you would have been true to her. You wouldn't have wasted your time on trash."

"Damn it, I *did* love her."

A gruff, bitter laugh jerked from his chest. "No, you didn't. You loved the way she made you feel. The way *her love* made you feel. Powerful. Strong. Worthy. But that was her mistake. She should have ran the instant she ever set eyes on you."

"Just because we never completed the blood bond doesn't mean she didn't belong with me. She was my wife, Cian! Her place was at my side!"

He shook his head, his tone thick with revulsion. "She always said you couldn't bond with her because of the darkness in your heart. The evil flowing through your veins. But I know differently. I know firsthand," he growled through his gritted teeth. "You. Lied."

Leaning forward in his chair, his father gave him a penetrating look. "You're not bonded. I would be able to tell."

"You're right, I'm not. But not because I *can't*." No, he knew damn well that if he'd lived his life differently, he would have already claimed the hell out of Sayre Murphy and forged a bond with her that was more powerful than anything their world had ever seen. "I haven't bonded with my woman yet, because unlike you, I'm willing to put her first."

Colin's thick brows rose. "And is that why you're here? Because you're putting her first?"

"I'm here because I'm ending this thing between

Aedan and me once and for all. This is where it began, and this is where it will end."

Those thick brows pulled together in a frown. "You really intend to kill your own brother?"

Shaking his head again, he said, "The monster walking around with Aedan's face isn't my brother. The boy we both loved was lost a long time ago. There's nothing of Aedan left in him."

Colin's chest lifted with a deep breath, the look in his dark eyes almost painfully piercing. "I know you blame me for not helping you before."

"I blame you for a hell of a lot more than that. But I'm not here to ask for your help. The only purpose of this visit is to make my position clear. I *will* fight Aedan to the death when he comes, and I *will* kill anyone who tries to stand in my way. *Anyone.* So if you want your bloody family safe, tell them to stay the hell away from me."

He pushed off from the door frame and started to turn away, when Colin's next words stopped him. "I...I made a mistake." At Cian's look of disgust, Colin grimaced. "All right, *many* mistakes. We've already been over this, but your mother—what I did to her—is the greatest of my failures. I had something...something unique, and I tossed it away for what amounted to nothing."

Cian narrowed his eyes. "If you knew what you had to lose, then why did you do it?"

"Because I was..." He paused to clear his throat, and then went on, looking as if the gruff words were being torn out of him against his will. "I didn't handle the things she made feel at all well. After you were born, those feelings grew. And she was somehow even more beautiful. More precious to me. I didn't know how to embrace that, and it wasn't long before I started to resent the pull that she had on me."

"That's why she could never bond with you," he muttered, his insides churning. "What you felt for her, you never allowed it to take hold. You fought it every step of the way. But you were too selfish to let her walk away and be happy without you."

Colin gave a weary nod, and for the first time that he could remember, his father actually looked his age. He looked old. Hollow.

"And your loyalty to Aedan?" Cian asked. "How do you explain that?"

Sighing, Colin said, "Despite what he became, he's still my son."

"Not for long," he grunted, turning away again.

"By the way," Colin called out, "I have the bachelor's house ready for you, and your guests are in the lodge."

Stopping dead in his tracks, Cian slowly turned back around, his hooded gaze locking with his father's through the open doorway. "My *what*?" he asked in a low, ominous tone.

Studying him with a deep, measuring stare, Colin said, "Your guests."

"Aw, fuck!"

Without another word, Cian turned and slammed out of the house, stalking across the lush lawn as he headed toward the massive stone-and-timber lodge that sat near a thicket of trees. Fear sat in the back of his throat like something threatening to choke him and his pulse thrashed in his ears like the straining roar of an engine. He knew exactly who his goddamn *guests* were, and he was furious that he hadn't guessed they would do something this outrageous. God only knew how long they'd been here waiting for him. His trip had taken longer than usual because he'd flown directly into Dublin so that he could stop by his apartment and arrange to have his things packed and ready to ship out, once he provided the moving company with an address. He knew where he *hoped* he would be going after this nightmare was over, but he wasn't going to presume until things were settled. He just knew he wasn't going to keep hiding in Dublin, pretending his entire world wasn't back in Maryland.

You know damn well where we're going, his beast rumbled. *If we have to camp on her doorstep until she gives in, we're going back. Going after the girl!*

"Yeah, well, the bloody girl is already here," he bit out, catching Sayre's mouthwatering scent as he neared the lodge.

Oh, hell no. I'm putting her over our knee for this and swatting her little ass!

"Not if I do it first," he snarled, throwing the front door of the lodge open and letting out a thunderous roar. *"Sayre!"*

A group of people walked into the high-ceilinged entryway from various rooms, and his jaw clenched as he took them all in. The mercs must have been handling things back at the Alley, because nearly everyone else was standing in front of him. All the Runners and most of their mates. Even Max and Elliot were there.

But there wasn't any sign of Sayre.

Scraping the words from his tight throat, he demanded, "What the hell are you all doing here?"

Jillian came toward him, and for a split second, he thought she was going to slap him again. But she didn't. Instead, she shocked ten years off his life when she threw her arms around his middle and hugged him so damn tightly he could barely breathe.

"Uh…"

Tilting her head back, she looked up at him and said, "You left before I got the chance to talk to you."

His right eyebrow slowly lifted. "You came an awfully long way for the two of us to talk, lass. You could have just used my number."

She smirked, the spark in her brown eyes telling him that she'd figured something out. He just didn't know what it was.

"Jillian, what's going on?"

She gave him another hard squeeze, then let him go and moved back to Jeremy's side, before she said, "I knew I couldn't have been as wrong about you as it seemed."

As relieved as he was that Jillian no longer looked like she wanted to kill him, he needed to find Sayre. Cutting a sharp look toward Jeremy, he growled, "Where's Sayre? And for the second time, what the hell are you all doing here?"

"What do you think we're doing here?" Jillian asked, looking at him as if he were being ridiculous.

He tried to catch Brody's eye, but the Runner was purposefully avoiding his gaze. The bastard. Cian knew that Brody had told them all where he was headed, even though he'd asked the Runner not to say anything until he'd contacted him.

And if he hadn't heard from him by the end of the week, well…he'd given the Runner strict instructions on what he wanted to happen then.

Struggling for patience, he cast another frustrated

look over the group. "Would someone *please* tell me what the hell is going on?"

Eli Drake, who was mated to the only female Runner, muttered something under his breath that sounded like *stubborn jackass*, but it was Cian's old friend Wyatt Pallaton who finally took mercy on him. "We're here to help you, man."

"I don't need anyone's bloody help," he argued. "I have a plan."

Brody finally looked him right in the eye and snorted. "You have an invitation to the psycho to come and face you, knowing damn well he's going to be foaming at the mouth. But you don't have the answer." His partner's green eyes narrowed with suspicion. "At least not one that you've shared with the rest of us."

"I know what I'm doing. That's all you need to know."

"What the hell, Cian? You never used to be this stupid," the Runner yelled, taking an aggressive step forward. "You really think that's how we're going to let this play out?"

"You aren't letting anything happen one way or another. This is *my* fight."

"That doesn't mean we can't be here to support you," Mason said, speaking up for the first time.

Cian rubbed his tongue over his front teeth and seethed with frustration, a goddamn red haze falling over his eyes as he snarled, "You're not doing jack shit but getting in my way."

"Even me?"

He flinched, that soft voice dragging his gaze up to the top of the stairs at the back of the entryway. And there she was. Sayre. Dressed in jeans, sandals and a summery white blouse, she kept those storm-dark eyes locked tight on his as she walked down the stairs, the group parting to make way for her as she came toward him. She was so beautiful to his starved senses, he didn't know how to take it all in. Luminous skin, fiery hair in a wave of curls that fell around her heart-shaped face. Those eyes…her pink, glossy mouth…and that pale, tender throat that he wanted to bite so badly it was a physical pain that ripped through his insides and twisted him into knots.

"We'll let you two have some time alone," Mason told him, "but you need to know that we're not going anywhere, Cian. Jeremy and Brody have been keeping us updated on what was happening, and we wanted to be there. The only reason we stayed away was because we didn't want to make things harder for Sayre. But we're here to stay for as long as you need us."

The group filed out then, going back to whatever they'd been doing before he barged in, and he found himself standing alone with Sayre.

"Baby," he breathed, shaking with fear and anger and too many other explosive emotions to put a name to. "I can't believe you're here."

Crossing her arms over her chest, she arched one of her golden brows and smirked. "Did you really think I was going to let you bring me back to this crazy bunch and then just let you leave me? That hardly seems fair, Cian."

"Who the hell cares about what's fair? You have no reason to give a fuck what I do. I left you. *Again*, Sayre. As far as you know, we're over."

Instead of bursting into tears, she looked like she was fighting back a grin, her big eyes shimmering with humor. "Yeah, that's not really going to work for me."

"S-aa-y-re," he growled, drawing her name out with a healthy dose of frustration.

Trapping him in that smoldering, breathtaking gaze, she said, "You've got some weird hang-up about your past and your jerk-face of a father, and that's fine. I get it. But I'm not willing to give up our future because of it."

"You're being unreason—"

"Why?" she asked, cutting him off. "Because I refuse to let you go? If I really thought that was what you wanted, then I would." Taking a step closer to him, she lowered her arms and straightened her spine, looking like a regal little goddess as she faced him down. "So go ahead, Cian. Look me in the eye, right now, and tell me you don't want me."

"It's not that simple," he snapped.

She lifted her chin, her sharp gaze burning with determination. "Tell. Me."

He opened his mouth, but couldn't force the words out.

She waited, her breath held, and then her gaze softened, the corner of her lush mouth tipping up in a heartbreaking smile of relief. "I knew it. I knew I couldn't be completely alone in this. Fate isn't *that* cruel."

"You might not feel that way when this is all said and done," he muttered, knowing there was no way in hell he could stay away from her now, and wondering if she were truly ready for him. For what he'd want from her. He'd missed her more with each second that went by since he'd walked away, and now…damn it, he was done. "God, Sayre. You have no idea how badly I want you."

"That's why you don't get to touch me until it's over," she told him, her voice dropping to a soft, provocative murmur.

"Wait. *What?*"

Her big eyes were beginning to sparkle with mischief. "You need incentive, Cian. Beat Aedan's ass down when he shows his ugly face, and then you can you do whatever you want to me. We're talking a completely open menu. I'm ready for your A game, big guy."

"Jesus," he hissed under his breath, squeezing his eyes shut as he covered them with his hand. If he'd ever been this painfully hard before, he'd blocked it from his memory. "Have you lost your friggin' mind?" he growled.

"Nope," she replied, popping the *p*. "But I've finally found my backbone. I thought that to be strong, I had to hold myself back from you. From what I wanted. But that isn't strength. That was nothing but fear. And fear doesn't have any place between two people like us."

Lowering his hand, he opened his eyes, needing to see her more than he needed to hide. "And what kind of people are those?" he rasped, forcing the words from his tight throat.

"Ones who *belong* to each other. Who *need* each other." Her lips trembled, then curved into a sexy, breathtaking smile. "Ones who are ready to spend the rest of their lives, every day and night, getting lost in each other."

"Christ," he groaned. "You're wrecking me, baby."

Unable to wait a moment longer to have her in his arms, he started toward her, but she held up her hands and said, "Stop right there, Cian."

He exhaled a sharp breath. "Damn it, Sayre. I *need* you."

She kept that beautiful, luminous gaze locked tight

on his. "I need you, too. But I need *all* of you, not just the parts that you're willing to share with me."

"I'm using everything I have to protect you, lass. *Everything.*"

"But you're not *giving* me everything."

He couldn't believe she was being this stubborn. "I *can't*. Not yet."

Taking a step back from him, she said, "Then I guess we're at a stalemate. Because until you share your soul with me, Cian, I can't share my body. And no, before you look at me like that, it's not because I don't want you to see what's inside me. All you have to do is look at me to know that I love you. That I'm *in love* with you. So, so much."

He shuddered, unable to believe what he was hearing. Yeah, he'd known that she lusted for him—but he'd been too goddamn terrified to let himself believe that she might already be in love with him. And while it was what he wanted most, he couldn't accept it. Not now, when God only knew what would happen when he faced off against Aedan.

So he forced himself to bite out a foul-tasting response. "You shouldn't."

"Shouldn't what? Tell you? Love you?"

"Yes! Damn it, I don't deserve it," he snapped, feeling the weight of his old self-loathing climbing over his back like a clinging demon. He wanted to shake off that fucker, but he didn't know how.

"*I* deserve it, Cian. I deserve *you.*"

"You have no idea how badly I wish that was true. But you deserve a hell of a lot better than me."

"Stop!" she shouted, and he knew she was pissed

when those sparks started pinging around in the air. "I won't listen to you talk about yourself that way."

"Sayre."

"No, just stop it, Cian. I'm so sick of hearing crap like that. No more. You don't get to keep spouting that same old bullshit. It's *done*. Do you understand me?"

"I...*fuck*."

Bright eyes flashing with anger, she said, "You either believe that we belong together or you don't. And if you don't, then it's already over. All of it. You won't walk away from this thing with Aedan if you don't believe."

He froze, something in her tone telling him that she was keeping a secret. "What is it, Sayre? What aren't you telling me?"

She quickly tore her gaze from his, but not before he'd seen the confirmation in her eyes. Already turning away from him, she said, "Goodbye, Cian. I'll see you tomorrow."

He got it then, figuring that she must have had a vision—a moment of insight where she saw into the future. He didn't know if it'd ever happened that way for her before, but if any witch were strong enough for a premonition, it was this one. *His* witch. "Damn it, Sayre, what did you see?"

Still making her way toward the stairs, he could have sworn there was a smile in her voice as she said, "Sleep tight tonight. I wouldn't want you to tire yourself out with a bunch of dirty dreams about everything you're planning on doing to me. An old guy like you needs his rest."

Torn between wanting to kiss the hell out of her smart-ass little mouth and the sudden urge to put her over his goddamn knee, he growled, "Get back here!"

"Can't," she said over her shoulder. "And just so you know, the next time you touch me, this *is* finally happening. I don't care if I have to tie your sexy ass up, you are *mine*."

For a moment, all he could do was watch her walk away from him, wondering what she'd done to him. How she'd so completely turned his entire world around until he didn't even know which way was up anymore. And then he heard himself say, "Sayre."

She watched him over her shoulder as she slowly made her way up the stairs. "Yeah?"

"You…" His voice trailed off, and he ran a shaky hand down his face before continuing. "You mean everything to me. If it all goes to shit tomorrow, I just want you to know that."

She stopped about halfway up the staircase and turned around, one hand gripping the railing as she stared down at him. "You know, you've spent so much time worrying about what I deserve, but what about you?"

He gave a hard swallow. "What about me?"

Her precious face was flushed with color, and her bright eyes gleamed. "What do *you* deserve, Cian? What do you *want* to deserve?"

"Just you," he managed to choke out in a husky rasp. "I want to deserve *you*."

She turned around again, but not before he caught the beautiful smile that touched her lips. "And nothing's going to go to shit," she called out, looking back over her shoulder to give him a wink. "Just get your head out of your ass and try not to do anything stupid tomorrow."

Crazy, beautiful, kick-ass little witch. God, she was going to be the death of him.

I just hope you don't mean that literally, his wolf grumbled, and he had to bite back a sharp bark of laughter, in complete agreement.

Grinning like an idiot, Cian watched the sway of her hips as she climbed the stairs for a few more seconds, then forced himself to turn and walk away, knowing damn well that he couldn't stay in the same building as Sayre and not be all over her. It struck him, then, like a physical force that knocked the smile right off his face, that he was always turning and walking away from her, when all he really wanted was to have her in his arms, holding her as close as possible.

But fate was always working against him, blocking his shot, and he was tired as hell of it. He was ready to teach that bastard a lesson and make him bleed.

Then he wanted to grab up the girl, bare his fangs in a vicious snarl to anyone who tried to get in his way and carry her off into the night.

He wanted his own goddamn happily-ever-after. And he wanted it *now*.

He just had to get rid of the bastard standing in his way.

And that meant that it was time for Aedan Hennessey to finally meet his maker in Hell.

Chapter 16

Cian had spent the entire day doing his best to avoid Sayre, knowing he needed to be sharp for when Aedan arrived. And now that time was almost here. A violent storm loomed out over the churning sea, keeping company with the crimson sun as it made its final dip beneath the horizon, while a million stars looked down from above, the sparks of light like curious eyes, eager to see what would happen.

He'd known his brother wouldn't make him wait long. As soon as Aedan sensed that Cian had taken Sayre's blood, he would have been driven mad with frenzy. Aside from the fact that she tasted like friggin' nirvana, sumptuous and hot and rich, *that* was the reason why Cian had licked her blood from her body the night he'd left the Alley. Because he'd known it would turn Aedan into his puppet, ensuring his brother followed after him like a faithful bloodhound. And with Sayre safely under lockdown in Maryland, there'd been no reason for Aedan to think she wasn't traveling with him. Cian had even purchased an extra ticket in her name for the flight, just in case his brother had checked.

But she wasn't under lockdown in the Alley. The

headstrong girl had followed him to Ireland, putting everything he'd planned in jeopardy.

In fact, she was there with him now, standing at the far side of the cliff-top clearing, the Runners flanking her sides. She looked so insanely beautiful it was difficult not to stare, the golden glow of one of the swinging oil lamps that had been placed around the perimeter making the red in her hair burn like a flame.

The only bright spot in his day had been when Brody came to see him at the bachelor's house where Cian was staying, and handed him a flask of Sayre's blood. According to the grim-faced Runner, she'd wanted him to have something to drink for *luck*. Of course, there'd been the added benefit of how her blood affected him, hitting his system like a shot of pure, high-voltage adrenaline. He was ready for this fight, and knew it wouldn't be long now. Moments ago, Colin had received word that Aedan was nearing his land.

"I know why you chose this place to face him," his father called out, standing on the opposite side of the clearing from Sayre and the Runners, surrounded by a sprawling group of people who Cian refused to look at too closely, not wanting to see his same features staring back at him. "And I spoke with Simone this morning. I know what you bought from her."

"What's he talking about?" his friend Eric asked him, but Cian shook his head, making it clear he didn't want to talk or make explanations. He knew the Runner was asking about Simone, because Cian had already explained to Brody why it was imperative that he fight Aedan in Ireland, on their father's land. It had to do with a unique spell Colin had paid to have cast over the grounds decades ago. A spell that ensured Colin remained the dominant male by weakening the power of any other male once they set foot on Killian's Mount. He didn't see it having much effect on males as strong as he and Aedan were, but given his brother's physical power these days, Cian was willing to take any advantage he could get, no matter how slight.

And as for Simone—well, if things went badly, the Runners would learn soon enough what he'd purchased from the elderly witch the previous day, when he'd first arrived at his father's estate.

They waited another breathless span of seconds, while lightning thundered and crashed out over the violent sea, the winds so strong they whipped at people's clothing and lifted their hair, shaking the trees like invisible monsters. And then the monster they'd all been waiting for finally made his appearance.

"Are we having a party that no one told me about?" his brother drawled, moving so quickly that he seemed to have come out of nowhere and assuming a place not five yards from where Cian stood. He could hear the Runners talking in quiet, worried voices, since this was the first time they'd set eyes on Aedan. But Sayre remained silent, her steady gaze giving him strength.

Come on, you bastard, he thought. *Let's do this.*

He didn't bother to respond to Aedan's inane question, determined to get this nightmare over and done with as quickly as possible. Unlike the last time he'd seen his brother, tonight he was facing Aedan beneath the full light of the moon, and as he pulled in a deep breath of the sea-scented air, Cian gave himself over completely to its power, letting it call not only to his beast, but also to that dark well of strength he always kept so firmly locked inside him. Within seconds, his clothes had shredded as his body expanded in height and muscle mass, bones cracking and reshaping themselves into the predatory shape of a killer, his fangs dropping as his claws burst through the tips of his fingers. Even his face reshaped itself into the intimidating muzzle of a wolf, complete with razor-sharp teeth that could tear through flesh and bone like a knife slipping into warm butter. And instead of the fur that normally covered his body when he shifted, his skin darkened to a sinister blue-black, while his eyes changed from gray to crimson.

This was the first time the Runners had seen him in his "true" vampire-wolf form, and he could hear their collective sounds of surprise, as well as Brody's guttural *"What the ever-loving fuck?"*

Before he could give his former partner a hard time about his reaction, Aedan let out a vicious snarl, allowing his own transformation to take place. Long, sinister fangs dripped with saliva from beneath his thin upper lip, his talons curling longer around his fingers as his body turned that cadaverous shade of white again, his bones popping and extending until he was nearly Cian's height.

They waited for a heaving, weighted second, then bared their fangs and charged. Their bodies met in mid-air, slamming together with a brutal sound of flesh hitting flesh as they spun, twisting, delivering blows that had the night quickly smelling of blood. They'd traveled nearly twenty yards by the time they hit the ground, rolling dangerously close to the edge of the craggy cliffs. As they sprang to their feet, a lightning-fast kick to Cian's back sent him careening precariously close to the edge again. Aedan's maniacal laughter rang out, and from the far side of the clearing, he could hear the Runners shouting. Someone had apparently tried to join the fight to help him, only to realize that Colin had put a shield in place to keep everyone out until either he or Aedan had fallen.

"It will be a fair fight or there will be no fight at all," his father called out across the clearing, while he and Aedan circled each other, searching for a weakness.

A muttered collection of curses filled the air in response to Colin's words, and Brody sounded angry enough to shift into the shape of his beast then and there. "The vampire's a goddamn psycho! How the hell is that fair?"

"My sons are *both* strong," Colin responded, which made Aedan laugh.

"Aw, isn't that sweet, Cian? Dear ol' Daddy actually thinks you have a chance. What a fucking moron. You and I both know I'll be the one pounding inside your little witch tonight."

He snarled, and then they were at it again, fighting with a ferocity that brought constant gasps and curses from those around them. But their father simply watched in silence, standing tall and proud, as if he thought he was a god among men. Arrogant bastard.

When Cian looked back on this day, if he survived, he had a feeling he wouldn't recall the gruesome individual details. Instead, he would remember the spray of crimson that constantly filled his vision, the blood both his and Aedan's, while pain seared his system, burning him from the inside out. Dark, engulfing, savage waves of pain that came like the raging of the off-shore storm, hitting him one after another, until he couldn't even catch his breath.

As if she sensed that he was reaching the end, Sayre's power was unleashing with a force unlike anything he'd ever witnessed. Hawks and gulls swarmed overhead, their stark, constant cries echoing over the crashing sound of the waves, almost as though she'd called them to bear witness to her rage. But it wasn't just the animals falling under her spell—the tall trees that surrounded the clearing leaned eerily toward its perimeter, as if they'd been bent by a violent wind. Snakelike, meandering vines slithered across the ground, thumping repeatedly against the metaphysical shield that Colin had put in place.

She was desperately trying to reach him, her husky voice screaming in his head for him to keep fighting— but he knew if he didn't make his final move now, it would be too late. And there wasn't a chance in hell he was letting Aedan walk away from this, knowing the bastard would make Sayre suffer long and hard before he killed her.

"Tell me, brother," he panted, when they'd broken apart to gain their bearings after another brutal bout of combat. "Was your little Elizabeth really worth all of this?" he asked, deliberately taunting the monster as he carefully made his way toward the spiky patch of broken limbs and rotting tree trunks that sat clumped together at the eastern edge of the clearing. "Was she really worth all the hate? Because all I recall is a broken little girl who detested even the sound of your name. She didn't love you. She despised everything about you!"

Rising to the bait, Aedan let out a bloodcurdling roar and slammed into Cian so hard that it sent them both crashing to the ground—but the bastard was already too late. After wrapping the "binding tie" that he'd hidden earlier that day in one of the rotting trunks around Aedan's wrist, Cian quickly looped it around his own, the simple-looking strip of black leather instantly searing its way into their flesh. Then he locked his burning gaze with Aedan's, and gave him a chilling smile. "Thanks to Simone's witchcraft, you're bound to me now. Which means it's time for you to die."

"You *can't* kill me," Aedan scoffed, looking at him as if he were the one who'd been lost to madness. "Not when we're bound, brother."

"Just watch me," he snarled, and it was almost enough to make him laugh, the look of shock that spilled over Aedan's face like a stain.

Shaking his head with disbelief, Aedan's pierced brows pulled together in a deep frown as he looked toward Sayre, who was watching them with wide, terrified eyes. And then he slowly brought his crimson gaze back to Cian. "Is this real?" he asked, and there was something in his tone that reminded Cian of the boy he'd known all those years ago, and it broke his fucking heart. "You're willing to do that for her?"

"I'm willing to do *anything* for her," he rasped, his goddamn eyes filling with tears. "Whatever it takes." And with those final words, Cian shot one last, smoldering look at Sayre, drinking in the breathtaking sight of her until it fueled him with the strength he needed for one final burst of energy—and then he launched both him and Aedan through the air. They crashed into the middle of the rotten, broken trees, both of them crying out from the shared pain of their landing. Blood gurgled on Aedan's lips from the gaping wound that had been made when a jagged, protruding branch pierced through his upper back and tore straight through his chest, the spearlike tip hovering just beneath Cian's throat. But as brutal as the wound appeared, it wasn't enough to kill him, and Cian knew what he had to do.

With Sayre's screams echoing in his head, he whispered, "Time to die," and shoved himself onto the branch, the wood puncturing his throat and driving straight through to his spinal column, severing it in two.

After that, there was nothing but a hazy, icy darkness, as if he were floating through the nighttime sky. He could hear arguing, but it was far away. Someone was shouting that he was dead, that Sayre was going to kill herself trying to save him, and he struggled to tell her *no*, not to risk herself, but she was screaming for everyone to stay away from her, threatening to zap them over the side of the cliffs if they tried to stop her. Then a strange, shimmering vein of warmth started to snake its way through his weightless body, growing steadily hotter and more brilliant, until it felt as if he were lying in the center of a burning flame.

Only…he wasn't burning. Yes, there was pain, but his skin wasn't charring, or turning to ash. Instead, it was his throat and spine that seared as though lava had been poured directly into his wounds, and he suddenly realized that it was Sayre's healing powers being injected into his broken body.

"Did you make sure that goddamn binding tie is off him?" someone grunted, followed by a voice that sounded like Jillian's still screaming, "Jesus, someone stop her. She's going to kill herself!"

"Don't you understand what's happening?" Sayre growled, sounding like an enraged goddess. "He was tied to that asshole when he died, so he goes where his brother goes. If I let go of the hold I have on his soul, he's going to follow right behind him, straight into Hell!"

"And if you're linked with him like this, then so will you!" Jillian sobbed.

"I don't care!" Sayre shouted, her voice cracking at the end. "He doesn't get to come back, make me fall in love with his cocky ass and then leave me. Screw that! I won't let him! I know I can save him. Why the hell do you think I came here after he walked away from me all over again? I *saw* this, Jilly. I knew he would need me!"

"Whatever you saw, it's impossible to bring back a soul once it's gone. You know that, Sayre. You're not thinking straight."

"Maybe it's impossible for most," he heard Jeremy murmur. "But you Murphy girls are special, sweetheart."

Murphy girl? No! She needed his name, damn it. Needed to be a Hennessey.

And why in God's name was he just lying there, listening to them argue, when he needed to fight for her? When he needed to fight his way back to her, so that she didn't end up following him into the *after*? And while he was all for having this woman by his side for eternity—*though preferably not in Hell*—he wanted a lifetime with her first. He wanted the wedding and births. The holidays and family vacations. He wanted the whole goddamn package!

Scraping onto every ounce of strength he could find, Cian finally managed to force his heavy eyelids open. He found himself staring up at the tearstained face of the most beautiful girl in the world—but he didn't know what he'd done to deserve her. All he knew was that someone out there had given him a second chance, and he was taking it. Grabbing on with both hands and taking the hell out of it.

"Shh," she whispered against his ear, when he tried to speak. "Shh. Just lie here and heal for a moment. You're almost there."

Against his will, his heavy eyelids drifted shut again, and he existed in a strange dreamlike state, not asleep, and yet, not completely awake. Sayre's mouthwatering scent was all around him, soothing and warm, and he knew his friends were close by, their voices reaching out to him in soft murmurs and broken phrases.

"So she knew he was going to die for her?"

"Never thought it would happen to him."

"About damn time that it did."

No shit, his wolf grunted, its gruff laughter echoing in his head.

With a smile on his lips, he let himself go back under, no idea how much time had passed when he next opened his eyes. But he could tell that someone had put a pair of jeans on him, since he was once again in his human form, and Sayre was no longer holding him on her lap. Instead, he was lying on the blood-soaked ground in the middle of the clearing with something soft under his head, and Brody was crouching down beside him, a fierce scowl etched onto the Runner's scarred face.

"Hey, would you look at this," Cian croaked. "It's Broody Brody to the rescue."

Brody snorted, his green eyes glittering with relief. "Shut up, you lucky jackass."

Surprised by how good he felt, he managed a lopsided grin. "I know that look. You want to hug me now, don't you?"

"I think I'll leave the hugging to your woman," the

Runner muttered, shaking his head. "But I'm thinking I could probably welcome you back home now without constantly wanting to kick your ass."

"Thanks, man. You're all heart," he said drily.

Brody laughed, and Cian sniffed the air, searching for Sayre's scent. "Speaking of my woman, where is she?"

Jerking his chin toward his right, Brody said, "Right over there, giving your old man hell."

"That's my girl," he rumbled with pride, pushing himself up into a sitting position. He purposefully kept his head turned away from Aedan's body, not wanting to see it. Though he definitely didn't regret what he'd done, knowing it was the only way, it wouldn't be a sight he could stomach.

As if he'd read his mind, Brody lowered his voice so that no one else could hear him. "She saved you, man. Brought you back from a one-way trip to Hell. And you were ready to spend eternity there to protect her. I...I don't know what to say to that exactly, except that I'm happy for you. You went all in, Cian, and you came out breathing on the other side. Now you can leave the past in the past, where it belongs, and move forward by having a kick-ass life with your little witch."

"You know, when you put it like that, I'm pretty fucking happy for me, too."

"Yeah, I can see that you are." A low laugh rumbled up from the Runner's chest as he eyed Cian's smile. "Christ, that girl has you *so* wrapped around her little finger."

"That's only fair, since I plan on keeping her wrapped around certain parts of me pretty much twenty-four seven."

"Watch it, Cian." Jillian's laughing voice came from

somewhere behind him. "That's my baby sister you're talking about."

"And she's *my* woman," he said with a wealth of satisfaction, watching her giving his old man absolute hell for not doing anything to help him during the fight. No matter what, the little witch was always fighting for him—fighting for *them*—and he knew there were going to be some serious changes taking place in his life, the first being that he was going to stop buying his own bullshit. Because he finally got it.

Anyone could walk away. *Anyone.* But it took a real man to face the truth and accept that one little slip of a girl held his entire world in her hands. The smartest, sexiest, most incredible girl there was.

"And she's ours," he growled under his breath.

About. Fucking. Time.

He gave a low laugh, agreeing with the beast completely.

Needing to hold her more than he needed his next breath, he managed to push himself up on his knees, and while he was a bit shaky, it was a goddamn miracle he was alive. Suddenly, kneeling in the middle of that godforsaken clearing, he realized something that was pretty damn important. For the first time, he saw, and actually *believed*, that everything really did happen for a reason. All the pain and heartbreak and fear and loss. He'd spent so many years wishing he could undo it all, but it was those things that had brought him here, to this point. Made him who he was. If he'd been different, fate might have never chosen him for Sayre at all, because it was the sum of all those parts of him that made him hers. That put the two pieces of them together, clicking them into one.

Each decision and step they'd made had led them to this point.

Every single goddamn one of them.

It was the kind of thing that could twist your brain into a pretzel if you thought about it for too long, and he didn't need to waste his time. He wasn't fighting this outcome. No, he was grabbing on to it as hard and as tight as he could, and holding on forever.

Holding on to her. His woman. His beautiful little bad-ass witch.

He didn't care what Colin Hennessey or anyone else thought of what he was about to do. The only person who mattered was Sayre, and Cian knew she would understand the symbolism behind the way he started crawling toward her on his hands and knees. Before his father and friends and God, he was humbling himself for her, making it clear to one and all that he would crawl after her over any distance, for any amount of time, until he finally had her in the end.

She ran toward him the instant she caught sight of him, tears streaming down her flushed face, and he moved to his knees again so that he could catch her against him, his head tilting back as he stared up at her, getting lost in those big, beautiful eyes. "You're *mine*," he told her, his big hands gripping her hips. "That means I'm never letting you go, Sayre."

He couldn't stop the slow, satisfied smile that lifted the corner of his mouth when she dropped to her knees before him. "It's about time you said that."

"And?" he murmured.

She blinked, looking adorably confused. "And what?"

"There's something else it's about damn time that I said to you." Looking her right in the eye so that she would know just how much he meant it, he cupped her precious, tear-drenched face in his palms, and told her, *"I love you, Sayre."*

"Oh, God," she whispered, crying even harder. "I can't believe you just said that."

He could hear his father bitching from somewhere behind her about how he was making a spectacle of himself and that real men didn't grovel, but Cian just tuned out the jackass, unwilling to let him intrude on this moment. Then he heard Jeremy mutter, "You know, I didn't think it was possible for someone to be an even bigger pain in the ass than Cian. But I was wrong. His old man *sucks*." He snickered under his breath. "That's kinda fitting, I guess, seeing as how he's a vampire."

"Seriously?" Carla asked. "You're making jokes *now*?"

"You know what Jeremy's like," Mason murmured. "The End of Days could be here and he'd still be laughing it up."

"Speaking of jokes," Cian said, raising his voice so the group could hear him, "when we get home, I want my cabin stripped down to the baseboards, ready for Sayre and me to make it the way we want it."

Jeremy snickered again. "I think we can manage that. But what do you want us to do with all the green shit?"

Keeping his eyes locked tight on Sayre, unwilling to look away from the love he could see shining there in that smoky, smoldering blue, Cian grinned as he lowered his voice and said, "Let's ship it over here. I'm betting my old man would love it."

The others all laughed, but he was already sipping from Sayre's soft lips, her sweet taste fueling him with energy, making him feel like he could take on the entire bloody world. But the world would have to be taken on by someone else. All he cared about taking was *her*— as hard and as often as she'd let him—and he couldn't wait a goddamn second more.

"Let's get out of here," he growled against her hot little mouth as he quickly moved to his feet with her in his arms and carried her away from their cheering friends, up to the bachelor's house, his body growing stronger with each step that he took. He felt as though he'd existed in two parts: the man he'd been before he started to see clearly, who wanted to put his hands around fate's throat and squeeze the life out of him. And then this one, who was ready to embrace the shit out of that fucker and thank him for making this incredible woman a part of his life, because he wouldn't change it for anything.

Seriously. Not a single goddamn thing.

Though they managed to make it through the front door, they didn't get any farther than the entryway before their desire got the better of them and they went wild on each other.

"Shit," he muttered, dropping down on his knees, his hands digging into her sweet little ass as she wrapped herself around him like a vine. "I'm still covered in blood, baby."

"Don't care," she gasped, kissing her way up the side of his throat, her lips and tongue driving him mad, while practically all the blood left in his body shot south, hardening his cock to the point of pain.

"Damn it, Sayre." His voice was raw and graveled with need. "You deserve better than this."

She pulled back just far enough that she could smirk at him. "Blood is a part of your life and it always will be. Which means it's a part of mine, too. So I doubt this is the last time we'll go to bed bloody."

"We're not even in a bed," he grunted, coming down over her as he laid her back on the hardwood floor. His right hand fisted in her silky hair, while his left one settled on her waist, his thumb stroking the soft skin on her belly.

With a devilish light in her eyes, she said, "I don't care about that, either." Then she lifted her head, nipped the edge of his jaw with her teeth and asked him, "Are you hungry for me, Cian?"

"Starved," he groaned, ripping at her clothes so that he could get to that soft, bare skin underneath. "And too damn desperate to wait, Sayre."

"Good," she said with a wealth of satisfaction that made him feel like he could level a bloody mountain for her, if that's what she wanted. What she *needed*.

"Tell me you're happy, and mean it," he said in a rough, breathless rasp, as he shoved her shirt up over her head, then quickly got rid of her lacy bra. "Because I can't let you go, Sayre. I did it once and it killed me inside each day. I can't do it again."

"You won't have to," she told him, running her greedy hands over every part of him she could reach, her delicious scent only getting richer with the rise of her need. "You aren't ever getting rid of me, and happy doesn't even begin to describe how freaking good I feel."

"Thank God," he groaned, pressing his parted lips against the center of her chest.

Lifting his face with her hand cupped under his chin, she waited until his molten gaze had reconnected with hers, before taking a quick breath, and saying, "I want this—want *you*—but I need to tell you…I mean, you probably figured it out…but I never actually fooled around with anyone else. So this is my *first*. My first time."

His breath jammed in his throat, and he blinked as he touched his tongue to his lower lip, letting those husky words work their way into him. It didn't change how he felt about her, or how much he wanted her, because he was in this no matter what. Whether she'd had fifty lovers…or none. But he'd have been lying through his teeth if he'd said he wasn't happy as hell about it.

"Mine, too," he finally managed to choke out, while his blood pounded in his ears, his heart damn near jerking its way through his chest. "It's mine, too, baby."

"Cian!" she gasped with a laugh that felt like pure, white-hot sunshine being injected straight into his veins. Then she smacked him in the shoulder for making what she thought was a joke. But it wasn't. Stripping away the rest of her clothes as quickly as possible, along with his jeans, he lifted his head and looked at her. Watched her luminous eyes go heavy with need as he lowered his hips between her parted thighs and rubbed his hot, granite-hard erection against her slick folds, his own eyes no doubt burning red with the ferocity of his need.

"I mean it," he told her, his deep voice as low and fervent as a vow. "This *is* a first for me, Sayre, because I've never *made love* to any other woman in my life."

"Then do it now," she whispered, slaying him with her beautiful smile as he reached between those slender thighs and pushed a long finger into the tight entrance nestled there, finding her deliciously hot and slick, melting for him like sun-warmed honey. "Make love to me, Cian. Don't make me wait."

"Gotta make sure you're ready," he groaned, squeezing a second finger into that tender, cushiony sheath, the way she clasped him, so tight and hot and wet, shooting a jolt of heat up his spine that had him gritting his teeth, fighting for control.

Then her next words shot it to hell.

Chapter 17

"Please, Cian. We've had freaking days of foreplay. I need you *now*," Sayre begged, thinking that he felt so much harder against her inner thigh, than he had the other times that they'd done this. Well, not *this*. But the lead-up. The slow build of their lust and love and need that was *finally* going to have its day. Hopefully before they detonated from the heat.

He felt bigger, too, and she knew this was going to be anything but easy. But she didn't care. Nothing worth keeping ever came easily, and she was keeping this man with her for...well, forever.

Suspecting he was worried about hurting her, she was ready to start pleading again, when he pulled his fingers free and notched the thick, heavy tip of him against her opening. Digging her nails into his shoulders, she panted with excitement as he started to carefully push forward, forcing her to stretch open for him, her power bursting free in a glittering array of sparks, letting him know exactly how desperate she was for this moment.

"So bloody tight, Sayre." He muttered the words directly into her ear, his voice so low and sensual it made her shiver even harder, her hands clasping his hips as she tried to pull him closer. "I *knew* you would be like this, lass. So damn perfect it blew my mind."

"Please," she gasped through trembling, tingling lips, not even sure what she was begging for. More? Faster? Deeper? All of them? *Yes!* All of them. She needed *everything*.

As if he heard her silent demands, he put one of his big, hot hands under her ass, tilting her up to him so that he could wedge more of that broad shaft inside her, keeping his rhythm slow and easy, rubbing and stroking all those wickedly sweet spots that were making her slippery and hot and so damn desperate for him she was digging her nails into his hard, gorgeous skin and moaning her head off.

Then he finally bit out a gritty curse, gripped her hips in his strong hands and shoved himself impossibly deep, forcing every single inch of that massive erection inside her. She cried out as he hit the end of her, his cock throbbing against her sensitive tissues, so big she couldn't breathe around the shocking sensation. But who needed air when she was full of this magnificent male, his teeth nipping her tender earlobe as he breathed in a harsh, ragged rhythm, his powerful, bad-ass body buried deep inside hers? Then he started to move, their heat-glazed stomachs and chests sliding against each other, his mouthwatering muscles flexing beneath his tight skin as he rolled his hips against hers, thrusting in a breathtaking rhythm that was getting better each time he pushed inside her.

"How's that feel?" he asked, his husky voice low and intimate at her ear.

"Insanely freaking amazing," she gasped, arching her

back so that she could press her swollen breasts harder against his chest.

He breathed a dark, devastatingly sexy laugh into her ear, but she meant every word. He was so big that it kind of felt like she was being split in two, and yeah, that hurt. But there was something beautiful behind the pain—a fullness and need and sense of rightness that overshadowed the discomfort and made her want *more*. Made her need it...*crave it*. She ran her palms up his sleek back, loving the play of powerful muscles beneath his hot skin and the hunger she could feel burning inside him as he used that magnificent body to claim her. Each time that he withdraw, her body fought to hold on to him, and he came back into her even harder, the sounds he made and the way he moved letting her know he needed her just as badly as she needed him. If not more.

"Ah...*fuck*, that's so sweet," he groaned against her temple. He nuzzled her hair with his nose, his right hand curled possessively around her breast as he drove inside her. "So goddamn *perfect*."

"What is?"

Pulling his head back, he locked his scorching, molten gaze with hers. "You're opened up to me, lass. *Completely*. I can feel everything. Everything that's in your heart, and it's... Christ, Sayre, there aren't even words."

Her throat shook, melting with emotion. "Love you so much," she whispered, pushing her fingers into the thick, damp strands of his hair.

Staring down at her as if she were a miracle, something cherished and infinitely precious, he said, "I know, Sayre. God, baby, I know. And you are so bloody beautiful, inside and out. The most beautiful woman in the world."

She couldn't help but smile with pleasure, because even though she knew it wasn't true, he made her feel that way. Because she knew it was how he saw her. Even when she was old and gray, she knew she would be able to see this same devastating level of devotion in his eyes, and *God*, that was so freaking sweet.

"I want it harder," she moaned, curling her hands around the back of his neck, his skin feverishly warm to the touch.

Something hot and wicked moved through his eyes. "Good, because I'm about to take you so hard you won't be able to walk up to bed, and then I'm taking you even harder."

"Do it," she gasped, unable to keep the smile off her face when she noticed his fangs, gleaming and white, drop beneath his upper lip. They definitely weren't his wolf's fangs. They were sharper, deadlier. But she didn't care. If she'd wanted easy, she'd have fallen in love with another man. But she'd chosen *him*, because he was everything she could ever want or need or desire, and she wanted the full experience. Every single scream-inducing thing he could do to her.

"Do *all* of it," she moaned, turning her head so that the tender side of her throat was left vulnerable and exposed, her blood thundering through her veins. "Make the bite, Cian. Make me yours."

"Don't," he grunted, his gaze immediately narrowing to sharp, piercing points of gray beneath his lowered brows. "Don't tempt me."

"But it's time."

Shaking his head, he argued, "I've lost too much fucking blood tonight and you smell too damn good. It's too dangerous right now, Sayre. We need to wait until my control isn't shot to hell and back."

"I don't care about your control. I trust you and it needs to be *now*, when we're finally together like we've been meant to be for so long. This is perfect."

"Sayre," he growled, his hammering thrusts getting rougher...deeper, driving her deliciously close to a powerful release she knew might damn well make her faint, it was going to be *that* intense.

Clutching his hard, slick shoulders, she stared up at his beloved face and said, "You've *died* for me, Cian. Do you really think there's any way any part of you would let me come to harm?"

"No," he grunted, and she figured she'd finally managed to convince him, because his hand was suddenly in her hair, wrenching her head to the side, exposing the tender column so that he could drive those sharp fangs deep into her throat, piercing her tight flesh and making the bond. That unbelievable, tilt-the-world-on-its-axis bond that had her fighting for air, so filled with emotion there wasn't room for anything else. Just love and trust and hope. Joy and happiness and a soul-deep need for this man who was the other half of her heart.

When he tried to pull his head back, she fisted her hands in his thick hair and held him to her, saying, "More. Take more, Cian. Drink from me."

He stiffened at the end of a hard downstroke, packed up thick and deep inside her, his powerful frame shuddering. "No," he snarled against her throat, pulling his fangs back with a wet pop. "I won't use you like that."

"You will," she breathed, keenly aware of the hot blood streaming from the bite he'd made, the two puncture wounds flowing freely. "You promised me every-

thing I'll ever want, and I want this. I want as deep inside you as you are in me."

"It's wrong," he rasped, his body rigid with tension.

"I belong inside you, Cian, pumping through your veins. Filling your belly." She arched her back, pressing up against him, loving the way their damp bodies rubbed together. "Nothing between us is wrong. Nothing is a sin. I offer this freely, and I'm even begging you for it. I want to be the thing that nourishes you. That gives you what you need."

"Shit," he growled, already lowering his head again, his warm breath rushing against her. "You're too damn perfect to be real."

She screamed in ecstasy only seconds later, holding him to her tighter as a lush, breathtaking orgasm pulsed through her, her hands fisted in his hair as his open mouth closed over the punctures and he started to suck on her. Driving himself inside her with a thick, aggressive rhythm, he devoured the hot blood that flowed through her veins as if it were the most exquisite thing he'd ever tasted. "Oh, God! That's so amazing, Cian."

He gave a low, animalistic growl against her flesh, and she grinned, knowing it was because he'd liked hearing her. When he finally pulled his mouth away, he pressed a gentle kiss to her throat, lapping at the tender skin where he'd bitten her, and she hissed from the pleasure. "Come for me again, lass. Give me one more. *Now*," he growled, dropping his forehead against hers, "'cause I'm about to come for you so bloody hard."

As if her pleasure were his to call and control, they crashed over that dark, devastating edge together, his hips slamming and grinding against hers as he pulsed inside her, his hands gripping her body hard. His raw,

guttural curses and her keening cries filled the air, while
her power consumed them, fueled by the bond that now
flowed so strongly between them. To another's eyes, they
would have no doubt looked as if they'd been engulfed
in crackling, crimson flames, yet they were thankfully
unburned, if not completely shattered when he finally
collapsed in her arms. He was still gently thrusting inside her, as if he couldn't bring himself to stop, his hot
face resting against the cushion of her breasts as they
struggled to catch their breath.

"God, Sayre. I could feel that sweet burn *inside* you,"
he groaned, sounding drowsy with satisfaction. She let
her eyes drift closed as she stroked his head, running
her fingers through his hair, and had no idea how much
time had passed when he carefully withdrew from her.
Then he pushed himself to his feet, lifted her into his
arms and carried her upstairs to the bathroom, where
he put her in a hot, steaming shower.

Holding her face in his hands, he took her mouth with
lush, drugging kisses, while the water sprayed down on
them from above, washing them clean.

"It's never been like that for me before," he told her,
when they finally had to stop kissing long enough to
breathe. Keeping his head bent over hers, he held her
face as he stared deep into her eyes, saying, "Nothing
ever even came close. And now you own every part of
me. *Own* it, Sayre. And I'm so damn sorry. Christ, I'm
so sorry, for everything, baby. I told myself for so long
that I couldn't love you because I was too much like my
father. Because his blood ran through my veins. But
the other night, after Aedan came to the Alley, I finally
started to figure out that it was just a lie. The truth is
that I've been too afraid to let myself love you because

I was terrified of ending up like my mother. Of losing…
everything. What if you didn't love me in return? What
if I gave you my heart and you broke it?"

Clutching his strong wrists, she blinked the water
from her lashes as she said, "I wouldn't. I won't. I'll
protect it with my dying breath, Cian."

"I know, baby. I know. I'm just sorry it took me so
long to figure it all out. To see that love doesn't make
you weak, so long as you're giving it to the right person. When that happens, it only makes you stronger."
A wry, lopsided grin started to twitch at the corner of
his mouth as he added, "And I'm probably going to have
my man card revoked for babbling like this, but even if
you didn't love me back, I would still love you like this,
Sayre. With everything that I am and will ever be. With
every part of me."

"But I do love you. I love you so much. More than
anything."

Touching his open mouth to hers, he smiled as he
nipped her bottom lip. "I know, lass. I could feel every
breathtaking part of it when I was buried deep inside
you. So deep I was practically coming out your mouth."

She couldn't help but laugh against those sexy, smiling lips. "Keep talking like that and I think your man
card is gonna be just fine."

"Face it, witch. You love my dirty mouth."

"I do," she gasped, already shivering with need for
him. "I love everything about you, Cian. And that's why
I'd like to come back here. I'd like to split our time between the two countries."

"Why the hell would you want to do that?" And then
in a drier tone, he said, "Are you sure you're not just

trying to avoid your mother? Because *that* I would actually be okay with."

She shook her head as she laughed. "Don't worry about Mom. She'll come to love you, I promise."

He still looked skeptical, so she leaned closer, pressing her lips to his for another kiss, this one brief and sweet. When she pulled back far enough to see his eyes, she said, "I want to spend time here because I can sense how much you love this country. Maybe not *here*, where your father is, but you love Ireland, Cian. This land, it's in your blood."

"*You're* in my blood."

"And this place is, too. I want to make happy memories here for you. I want the children we'll have one day to know both our countries." She could see the fear that darkened his gaze at her words, and so she said, "Not all wolves and witches are good, and not all vampires are evil. You're proof of that, Cian. It's love that builds a person's heart, and we'll give our children so much they'll glow with it."

He swallowed so hard that she could see the movement in his throat, but he didn't say anything. Just stared down at her with those dark, smoldering eyes.

"Unless you don't want that with me," she murmured, stroking the rigid muscles at the back of his neck.

"God, don't think that," he rasped, the husky words sounding torn out of him. "I want it more than anything. I want to put a baby inside you right now. But…Christ, Sayre. The idea of having all that, everything I want… it still scares the hell out of me."

"Cian, use the bond. *Feel* my love for you. It's okay to be happy," she told him, understanding his fears even better than her own. "It's okay to look forward to the future. To our life together. And I promise I'll help you. I'll be here for you, every step of the way."

And she was—for every single step—changing Cian's life in ways he'd never even imagined. Each one making it richer, brighter and filled with so much love he knew he was the luckiest son of a bitch on the planet.

After that night, they couldn't keep their hands off each other, and a week went by before they finally left the bachelor's house and headed back home.

Then he had her on the plane, on their way back to Maryland.

And in the car, on their way up to the Alley.

And when they reached his cabin, he took her right back to bed, and kept her there.

In short, he'd become completely insatiable when it came to his woman. Not just for her body, but for every part of her. Those smiles that brought him to his knees and the snark that never failed to make him laugh. They'd talked constantly the past week, when they weren't making love, making plans for the future… sappy and sweet and so filled with hope it was impossible to stop smiling. He would have felt like a lovesick fool if not for the fact that his little witch was the same.

And, damn, did she wear happiness well. As gorgeous as he'd always thought she was before, it was nothing to how stunning he found her now. Cian realized that what he'd thought of as love when he'd first accepted that Sayre meant something to him had only been the beginning. Powerful and strong, but too new to be fully in its own, like the first flake of snow in the world's greatest blizzard. Or the first grain of sand in a never-ending desert.

And what he felt for her now. God, there simply weren't words.

The night was sultry and sweet, the woman in his arms, snuggled against his body, even sweeter. Her heart was pounding, rushing the blood through her veins, and he could feel the darkness in him quickening with awareness, eager for the hot, rich spill as he pierced her flesh. Even his wolf had become addicted to his blood feedings, the intimacy of the act appealing to the beast's primal, possessive nature.

After long discussions on the matter, Sayre had finally convinced him to keep feeding from her until she reached his age, since she wanted them to be able to grow old together. Like the miracle she was, she was teaching him to not only accept that brutal part of his nature, but also to embrace it. And the way she called him her "blood wolf" when she wanted to feel the bite of his fangs made him steel-hard every single time. They indulged often, and he loved how close it made him feel to her, only strengthening their bond.

"Already?" she asked with a soft catch of excitement in her voice, when he rolled back on top of her, pushing his way between her thighs. His cock was hard as a rock as it brushed against her slick, swollen folds.

"I have a lot of time to make up for," he told her, pushing inside her, working his hips in careful nudges until she'd taken every inch. When he was buried deep, her soft little body gripping him like a tight, wet glove, he lowered his head and took her mouth with hot, hungry kisses that curled her toes.

"So this whole making-up-for-lost-time-in-the-sack thing we have going on. Does that mean you'll eventually stop wanting me so much?" she gasped, when she

finally had to break away from the ravenous demands
of his mouth so that she could catch her breath.

"I should say yes, but I honestly don't see that happening, lass. Each time, I want you even more…and it
somehow just keeps getting better." And it was true. Not
just on a physical level, though that was unlike anything
he could have ever dreamed of. The way she clasped
him in her tight body, the way she moved with him and
smelled and tasted and felt in his arms—there was simply no comparison. But the emotional aspect was just as
intense, if not more so, adding a richer, deeper layer to
the act that was impossible to explain. He just knew that
he needed it, *needed Sayre*, more than he needed water
and air. Hell, he needed her more than he needed blood
or the moonlight. His hunger for her had become more
a part of him than either his wolf or his "dark" blood
could ever be, and he wouldn't have it any other way.

"At this rate, we'll probably kill ourselves with sex,"
she teased, pushing against his shoulders until he'd
rolled to his back and she'd ended up on top, straddling
his hips.

"You won't hear me complaining," he growled, mes-
merized by the sight of her as she started to move. "More
like begging for more."

Eyes gleaming with pleasure, she gave him a beautiful, breathtaking smile. "I love how you do that. How
you always tell me how much you want me. You're going
to spoil me rotten, aren't you?"

"You bet your sweet little ass I am. Before and *after*
I get my ring on your finger." He was ready to pull her
down to him so he could take that sweet mouth of hers
in another greedy, scalding kiss. But she had other ideas.

"I promise to spoil you back," she whispered, pulling her hair over her shoulder as she turned her head, exposing the vulnerable curve of her throat. It was the signal that she was ready. Ready to give him all that he needed. To nourish his body, as well as his soul.

"Baby," he groaned, his abs flexing as he sat up and buried his face against that warm, tender skin, his mouth watering for the taste of her and his heart thundering like a drum, "you already do."

Then Cian buried his fangs hard and deep, and as he lost himself in the intoxicating taste of his woman, the feel of her reaching into the very heart of him with that burning, blinding light that was pure Sayre, he knew a sense of peace that reached all the way down to his soul. A sense of being *home*, exactly where he belonged.

He no longer feared the present or let the past consume and define him. He didn't have time for that kind of nonsense, because he was too busy looking to the future. To a life that was so much more than anything he could have ever hoped for.

A future he wouldn't give up for anything in the world.

And he couldn't wait to get started.

* * * * *

MILLS & BOON®

Need more New Year reading?

We've got just the thing for you!
We're giving you 10% off your next eBook or
paperback book purchase on the Mills & Boon
website. So hurry, visit the website today and type
SAVE10 in at the checkout for your exclusive

10% DISCOUNT

www.millsandboon.co.uk/save10

MILLS & BOON®

nocturne™

AN EXHILARATING UNDERWORLD OF DARK DESIRES

A sneak peek at next month's titles...

In stores from 16th January 2015:

- **Sentinels: Alpha Rising** – Doranna Durgin
- **Wolf Born** – Linda Thomas-Sundstrom

Available at WHSmith, Tesco, Asda, Eason, Amazon and Apple

Just can't wait?
Buy our books online a month before they hit the shops!
visit www.millsandboon.co.uk

These books are also available in eBook format!